D0761564

Books by Sharon Duncan

The Scotia MacKinnon Novels

Death on a Casual Friday

A Deep Blue Farewell

The Dead Wives Society

The Lavender Butterfly Murders

Quantum of Evidence

The Officer St. Claire Novels

Going Dark

Our Agent in Mayfair

sharon duncan
quantum of
evidence

a scotia mackinnon mystery

Western Isles Press
Gig Harbor, Washington

westernislespress@gmail.com

Quantum of Evidence

Cover photograph and logo by Getty Images
Interior and eBook design by W. Bruce Conway

First published in the United States by Western Isles Press in
2017. Second edition published by Western Isles Press in 2018.

Print: ISBN 978-0-9993949-6-0
eBook: ISBN 978-0-9993949-1-5

Distributed in the United States by Kindle Direct Pubishing

*To die, to sleep - to sleep, perchance to dream -- ay,
there's the rub, for in that sleep of death what
dreams may come . . .*

William Shakespeare
HAMLET, Act III

EASTSOUND, ORCAS ISLAND, WASHINGTON STATE

January 15, 1982

The worst nightmare isn't the one that attacks while you're asleep, twisting your gut, slicking your body and cutting off your breath. That kind you wake up from.

The ultimate nightmare is waking to face down a monster that's real and twisted and may stalk you forever.

When Peder Gundersen stumbled out of the farmhouse into the cold sleeting rain, he knew the bloody face peering over the edge of the old wooden table would haunt the remainder of his days and nights. His left arm was virtually useless and he struggled to pull on the canvas barn jacket. He fumbled for the keys in the pocket, realized with horror that he was still clutching the gun. He halted at the edge of the porch, holding the .38 out in front of him as if it were a viper. Shuddering with cold and shock, he tried to make sense of what had just happened, felt bile coming up into his throat. Then, abandoning any attempt at sanity, he hurled the weapon into the dense thicket of Oregon Grape and made a staggering run through the downpour to the car he'd left in the driveway when he and Hazel had gotten home last night.

He'd like to think that's where the nightmare began. With the argument at the bar in Eastsound. It was Hazel's usual tirade. About how he was a pathological womanizer and didn't love her and never had and was always sending money back to that bitch in Norway. When he accused her of bankrupting them with her horse expenses and stealing his pension and spending more time with Brenda Sue than she did with him, she called him a psychopath and picked up her big leather purse and walloped him right in the face. His nose had spurted blood. Both their drinks went careening onto the tile floor and they were asked to leave. Back at the house the fight continued far into the night, growing more vicious with each pour of vodka, until the two combatants had simply passed out. Then the next thing he heard was the loud, aggressive knock on the front door.

He slid into the car, managed after three tries to insert the keys into the ignition, and knew in his heart that the nightmare began a long, long time before last night. It started the day he brought Hazel into the house more than twenty years ago. And everything had gone straight to hell from there.

Now all he could think was that he had to get away. Far, far away. He shifted into reverse, lurched out of the driveway onto Old Orchard Lane. The air was dark and heavy and he came within inches of hitting the battered red pick-up parked along the side of the road. The car stalled and it took several tries to restart the engine. He took a deep breath, drove slowly past the neighboring Benton place shrouded in the sheeting rain, made a left turn onto Dolphin Bay Road. He had to make it to the mainland. Then where? Then what?

The pounding in his head was worse, a relentless thrum that intensified the vodka-induced nausea. The blood from his shoulder was leaking down under the jacket, onto his trousers and the seat. He turned onto McNary Lane, nearly colliding with a small white Honda whose driver was navigating as blindly as Peder was. The sleeting rain had turned to snow, big wet flakes that stuck to the windshield. God, how he hated Pacific Northwest winters with days and weeks and months of endless gloom. He would gladly sell what was left of his soul for just one day of golden sunshine.

Peder could think of only one safe haven. Only one person who might make the nightmare disappear. But first he had to make it into town. Clueless as to the winter sailing schedule and how long he'd have to wait for the next freakin' ferry, he drove more by memory than sight, peering around each blind curve, hoping against hope that he wouldn't see the big black truck barreling toward him.

Please, God.

Chapter 1
PORT OF FRIDAY HARBOR

San Juan Island

Present Time

Secrets are rampant in small towns and small islands. There's no privacy. No anonymity. No place to hide. The grapevine rules and rumor distribution is exponential. The small town of Friday Harbor on San Juan Island, located halfway between mainland Washington State and the Canadian province of British Columbia, is no exception. So it wasn't a surprise that Tina Breckenridge didn't want to be seen walking into the office of a private investigator.

She called late Friday afternoon. I was hurrying back to *DragonSpray*, cutting through Fairweather Park where two large ravens were conducting a somber croaking dialog atop the big wooden crossbeam of the Pillars of Welcome. The ravens were shiny and black and apparently had declined to follow their avian brethren south. Or maybe ravens didn't migrate.

The fog was dense and the rain was cold. I'd been back on the island only two days after spending four months with Falcon in Porto Sollér. The chill of the rain was a surprise on my face that had recently been basking in Mediterranean sun. I answered the phone call and continued down the main dock past the Harbormaster's office, treading with care on the old wooden planks I knew would be slick from the rain.

"McCready is accusing me of being a *murderer*, Scotia. Have you seen his campaign posters? Can we get a restraining order against the SOB?"

I heard the desperation in her voice and peered into the falling darkness. Tina Breckenridge, an island sailing instructor, was running for San Juan County Commissioner against Lochlan McCready, a newcomer from California. The special election was two weeks away. "If you get a restraining order, Tina, you have to be prepared to file suit against him. Given the First Amendment, that won't get you very far. Where'd the murder stuff come from?"

"It's about my great-aunt. Hazel Gundersen. The one who was convicted for murdering her husband. Since McCready put up the posters, the kids have been making life hell for Stephan."

I vaguely remembered a horrific tale about some island woman who'd killed her husband and ground him up into sausage. The husband was a ship's pilot, Swedish or Norwegian. "That was your *aunt*?"

"My great-aunt. Can we talk? Stephen got into a fight at school. Zelda says McCready's an assassin."

"My officemate frequently exaggerates."

"Paul will use any excuse to take him away from me."

"How about Monday? I'll be in the office at nine."

She hesitated. "Could we meet somewhere else? Like the Netshed? Maybe a little earlier?"

"The Netshed at 8:30 on Monday."

My name is Scotia MacKinnon. I'm a licensed private investigator. I have an office in the Olde Gazette Building in Friday

Harbor where I share space with a graphic artist /events arranger named Zelda Jones. My usual scope of work is assignments for local attorneys or insurance companies: Locating hid- den assets, investigating arson, doing backgrounds on internet Lotharios. I live aboard a 38-ft. sloop-rigged sailboat named *DragonSpray*, a replica of the vessel Joshua Slocum sailed singlehandedly around the world at the end of the 19th century. And, like the intrepid Captain Slocum, I was born in a small town in Nova Scotia.

My recent sojourn in the Balearics was the result of a case I cleared on an international sweetheart swindler. A case so sensational that it lured an MI6 agent all the way from London to our hillside village at 48 degrees 53 minutes north.

The MI6 agent was Michael Farraday, alias Falcon. I don't believe in coincidences, but Fal-con's appearance coincided with the decline of my romantic relationship with a Seattle maritime attorney. One thing led to another and I accepted Falcon's in-vitation to fly to the Iberian Peninsula. Mission: Sail *S.V. Aphrodite* from Lisbon to Mallorca. The mission was accomplished and the summer slipped away in a blur of sun, blue water, Italian wines and lingering embraces.

Now, on a gray Monday morning in early October, I huddled in *DragonSpray's* warm cabin in my pajamas, sipped my French Roast, and listened to the

NBC news anchor cover the latest riot in Cairo while a few tentative rain drops pattered on the overhead hatch covers. I tried not to dwell on the fact that a month earlier I'd been soaking up sun on the balcony of a whitewashed, red-roofed villa on the West coast of Mallorca. And that if Falcon hadn't received the phone call from the U.K., I would still be there. But he had and I wasn't.

The NBC newswoman moved on to a terrorist massacre in Peshawar of 145 students and teachers. Shaken by the evil that had been unleashed against the world in the name of religion, I turned o the TV. I dressed in my usual rainy day working attire: warm sweater, blue jeans, boots. I retrieved my parka from the hanging locker in the a stateroom, grabbed my cell phone from the galley counter. I checked for a text message from Falcon.

Nothing.

As I closed the companionway, Henry, my dock-side neighbor, was leaving *Pumpkinseed*. Henry is a gloomy fellow who manages the local branch of a major mortgage company. At one point he'd been engaged to a redheaded bartender named Lindsey. Henry muttered a curt "Good morning," and hurried up the dock toward the Port administration building before I could ask about Calico, the tabby cat we share. I hadn't seen her since I'd been back. at worried me. It also sort of worried me that Henry and I used to be good neighbors and now he barely spoke to me. Maybe was even avoiding me.

Chapter 2
The Netshed

San Juan Island

As I strode up the dock past the Port offices, I inhaled the briny smell of the harbor and heard the three short soundings of the horn that signaled the departure of the 8:05 ferry for mainland America. In the upper parking lot I unlocked the Alfa Berlina, slid inside. The motor turned over immediately. I settled into the bucket seat, slipped a Luther Vandross CD into the player, and watched the *Sealth* back to port away from the ferry dock, do a slow turn, and move smoothly past Brown Island and out into San Juan Channel. During the 'shoulder seasons' of spring and fall, the Sealth was one of two vessels making the 16-nautical mile passage, carrying vehicles and foot passengers from Friday Harbor to Flounder Bay on Fidalgo Island. And then back again on the reverse run.

The rain was coming down heavier. Once upon a time, October on San Juan Island was a month of mellow sunlight and blue skies. A soft buffer between summer's golden meadows and the frigid rains of a Pacific Northwest winter. The best time to uncleat *Dragonspray's* lines and cruise up through the Canadian Gulf Islands to Telegraph Harbor or Nanaimo. Now, heading into a new Ice Age, summer here is foreshortened. Storms from Alaska or Siberia arrive earlier. By late September the Snow Birds have departed for Kauai or Phoenix or Nairobi.

I motored down the hill past the Drydock Restaurant and edged around the corner and uphill onto Spring Street, reviewing what I knew about my appointment at the Netshed. Tina Breckenridge is a tough island woman in her late 30's or early 40's who previously worked as crew on a crab fishing boat in the Bering Sea, then married a local fisherman, raised a son, and became a sailing instructor. Following a near fatal misadventure in Desolation Sound , she divorced her husband and moved with Stephan down to the Ballard neighborhood in north Seattle to live with an aunt. Located in an area bordered by both Puget Sound and Salmon Bay, Ballard's history included a lucrative lumber industry, followed by commercial fishing. Many of the fishermen were from Scandinavia. Tina Breckenridge had spent most of her adolescence in Ballard and became a boat builder before heading north to crew on a crab boat.

Uphill again, I continued on past houses cantilevered on the hillside above the harbor, then onto Turn Point Road. The only vehicle I met was a dark green restored Chevy pick-up turning out of the Netshed driveway. The driver waved and I pulled into the parking area.

The Netshed is owned by Peg O'Reilly. A long time ago, when San Juan Island's sustenance came from logging and fishing, the Shed was used to store nets for the local fishermen. Peg bought the dilapidated building with insurance proceeds after her husband perished in an Alaska storm. She remodeled the upper level into an apartment for herself and her Border Collie. The downstairs she transformed into a rustic L-shaped diner overlooking the harbor. She kept the original wooden plank floors and the big exposed ceiling beams. There are two rows of booths upholstered in dark red naugahyde. A 1940's vintage counter runs the length of the big room with a passthrough window behind. The Shed is open from 5:00 a.m. to noon. Only breakfast is served. It's a hangout for locals, mostly fishermen and contractors and a few retired geezers that shun the trendy spots in town. To the infinite relief of the patrons, the Netshed is sufficiently removed from the village watering holes for the mob of summer visitors that overflow the restaurants above the ferry docks.

There were three pickups and a small car parked next to the Shed. At the floating dock out front, two commercial fishing boats bobbed in the wind and current.

I hurried through the downpour and stepped past the recumbent Collie, into the warm space that smelled of frying bacon and coffee and cinnamon. I closed the door behind me, scanned the room for Tina Breckenridge. I didn't see her. Two booths in the far side were filled with men wearing overalls and flannel work shirts. I recognized several of them and nodded. No one was seated at the long counter. I slid into the nearest empty booth as Peg came out of the swinging door balancing four large white platters. She served the booth in the very back, kibitzed with the customers, refilled their cups, then headed in my direction with the carafe of coffee. I knew it was strong and black and definitely not de-caf.

"Nice to see you back, Scotia." She filled my cup. "Tina joining you?"

Peg is 60-something, tall and sturdy. She has curly iron gray hair and her face shows a lot of mileage at high speed. Peg O'Reilly is Tina Breckenridge's godmother, and despite the difference in their ages, the two women are close friends. I nodded. "How's life, Peg?"

"The price of pork is going through the ceiling," she said grimly. "It's going to put me out of business. Goddamn drought. Nobody wants to raise pigs any more."

"Maybe you should buy a hog farm, Peg. Grow your own pork."

The door opened and Tina Breckenridge came in. She glanced quickly around, smiled at Peg, and slid into the seat across from me. "Thanks for meeting me here."

Peg's face softened and she patted Tina shoulder before filling her cup. Tina looked years younger than when I'd last seen her. She wore a purple parka over faded blue jeans. Her dark hair was wet and windblown. The short shaggy cut made her high cheekbones stand out and her violet eyes startling. She put a bulging manila envelope on the table and peeled out of her parka while Peg hovered. I glanced at the breakfast choices on the big whiteboard behind the counter and ordered #2, Peg's homemade cinnamon bun, as did Tina, along with a glass of fresh-squeezed O.J.

"You gals be careful what kinda of boxes you open up," Peg admonished before heading to the kitchen. I assumed she meant the Pandora variety.

"You and Stephan are back on the island," I said. "Is it for good?"

"Forever, I hope. I'm so not a city person. Stephan didn't fit in with the kids in Ballard. I tried home schooling him again, but it didn't work."

"Are you and Ian still together?"

A smile lit up her face. "We are. He's finishing a project in Seattle. It's a history of the Ballard fishermen. He plans to move up here by the end of the year."

"How does he get on with Stephan?"

"Not so good. He was up this summer. Stephan hated sharing our cottage and he went to spend a month in Alaska with Paul on *Pacific Mist*."

"How'd that go?"

"Paul got him a smarter smart phone than the one I gave him. And a GPS. Now he doesn't speak anything but lat-long. When he's not on Facebook he's geocaching."

"The age of social media."

"Better Facebook than drugs."

I recalled that Stephan had had at least one Minor in Possession and some charges of vandalism or truancy the previous year. "Is he back in the high school?"

"He's at the International School. Paul's paying for it."

I smiled. "So, no more Parker Benjamin."

"Please, God, no more Parker Benjamin." She rolled her eyes. "Stephan's learning Japanese. That's where his class is going for winter special project."

"Where are you and Stephan living?"

"We're renting a cottage on Wold Road. It's on Lily MacGregor's property."

"At the Secret Garden?"

"She sold that after Mac died and bought the place on Wold."

"She has a son, doesn't she?"

"Yes. Sean's doing an exchange student thing in Italy and Lily's niece, Sage, is living with her. There's a small caretaker's cottage on the property. Perfect for us until I find something to buy." She sighed and said, "I think Sage has a crush on Stephan. Or vice versa. He spends hours texting her. Not sure where that's going."

Peg brought the O.J. and the cinnamon buns to the table. I attacked the yeasty pastry as Tina continued. "I taught sailing here all summer. Not just adults, but kids, too."

"Can you do that year round? Make a living at it?"

"Nope. I'm selling boat stuff at West Marine for the winter. Life is calmer. Or it was until I decided to get into politics."

"You having second thoughts?"

"It was a terrible idea, but I don't want to be a quitter. And honestly, Scotia, San Juan County deserves someone better than that, that –" She hesitated and lowered her voice, glancing toward the booth in the back. "–that Nazi."

"Is he that bad?"

"That's what Zelda calls him. She thinks Mc-Cready's more conservative than Attila the Hun." She frowned. "And he has so much money."

"Is that the only problem? The money he spends on his campaign?"

"It's the awful lies he's putting out about Aunt Hazel. Lily says I should get an injunction against him." She reached for the manila envelope and pulled out a black and white poster. "Take a look at his latest."

The background on the poster was ghoulish and gray. In the upper right hand corner a haggard looking woman peered from behind bars. I felt a wave of dismay as I scanned the text.

Tina Breckenridge was a kidnap victim. Or was she a part of the set-up?
Tina Breckenridge doesn't think your public school is good enough for her son.
Tina Breckenridge comes from a family of criminals. What else do you need to know about Tina Breckenridge?

I took a deep breath. "Mama mia. And I thought the national elections were bad."

"Aunt Hazel was a total bitch. My Aunt Jeanette says she and Uncle Peder were always fighting, but she wasn't a murderer."

"Peder was the sea captain?"

"A ship's pilot, actually. Worked out of Port Angeles."

"Is that where they lived?"

"Aunt Hazel had a horse stable on Orcas. Raised and showed draft horses and rented out rooms to visiting horse people."

"What did Hazel and Peder fight about?"

"About money, about his girl friends, real or imaginary, you name it. And she was a mean drunk. But the family never believed she killed him. They never even found Uncle Peder's body. "

"You mean he just disappeared?"

She nodded. "According to Hazel, he took off one cold winter day and was never seen again." She shrugged. "Maybe he finally had enough of Hazel, went back to Norway." She paused. "Hazel said he probably committed suicide."

"Why would he do that?"

"A year or so earlier, there was a collision on a ship he was piloting. Or it ran aground. He lost his pilot's license and had to retire."

I glanced at the poster again. The man behind it very much wanted to be a County Commissioner. "Your Aunt Hazel had a jury trial?"

She nodded. "It went on for a month. She was convicted and sentenced to life."

"Was there an appeal?"

She nodded. "It was rejected." She shoved the poster back in the manila envelope and slid it across the table. "Aunt Jeanette was a legal secretary for some criminal lawyers in Seattle while the trial was going on. They said all the evidence was circum-stantial. Several witnesses changed their story. There was blood on the carpet and the ceiling and a blood spatter expert testified, but there was never any DNA testing."

"When did all this happen?"

"Twenty-nine years ago."

"Before DNA evidence was allowed in trials."

"Yes."

Technology for preservation of DNA wouldn't have existed back then, and even now only about half the states require automatic preservation of DNA evidence after conviction. Washington is not one of them.

"Is Aunt Hazel still in prison?"

"She died ten years ago."

"In prison?"

She nodded.

I pulled apart the cinnamony heart of the bun with the brown sugar and raisin filling. "Maybe the smart thing is to withdraw from the race. Politics is dirty. And getting dirtier."

"One of the town bullies, a kid named Gorv, has been posting nasty stuff on Facebook, that Stephan's family are criminals. I'm afraid it will get worse. Can you help me?"

"Who was your aunt's attorney?"

"His name was Jarvis. It's in the envelope."

"A local?"

"From Tacoma. His family had a horse farm on Orcas. That's how Hazel knew him."

"It's been 29 years. Your aunt is gone. What could we accomplish, Tina?"

"Read the stuff in the envelope. I have to let people know she didn't do it. Or remind them that there was no actual proof." She hesitated and stared out the window. "There's another thing."

"And that is?"

"Paul's on his way back from Alaska. He doesn't want Stephan living with me. When he sees the stuff

McCready's putting out about me and the family, he's going to go berserk."

"Do you have custody?"

"It's joint, but we agreed Stephan would live with me during school term. Now Paul wants him full time. And he wants to take him to Alaska."

"In the winter?"

She sighed. "He's talking about moving there permanently with his girl friend. She's from Sitka. He's going to sell our old place."

"Paul can't take Stephan out of the state without your approval."

"I know. But that's a legal battle I can't afford."

"What does Stephan want?"

"He wants all of this to go away."

We sat in silence for a few minutes. I finished the cinnamon bun and drained my cup. "At the end of the day, McCready can say and write anything he wants, even if it's dirty and hateful and mean spirited. Constitutional First Amendment rights, and so on. Maybe you'll have to sweat it out. This island is pretty liberal. He probably won't get enough votes from conservatives to win, no matter how much dirt he tries to dig up on your family. Or you could get out of the race before you get *really* beat up. Think about it."

She shook her head. "I have to do something *significant* with my life, Scotia. A lot of people here think I'm just a sailing bum. Or the crazy woman that went to work on a crab boat. I want to be a Commissioner and I want to buy a house where Stephan can bring friends, and I want my family's name cleared," she said fiercely. "So does Aunt Jeanette. She was one of the witnesses, you know. At the trial."

"What did she testify to?"

"Aunt Hazel used to call her when she was drunk. She'd tell her Peder was a philanderer and she hated him and she was going to kill him. When Uncle Peder disappeared, she thought maybe Hazel had made good on her threat, so she called the sheriff."

I picked up the bulging envelope. "Reviewing a 29-year-old murder trial. Could get expensive."

"Aunt Jeanette just sold an apartment building in Seattle she's owned for thirty years. On Queen Anne Hill, so she got a nice price. She'll pay whatever you need if you can do something to shut McCready up and we can find out what really happened to Uncle Peder."

She looked at me with pleading eyes. "I've been doing a lot of research on the trial." She reached into her rucksack and pulled out a second fat envelope.

I'd drawn on my investments to keep the bills paid while I was away sailing and vacationing with Falcon. *DragonSpray* needed a haul out and an upgrade in the electrical wiring. My daughter Melissa would need help with graduate school. Trying to dig up evidence in a cold case file might turn out to be futile, but the offer of "whatever you need" along with the possibility that an innocent woman had been convicted, was hard to turn down.

"I'll take a look at what you've got. If I can do anything, I'll need a retainer and a contract." I brushed the crumbs off my sweater, put the envelopes in my carryall. As I stood up, Tina made a final request.

"Please see what you can dig up on McCready.

He can't be as lily white as he appears. Two can play his game."

Chapter 3

Olde Gazette Building

Friday Harbor

By the time I got back into town, the rain was a steady downpour. I pulled into the only empty space in the Port parking lot above the yacht club and checked for text messages. There was one from my mother, Jewel Moon, who lives down on the northern California coast: *Congratulations! Talk soon.* I had no idea what I'd done to merit her felicitations, but Jewel Moon has her own eccentricities. I locked the car and trudged up the 78 steps to 1st Street and cut across the Court House parking lot, wondering why Falcon hadn't called.

Or texted. Or e-mailed.

I thought about the phone call he'd received from his brother that mellow afternoon in Porto Sollér: He was needed back in the U.K. to help unravel the settling of his mother's estate that included a house in Scotland that the sister was claiming despite a will that awarded it to him. It all seemed so far away and disconnected from my life in Friday Harbor that I might've dreamed it.

The downstairs area of the Olde Gazette Building houses Zelda Jones, doing business as New Millennium Communications. Zelda does occasional high-tech research for me when I can't acquire information through normal channels. The third office, formerly occupied by Soraya, a naturopathic physician from Orcas, had acquired a new tenant during my absence. A scientist and wildlife photographer from the U.K., Zelda said, who was trying to disprove Einstein's theory of relativity and save the foxes of London.

Inside, opera music filled the air. Something German, maybe Wagner. Along with the scent of burning madrona logs, there was the fragrance of really good coffee, but the Netshed brew had me sufficiently decaffeinated. Zelda sat in front of her huge flat-screen monitor staring at a display of exotic graphics. She twirled about as I headed for the mail cubbies. Her attire was contemporary tomboy. Man's striped shirt, black denim pants, black ankle boots. Her carrot-colored hair was styled Goth and small silver skulls dangled from her earlobes. While I was away she had acquired a new tattoo: a large reptile that bore striking resemblance to one sported by an infamous Scandinavian cyberpunk hacker.

"How was your meeting with Tina?" she asked. "Is she going to sue the Nazi bastard?"

"How did you know I was meeting with Tina?"

"Tina told Peg O'Reilly that you're going to help her clear her name. Peg called Abby. Business is slow. I can help you with the research on the old murder trial."

"It's probably a lost cause. What's to be gained? Hazel Gundersen died ten years ago."

"What's to be gained? Lochlan McCready is a total SOB. Abigail and I went to his fundraiser at the

Legion last night. His politics are Neanderthalian. He talks about "securing the islands" as if Friday Harbor's going to be the next Ground Zero. He wants to bring five thousand new jobs to the island. Give me a *break*! And he's glommed onto the old Gundersen murder case. He mentioned it three times in connection with his *opponent*, as if Tina was the one convicted. Abby says everyone knows Hazel got convicted just because she was a blowsy old drunk."

Abigail Leedle, an island septuagenarian who used to teach biology at the high school, is a talented photographer with seemingly endless energy to protect the wildlife of the 55-acre island she calls home. She and Zelda were founding members of a group of free-thinking island females who call themselves the Coronas.

Across the room, Dakota snored on the braided rug in front of the wood stove in Black Lab dreamland, oblivious to his mistress's diatribe.

I shrugged. "I can't rewrite history. By running for public office, Tina has become a public figure. McCready can say anything he wants."

"The Coronas are supporting her, but we don't think she's got a snowball's chance in hell of winning."

"You think McCready will win?"

"Abigail says the Nazi will buy the election. He's probably got his own super-Pac."

"I think the Coronas are underestimating the intellect of the San Juan Island electorate."

"With enough money you can buy any election. Besides, he used to work for the Company. Maybe still does."

"The CIA?"

She nodded. "Wet operations. In Columbia and Venezuela. And before that he was in Africa. "

"How do you know that?"

"I had breakfast at the Doctor's Office this morning. McCready was sitting at the next table waiting for the ferry with his cute little I-book." She chortled. "You'd think a spook would be smart enough not to use an unsecured network, wouldn't ya?" She produced her signature impish grim.

Zelda's previous work experience included ten years at a computer security firm in Seattle. "You're treading on dangerous ground."

"I didn't leave any footprints or do any damage. He'll never know."

As I sorted through the contents of my mail cubby, I pondered why a former or current CIA operative was running for the San Juan County Council. Or even why he'd chosen to live on a small island where the most contentious bit of daily life typically concerned someone's ex-Significant Other ending up at a party with the new Significant Other. But the Coronas were as accurate forecasters as any official pollster. If they thought Tina would lose the election because of McCready's smear tactics, she probably would.

"Hazel Gundersen was convicted almost thirty years ago," I said, riffling through the real estate flyers, a moorage bill from the Port of Friday Harbor, a postcard notice from my dentist, and three pink phone message slips. "Politicians can get just so much mileage out of ancient history."

"Hah! That didn't stop the Swiftboaters or the

Birthers. And people have long memories around here. By the way, Carolyn Smith called twice. I told her you were at a meeting so she didn't call your cell, but she said it's important."

Zelda will never admit to being anyone's Gal Friday, but she is not opposed to fielding my phone calls while I'm out. Mostly, I think, to maintain her reputation as Numero Uno Friday Harbor News Source. I dumped the junk mail in the recycle bin and glanced at the big whiteboard she had recently added to the office. She was using it to organize her design projects, and in one corner was posting pithy aphorisms. Today's was, "*I didn't say it was your fault.* I said I was blaming you."

Upstairs, I unlocked the door, hung up my parka, dumped the mail on my desk, and read the phone messages. One from Jared Saperstein, two from attorney Carolyn Smith. I've done a number of assignments for Carolyn and her associates. Small cases, except for one long-running case of a missing heir. Which was why she was calling.

"Thank God you're back, Scotia. Harrison Petrovsky's sister is on the warpath again. Petra says she's going to le to have the will nullifed if it's not settled by anksgiving. And then sue me for malpractice."

"She's threatened that before," I replied, glancing at the notice from my dentist. "Right a er she tried to get Harrison declared officially dead." Petra Petrovsky von Schnitzenhoff was the sister of a missing heir who'd left Friday Harbor in a gaff-rigged cutter named *Ocean Dancer* headed for Mexico and the Marquesas. In order to fulfill the 30 requirements of the bequest – something like six million dollars to be divided three ways with all beneficiaries physically present – we needed Harrison to return home. Ignoring our phone calls and e-mails, he'd spent months cruising the South Pacific, acquiring a Tongan or Tahitian girl friend, outrunning a typhoon, idling about in ports from Sydney to Singapore. Every time I located a local P.I. to nab Harrison, he'd managed to hoist anchor and disappear. Zelda had recently discovered that Harrison's disinterest in returning home had to do with a jilted pregnant fiancée.

"When was the last time anyone actually heard from Harrison?" I pulled the Petrovsky file from the side drawer of my desk.

"Sister number two – her name is Luisa – says Harrison left Thailand three weeks ago, and was going to stop in the Seychelles. Their plan was to come home by way of the Mediterranean."

"*Mediterranean*? He was supposed to arrive in *Trinidad* how many years ago? We hired a P.I. there. Remember? What happened to *that* plan?" I thumbed through the file, searching for the last exchange of e-mails. "And who is 'they'?"

"According to Luisa, Harrison's current crew is from Singapore. A female stockbroker. They sailed to Sri Lanka and then the Seychelles. Harrison has a blog and he was posting his locations on Facebook. But there haven't been any posts for two weeks. Luisa is worried. Since you're a sailor, I thought maybe you could figure out where he might be. Latitude or longitude."

" "Where do I start?"

"I'll forward Luisa's e-mail. Please reach out to her."

I put down the phone ruefully. I don't like dangling threads and Harrison Petrovsky had been dangling longer than I could remember.

My next call was to Jared Saperstein, editor and publisher of the *Friday Gazette* and one of my two island confidantes.

"Saperstein." Jared's voice was crisp and impatient.

"Scotia MacKinnon returning your call."

His voice lost its impatience. "Are you available for lunch?"

"Yes."

" Pablo's at noon?"

"See you there."

 I checked for incoming e-mail and deleted two offers of cheap air fares and one message from a gentleman with questionable French syntax advising me that I had won 500,000 euros and could claim it by e-mailing him my Social Security number and a copy of my passport.

I put away the Petrovsky file and sat for several minutes contemplating the two envelopes Tina Breckenridge had given me. Would delving into ancient history do anything to short-circuit Lochlan McCready's assault on Tina? I'd never met the man. Almost by definition, negative political ad campaigns are vicious abstractions, frequently taking a fact or statement out of context and converting it into an outright lie. What was McCready's motive for waging such a hateful campaign? As an Old Island Farmer once told me, *meanness don't just happen overnight.*

I dumped the contents of Tina's two envelopes on my desk: umpteen newspaper clippings, half a dozen photos, a true crime book on the murder. Most of the yellowed clippings and articles were from local sources: the various island rags, the *Seattle Times, Pacific Northwest News*, and so on. The case of the *State of Washington v. Hazel Gundersen* had also attracted national media attention, either because of the alleged gory details of the homicide – according to the testimony of Hazel's brother, the victim was chopped up with a butcher knife and the remains burned, but not ground up into sausage, the sausage tale was a myth –or because it was rare to have a conviction and a life sentence when there was no body.

I examined the hate poster I'd already seen and half a dozen other flyers and brochures of the same ilk, still puzzling over the meanness of the attacks. This was the San Juan Islands. For the most part, people were civil and peace-loving. I studied Lochlan McCready's image on the cover of a colored flyer. He was an older Daniel Craig. Late forties or early fifties. Tanned, lean, broad-shouldered. A strong face, unlined except for two vertical creases between his eyebrows. An unsmiling mouth halfway between thin and sensual. The eyes were blue, piercing and intelligent. Hair, straight and blond going gray, cut short but not military. White shirt open at the collar tucked into black trousers. Brown leather jacket. Black boots. He was leaning against a gray SUV, arms crossed over his chest. His demeanor was "no nonsense, let's just get the job done." If he had a sense of humor, it wasn't noticeable. Lochlan McCready was not a man you would get close to without his permission. Not at all cuddly.

The inside of the flyer had a one-page bio: Born and raised in Los Angeles, recruited to play football at the University of Michigan. MBA at UCLA. Army Special Forces from which he joined the Central Intelligence Agency. Posted to Chad and then Paris. Also worked in Hong Kong before he returned to D.C. Retired to raise grapes in Santa Barbara County. Moved to San Juan Island two years ago. No family photos. No mention of a wife or children. Nothing about Venezuela.

I turned back to the contents of the envelope, scanned the chapter headings of the true crime novel on the Gundersen case and studied the photographs Tina had included. One shot was of a tall slender woman of some fifty years standing beside a tall, sturdy man, probably in his 70's, apparently taken at a party. The woman was wearing an ankle- length print dress and had a wine glass in her hand. The man had his arm around the woman's shoulders. The back of the photo carried the inked notation, *Hazel & Peder's 15th anniversary*. The next image showed Hazel leading a large draft horse (*Hazel with Prince George at County Fair*). The third featured Hazel standing next to a short, plump smiling woman of probably the same age. Both women were wore blue overalls and checked shirts (*Hazel and Brenda Sue*). Hazel was not smiling in any of the shots.

My ancient grandfather clock was working itself up to chime the half hour when I heard Zelda's quick footsteps on the stairs and a knock on the half-open door.

"I'm taking Dakota for a walk and meeting Lily and Abby for lunch." She handed me a sheaf of papers. "I thought this might be useful. Stuff on the Gundersen case from the Washington State history link." She grinned. "It's a freebie. Event arranging is down just now, so I'm available for in-depth research. Like maybe the court records? By the way, I'm enrolling in a Citizens Police Academy Course. Twelve sessions. And if you're having lunch with Jared, ask him about the civil war over the wetlands." She gave me a toothy grin and before I could ask why the Police Academy, she was gone, pounding back down the stairs and out the door.

I stuffed everything back into the envelopes and locked it all away with Zelda's internet report, considering the possibility that Hazel Gundersen had been wrongly convicted and had spent her last years in a woman's correctional facility.

What if the alleged victim, Captain Peder Gundersen, had never been murdered at all? Supposing he'd disappeared voluntarily? Gone back to Norway. Or decided to commit suicide and jumped off the ferry when it was crossing Rosario Strait. Or supposing the Captain, fed up with the well-publicized fractious domestic situation, had maliciously set Hazel up to take a murder rap.

And that Hazel was convicted because she was a 'blowsy old drunk.'

Chapter 4
PABLO'S RESTAURANT

Friday Harbor

The restaurant was crowded, Jared waving from a back table, getting up to hang my dripping parka on a hook by the door and give me a long, lingering hug. He seemed to have lost weight. His embrace was strong and I wondered how I could have forgotten how comforting.

"Nice to have you back, love. You look . . . wonderful. Wow, short hair, suntanned, not an ounce of fat. Maybe I should go find *me* a Mediterranean island." He gave me a once-over, ruffled my hair.

I considered mentioning that sometimes appearances had more to do with companionship than geography. But I didn't. Because that would lead to chitchat about Michael Farraday and then I'd have to admit that I hadn't heard from him since he arrived in London five days ago. Instead, I studied the menu, chose the day's special. While Jared placed our orders at the walk-up counter, I noticed the book-size brown paper parcel on the table. A new first edition Sherlock Holmes? He returned with two tankards of ale.

"I know you don't usually imbibe during working hours, but it's been a long time. Cheers!"

We toasted, tasted, and regarded each other for

a minute or so over the foaming tankards. He handed me the brown wrapped parcel. "A little item for your bedtime reading." I opened it. A first edition of Mac-Donald's *The Lonely Silver Rain*. I smiled. "Haven't read it in at least ten years. You're turning me into a collector. And boat dwellers can't be collectors."

"Maybe it's time for you to have a real home."

"Excuse me? *Dragonspray* is a real home."

He looked ustered. "I found the book over in Port Townsend, thought of you."

"So. Bring me up to date, Jared. What's new?

"Zelda mentioned a brouhaha on Orcas."

"Ah, yes. It appears a farmer over at Eastsound may have *inadvertently* constructed some buildings on what his neighbor considers wetlands. Threats of lawsuits are in the air. Speaking of your office mate, did she mention that she and her sidekick livened up McCready's fundraiser last night?"

"How so?"

"They asked one or two questions that were viewed as unfriendly by the organizers and they were invited to leave?"

"She omitted that bit. What sort of questions?

"About McCready's military background. Was it true he was involved in some CIA regime change in Africa? What about an assassination in Venezuela? How the hell did she get her hands on stu like that?"

Pablo brought our platters of chile verde. I inhaled the scent of rice and black beans. Jared began to ll one of the hot tortillas with the steaming pork stew. "She and Abigail are as incorrigible as ever." I glanced around and lowered my voice. "She hacked into McCready's email."

Jared frowned. "Not smart. Not if he was actually involved in any of the stuff she was bringing up."

"Have you been following his campaign?"

"Lots of us have. He's an enigma. Moves up here from California and leaps into local politics. And from where I stand, his politics may be a bit East of most folks here."

"Many people at the fund raiser?"

"A good sized crowd. The Legion regulars loved what he had to say about security."

"Which was?"

"He said the islands are vulnerable to terrorism, given our location away from any actual land borders. at we have to be more vigilant, be better prepared to track illegals using the San Juans as a bridge to the mainland. He never came out and said we've got to have cell towers on all the islands, but it was there."

"How did the crowd react?"

"With that crowd, it was pretty much preaching to the choir, but the consensus around town seems to be that he's got a good chance of winning. His only opponent is the Breckenridge woman. And she's viewed as somewhat unstable."

"What do you mean, *unstable*?"

He finished off the tortilla and chile verde, swallowed, and shrugged. " The kidnapping. Her brother being murdered. Divorcing her husband and running off to Seattle."

"She didn't ask to be kidnapped, Jared." My voice was snappish. I hate trite generalizations. "Her brother's murder didn't have anything to do with her and at least 50% of the people on this island have been divorced. Some more than once." There was a long silence. "Have you seen McCready's posters?" I asked nally. " The ones labeling Tina's family as murderers?"

"Doesn't mince any words, does he? How is Tina connected to the Gundersen murder?"

"Hazel Gundersen was her great-aunt."

Another silence. then he asked, "Is Tina Breckenridge your client?"

"Tina is desperate to stop his smear tactics. Swears that Hazel was innocent. at all the evidence was circumstantial. She wants me to help her clear Hazel's name and shut down McCready. Her Aunt Jeanette will pay my fee."

Jared gave a low whistle. "Not a bad assignment for your first week back. Are you going to investigate the investigators?"

"Don't know yet. At first glance, the verdict rested on testimony given by a drunken brother and a neighbor. No real forensic evidence, even though the police virtually took Hazel's farm apart. The whole case seems bizarre. A grisly murder on Orcas Island."

"The evidence scene was a very different one 39 back then. I can make the archives in the Gazette's backroom available. And I'd bet there's a stack of moldy files over at the courthouse." He laid one hand over mine. "Remember, McKinnon, that the lowest and vilest alleys in London do not present a more dreadful record of sin . . ."

". . than does the smiling and beautiful countryside. Point taken."

"Now tell me about the sailing adventure. Are you in love? Is this chap Farraday coming here to live? Is he going to move aboard *DragonSpray*?"

Chapter 5
OLDE GAZETTE BUILDING

Friday Harbor

Are you in love?

Jared's question echoed in my head as I trudged through the wind and rain back to the OGB. I'd avoided a direct response, chattering about the sail from Lisbon to Porto Sollér, described the brother's hillside villa and the Greek neighbors' domestic dramas, and finally got off the hook when Jared was called away to cover a fracas out at Roche Harbor.

Dakota was back to snoozing in front of the wood stove, Zelda conversing on her phone about something called passage cairns. She waved and pointed dramatically at the white board, wriggling her eyebrows lasciviously. There was a message in the lower corner: Scotia: *Check your cubby. Nick called.* I retrieved two pink phone slips from the cubby, wondering why the hell Nick Anastazi was calling.

Nick and I had been an item since before I moved to Friday Harbor, back when he had a maritime law practice in San Francisco. After his divorce he moved to Seattle to be near daughter Nicole, where he opened an office with two former Bay Area colleagues. He bought a house here on the island, up on Mt. Dallas, for weekend getaways. I'd spent many steamy nights there and we'd shared occasional weekends aboard *DragonSpray*, anchored in one or another of our secluded island coves. It took me several years to realize that the romance was superficial, that Nick never disconnected from his ex-wife. She called or stopped by whenever she was in trouble and I never ceased to be anathema to Nicole. In fact, the proverbial last straw was Nicole's wedding: *It would really be awkward, Scotty. Nicole is just not comfortable having you there with her mother. You probably wouldn't enjoy it anyway*. At which point, Michael Farraday, a.k.a. Falcon, had entered, stage left.

The numbers on Nick's message were both his cell phone and the Mt. Dallas house. The other message was from Tina Breckenridge, with a call back request. Behind me, Zelda finished her phone call. "A voice from the past, eh boss? He sounded really anxious to hear from you. Made me promise that I'd give you the message soonest."

I shrugged and threw Nick's message in the wastebasket. "Zebras don't change their stripes. Or is it leopards and spots? Anyway, what was that about a Police Academy course last night? Are you going into law enforcement?"

"No, but I'm thinking of becoming a bail enforcement agent."

"You mean a bounty hunter?"

"Yeah. They can make really big bucks. I've learned all the stuff about investigations and surveillance from working with you, so it should be a piece of cake."

"How big are the bucks?"

"Sometimes they get a percentage of the bail, like ten or twenty percent, sometimes just a flat fee. I heard a really good one who will work multiple states to get in on high bail, high profile cases can earn around seventy-five grand."

"So you'd go traveling to track down the skips."

"Yes, indeed. I can go anywhere in the U.S. The skips could be from Montana, Florida, California, Colorado. By the way, Colorado has a whole lots of wanted bozos."

"How many bounty hunters do we have in the county?"

"None, that I can find."

"So, no competition. We don't even have any bail bondsmen here, do we?"

"Nope. Which means that the bondsmen in Mt. Vernon or Anacortes or Oak Harbor or some other state really need some-body to catch the skips that're hiding out here in the deep dark woods. Or living on a boat, or in any of the hundred or so part-time vacation properties."

"You've given this a lot of thought."

"Yes, ma'am. I found this bail skip software, where you can design your own Wanted posters." She chortled. "How cool is that?'

I agreed that designing one's own Wanted posters was way cool and headed upstairs. I dialed Tina Breckenridge and told her I would take her case.

"I found some new stuff," she said. "When can we meet?"

"Are you okay coming to the office?"

She was silent for a minute. "I know at least

three of the men at the Netshed recognized me this morning, so what the hell."

We set up a four o'clock meeting, which would give me time to do more reading and start devising a plan to keep McCready at bay, at least temporarily. I'd turned my cell phone off at lunch. Now I turned it on and found a new text from Jewel Moon. *Hv u talkd 2 to Melissa? I'm so excited.* Exasperated with my mother's cryptic communications, I dialed Melissa's number, got her VM: *I'm actually available but cannot find the phone. Leave a message. I'll call as soon as I find it.*

"Melissa, please call me so I can share your grandmother's excitement."

It was too early for news on admission to graduate school. Maybe a rich boyfriend?

I checked e-mail, looking for a forwarded message from Harrison Petrovsky's sister. It wasn't there. I pulled out the Gundersen file and began reading the internet report on the Gundersen case Zelda has produced. It was extensive, running to a dozen pages.

On January 15, 1982, Hazel Kortig Gundersen shoots her 80-year-old husband, Peder Gundersen, a retired Puget Sound ship's pilot, in the head following an argument and a fight in an Eastsound bar over his retirement fund. With the assistance of her brother, Fred Kortig, Jr., who was visiting from Wisconsin, Hazel disposes of the body by cutting up it up with an ax and passing it through a commercial meat grinder, and then burning the ground-up remains in a burn barrel, ultimately mixing the ashes in a pile of horse manure behind their Orcas Island stable.

The article recounted how the San Juan County Sheriff's Office had first o pened a missing persons investigation upon receiving a report from Arne Ormdahl, another ship pilot and a close friend of Peder's, that he was unable to contact Peder and that Hazel was claiming Peder was in Norway.

Two Orcas island deputies, Matthew Lion and Herb Vidrine, were sent to the Gundersen residence to investigate, and interviewed various neighbors, but found no evidence to dispute Hazel's story. In August 1984, Hazel's niece, Jeanette Gish, who lived in Seattle, contacted the authorities with a story that she had received a drunken phone call from Hazel confessng that she and her brother 'killed the SOB'. Gish provided a written statement that was forwarded to the San Juan County Sheriff's Office. Deputy Lion obtained a warrant to search the Gundersen residence and property. He was accompanied by two sheriff's deputies and a criminalist from the Washington State Patrol laboratory. The group searched for eight days and logged over 600 pieces of potential evidence.

Five years elapsed between the first call from Arne Ormdahl to the trial and sentencing. After weeks of testimony and eight days of deliberation, Hazel Gundersen was found guilty of first degree murder, and sentenced to life in prison. The attorney appealed, the appeal was rejected, and she died in prison nineteen years later.

There were a number of items I marked for follow up. What were the circumstances of the vessel grounding that caused Peder to lose his pilot license? Did the investigators hire a P.I. in Norway to track the Captain and the alleged girl friend? What was bothersome was that all of the evidence cited on the History link seemed to be hearsay, contradictory, or circumstantial. What happened to the carpet and floor pieces that had blood on them? Were they thrown out or preserved? Tina had mentioned blood spatters on the ceiling. Was the blood matched to Peder? With so many missing pieces, how had twelve people arrived at a unanimous verdict of 1st degree murder?

I stood up, stretched, and peered through my dirty window. Across the street high school had just let out for the day. The rain had stopped, the sky was still a battleship gray. The recent rain was denuding the maple trees outside the building. Students poured out onto the street, some alone, some in groups of two or three, some walking, some heading for waiting cars. Some laughing, some silent, some sullen. I remembered how public school had been for Stephan Breckenridge. The truancy, the drug temptations. I hoped the International School would provide better guidance. I was fortunate that Melissa's high school years had been mostly trouble-free. And then I wondered again what it was that Jewel Moon's congratulatory texts were about. I resolved to track down Melissa and solve the mystery.

My phone rang. It was Tina Breckenridge.

"Scotia, I'm not going to make it today. Stephan got in a fight with the kid who's been bullying him on Facebook. I have to go talk to the headmaster. Could we meet tomorrow? I found some stuff on the ship grounding." She was talking fast and her voice crackled with stress.

"Give me a call when you get things sorted out. Good luck."

"Thanks, I need all I can get." Her voice broke and then she cut the connection.

I hung up the phone. Was there more to Stephan's school problems than just his mom's political campaign? Was Tina over protective? I knew she'd home-schooled Stephan, but at some point you have to turn your kids loose. Now she had to deal with her ex-husband wanting custody. She sounded like she was at a breaking point. I decided to pack up all the Gundersen stuff, call it a day, and head down to the boat. I checked my e-mail before shutting down the computer and found a message Carolyn Smith had forwarded from Luisa Petrovsky.

Harrison left Mahe Island in the Seychelles 10 days ago. His crew was a woman named Michelle Yee. They were headed for Mafia Island (Somalia? Tanzania?) to do some diving. Michelle's sister and brother-in-law own an eco-resort there. I don't know what it's called. He was posting their daily position on his Facebook page and on his blog. The plan was to spend a month on Mafia diving, then head south around the Cape and across the Atlantic. I've tried to call him on his satphone, but I only get VM. I've texted him and e-mailed him. I'm really worried. How can we find him?

I'd never heard of Ma a Island and I'm not a social media person. Much to Melissa's chagrin. I Googled for Harrison Petrovsky's Facebook page, found a few photographs about *Ocean Dancer* and a shot of him embracing a petite, dark-haired Asian woman with long hair. I tried to view his postings, but learned that I couldn't do that unless he accepted me as a friend. And to be a friend, I had to have a Facebook page. *Merde*!

I responded to Luisa with a copy to Carolyn Smith. *I will try to locate your brother. Please send me the positions Harrison has been posting. I'll do some research tomorrow on Ma a Island, try to contact the resort. Maybe they've already arrived.*

Meanwhile, I wasn't going to lose any sleep over the matter. Knowing Harrison Petrovsky, he and Michelle Yee were probably lolling around on some atoll, sipping cocktails and watching the sun set over the Indian Ocean. Or were atolls confined to the South Pacific?

Chapter 6

S/V DragonSpray

Port of Friday Harbor

Empty parking spaces predominated along Spring Street and I counted nearly as many clerks as customers at the market. I picked up a hand basket, headed for the frozen foods section, found citrus spareribs, Mandarin chicken and two small frozen thin crust pizzas. Dinner covered for three days. From the produce department I garnered a package of organic Romaine lettuce, two limes, some ripened-on-the-vine tomatoes, and half a dozen small cans of pet food. Maybe Calico would put in an appearance tonight. If not, I would corner Henry.

As I considered adding catnip to the basket, my cell phone chirped. I glanced at the sender and a little butterfly fluttered in my solar plexis. *Miss you. Incredibly busy. Talk soon. Falcon.*

That was *it*? After five days? Too busy to pick up a phone for three minutes? The little butterfly stilled. I pocketed the phone and walked toward the checkout stand.

"Scotia!"

It was Angela Petersen. Sheriff's deputy, my best friend and second island confidante. Her tan face was full of smiles. "You came back. We were taking bets that you wouldn't. That you would ask us to auction off *DragonSpray* and wire the money to the Med." She came around the counter and we exchanged a hug. "Missed you," she whispered, then moved back to look at me. "You look gorgeous. I've got a meeting five minutes ago, but can we get together tomorrow? A swim? A drink? Both? Health club's under new ownership. Lots to tell you. I need some advice."

"Absolutely. Swim at four. Drinks after."

"See you at the club and I want to know everything," she flung over her shoulder as she grabbed her paper sack and dashed for the door.

Everything, of course, meant Falcon, and I wouldn't be able to put her off as I did Jared. I swiped my debit card, took the large sack from the cashier, and made my way out the door and down the street. A heavy mist had settled in, and I didn't run into anyone I knew. The real estate office had a lot of listings in the display window and I mused briefly what it would be like to live in a real house again. At thirty-eight feet *DragonSpray* was spacious enough for me, but except for brief visits from Melissa and my mother, and weekends with Nick, I'd never lived with anyone aboard. What if Falcon *did* decide to reallocate to Friday Harbor? Could I get used to sharing my space? Did I want to?

The marina was enveloped in fog. I exchanged nods with a liveaboard couple from "F" dock who were trudging up the hill toward the showers. Out on "G" dock, *Pumpkinseed* was showing a light in the main cabin window. I didn't see Calico about, so I slid the sack of groceries and my carryall with the Gundersen file onto *DragonSpray*'s deck and knocked on Henry's bulkhead. He opened the door on the stern deck and peered out. "Scotia. It's you. What can I do for you?"

"I haven't seen Calico since I've been back. Have you got her locked up?" I asked in a teasing tone.

He stared at me for a minute, frowned, and looked away. "I gave her away."

"What d'ya mean, you *gave* her away. She was my cat, too."

He shrugged. "You left. Not a word about when you'd be back. She sat on *DragonSpray* for a week after you left. Waiting for you."

"Who did you give her to?"

"To Lindsey."

"The redhead? The bartender at George's?"

"She moved over to the Legion."

"I thought you two got un-engaged. Are you and she still . . . ?"

" We're talking," he said curtly, backing through the door and closing it.

I felt a lump come up in my throat. I stared at the closed door, unreasonably sad. I loved Calico. It was true she'd just wandered in one day, dividing her time between our two boats. But I fed her, or Henry would when I was away. She would creep in at night through the open hatch cover and snuggle around my feet. Sometimes she was the only living creature on the dock that cared or knew whether I came home. How could Henry have done that? We used to be friends. How had that gone wrong?

I put away the groceries, got one of my green

Spanish highball glasses from the cupboard, added ice and dry vermouth, topped it off with club soda and a sliver of lime. I put on the local TV news with the sound muted, and settled down at the table in the salon, trying not to think about a small furry creature keeping a vigil for me. With a lined tablet at hand, I opened the Gunderson file and began making notes on anything that might help Tina, trying not to listen for little toenails scratching at the hatch covers. Two hours later I stretched, gathered up my notes and reviewed what I'd learned about *The State of Washington v. Hazel Gundersen.*

Neither Hazel's niece, Jeanette Gish, nor Hazel's friend and neighbor, Brenda Sue Benton, had witnessed the murder. When Hazel and her brother, Fred Kortig, Jr., were summoned to the Sheriff's Office, both denied under oath any knowledge of Peder being murdered. Both swore that Peder had either returned to Norway or had committed suicide because he was depressed about the vessel mishap, for which he lost his pilot's license.

The deputies found a .38 caliber Smith and Wesson revolver in the woods near the house. Both Hazel's and Peder's fingerprints were found on the gun, and there was nothing to prove that it had been used to commit a murder. Brenda Sue described places where traces of blood and other evidence could be found. The deputies did, in fact, cut out pieces of carpet and flooring and ceiling and found blood stains, but there was no proof the blood stains (in all three locations) were not created during the couple's endless domestic battles. The blood type on the carpet and in the concrete was Type A, which was shared by both Hazel and Peder. No forensic evidence was ever found in the septic tank or drain field or manure pile. The one piece of testimony that was based on evidence was given by a blood spatter expert: that the blood spatters on the ceiling were consistent with those made by a gunshot wound. He also testified that he could not say whether the blood was animal or human.

Aside from that testimony, there was no evidence, physical or demonstrative, that there had ever been a murder.

The question remained: how had twelve jurors been convinced beyond a reasonable doubt to send an old woman to prison for life? How had the evidence passed the *corpus delicti* rule?

The term comes from Western jurisprudence and is one of the most important concepts in a murder investigation. Corpus delicti, from the Latin, "body of crime," refers not to the deceased, but to the "body of evidence" which can be physical, demonstrative or testimonial evidence. It refers to the principle that it must be proven that a crime has been committed before a person can be convicted. There is a corollary to this rule: that an accused cannot be convicted solely upon the testimony of an accomplice. The best evidence that a murder has been committed is the physical body of the deceased.

Tomorrow I would see if I could get access to the court records and, if Tina brought it in, I would review the information on the ship incident that had caused Peder to lose his pilot's license. I replenished my drink, put the citrus spareribs in the microwave, and turned up the audio on the TV. The world had not improved since the morning news. A self-serve coffee kiosk was opening in Seattle that was viewed as a job threat to hundreds of baristas in the city. A high-tech Canadian company announced the development of a micro-UAV that was battery powered and GPS-guided and could be flown by anyone with only a few minutes of training. The Dow had lost 255 points.

I turned off the TV, refreshed my drink, switched on the old multi-disc CD player and loaded it with my favorites. Kitaro's *Silk Road* was a good accompaniment to the salad and spareribs. While I ate, I thought about the missing Harrison Petrovsky. Something Luisa said in her e-mail troubled me, but I couldn't quite identify it. Something about Facebook. I suppose one day soon I would have to succumb to social media, if only to keep up with my daughter. As I cleaned up the galley I reminded myself to track down Melissa and find out what her news was. And then I would do the same with Falcon. To hell with re-lationship protocol. I don't do well with unexplained silences. Or cryptic text messages.

Rain, accompanied by occasional gusts of wind that shook *DragonSpray* on her lines, had started again, pattering on the cabin top. I settled into the settee in the main salon and dialed Melissa's cell phone. After four rings I got her voice recording: *Thank you for calling the Oval Office. The President is not available at this time. Please leave your name, phone number, the name of the country you wish to invade, and the secret password you received with your SuperPac donation.*

I bit my lower lip and waited for the beep and recorded my own creativity. "Melissa, this is your mother who's been making SuperPac donations for the past twenty-one years. Call me back tonight, or I will disinherit you tomorrow."

Next I scrolled up Falcon's name on my People list, my index finger hovering over his mobile phone number. When he was packing for the flight back to London, he'd said he would probably be up to his eyeballs in negotiations over the estate for several weeks, that he would have to trade something to get the house in Scotland, but we would be in touch. When we parted at the airport in Madrid, he to catch the British Airways flight to Heathrow, me running for the Iberia flight to Seattle, he asked that I let him know when I got back. When I staggered off the plane at SeaTac it was the middle of the night in London, so I'd texted him. He'd replied with a text that included an abrazo and a promise to call soon. That was six days ago or maybe seven. I glanced at the clock on my phone, thumbed up the time zone converter app. It was 4:11 a.m. in the U.K.

Disconsolate, I put down the phone and stretched out on the settee. *Silk Road* was replaced by Enya's *Orinoco Flow.* I heard the last float plane from Seattle come in, then I felt *DragonSpray* rock gently in the wake. Above my head a halyard tap-

tapped against the mast in the wind. I tried ignoring it. Sometimes that worked. Enya exited and another CD snicked into place.

The rain came down hard, pounding on the cabin top. Wind rocked the boat. I fretted about Calico. Did she have a warm and dry place to sleep? Or did Lindsey leave her outside to fend for herself against marauding raccoons and predatory foxes while she was tending bar until 2:00 a.m.?

From what seemed a great distance I heard the float plane take off and sometime around the third track of Songs from an English Garden, I dozed off, slipping into a shadowy space of fog and wind, walking along the cliffs out at Lime Kiln. Up ahead on the rocky trail I glimpsed the figure of a woman. She was calling out to someone or something on the path ahead of her. I quickened my steps, saw that it was Henry's girlfriend, Lindsey the Redhead. The someone she was talking to was Calico, who was scurrying away from her. They approached a sharp curve in the trail and Calico darted away, out to the very edge of the crumbling cliff, Redhead in swift pursuit. I felt a black rage well up inside of me.

"Hey, you idiot, stop chasing her," I screamed and began running. "She's going to fall over."

Redhead glanced over her shoulder. "Shut your trap. I can do what I want. She's mine now."

Furious, I gasped as Calico disappeared. 56

I raced ahead, trying to grab Redhead by the shoulder. As we approached the edge of the cliff, I had only one intent. Ten seconds later I caught up to her and shoved her with all my strength and watched as she screamed and disappeared over the edge. I crouched down and peered over, saw Redhead's limp body resting on a huge jagged black rock below. I scanned the rock-strewn hillside and called to Calico. Silence. I called again and then I heard a faint "meow" and I saw her, tucked into a crevice just below the edge of the cliff and to the left. I lay down, grabbed onto a straggly branch of something, and reached out for her, felt her cold nose with my hand, heard a ringing behind me, and woke up.

I grabbed the phone. A new text message from Melissa. *Call u tmorrow. Luv u.*

Chapter 7
OLD GAZETTE BUILDING

Friday Harbor

On Tuesday I got to the OGB at the ridiculous hour of eight o'clock. The rain had stopped and thick wet fog shrouded the harbor. Following the unsettling dream about Calico and the Redhead, followed by the non-message from Melissa, I'd taken myself to bed, sleeping restlessly, waking when the first ferry from Anacortes arrived at six o'clock. Whereupon I gave up on sleep, dressed, located my swim gear, and went for a run out to the University labs. After a shower, I dressed in a clean pair of blue jeans and the white sweater Falcon bought me in Lisbon. An hour later, the market was just opening and beckoned me in to purchase two warm cranberry orange scones. Mini scones.

There was a thick envelope wedged into the front door of the OGB. The envelope contained a stack of newspaper clippings and internet printouts on the ship grounding back in 1980. A note from Tina was taped to the envelope: *Can't make it this morning, will call this afternoon.* I set up the coffee maker, considered making a fire and decided not to. Upstairs I added the clippings to the Gundersen file, turned on the wall heater, downloaded my e-mail.

Scanning past the *NY Times* latest headlines and the local weather, I found a message from sailing friend Ron Callahan imploring me to crew for the Harvest Moon Regatta on Saturday. My history with Ron was that several years ago I'd helped his attorney put together a case for allowing Ron to retain custody of his daughter after his wife ran off with a ferry boat captain. I had no better offers for the weekend, so I replied that I would crew as long as I didn't have to do foredeck.

The next message was a notification from my bank that my monthly online statement was available. I clicked up the website, looked up my secret password that was pasted to the back of a binder labeled Family Tree, and reviewed my checking account and two investment accounts. The market had taken a big dip while I was away. I'd monitored everything periodically from Porto Sollér, but only now did the reality hit me of how closely I would have to watch my spending until I picked up some new clients. I stared at the summary of my account and for the first time seriously considered the idea of creating a business Facebook page to lure in new business. I abhorred the idea of putting myself out there for millions of internet surfers, but Zelda could help me with firewalls or privacy levels or whatever.

Lastly, there was a message from Luisa Petrovsky: *I'm listing the positions Harrison posted before he stopped. The resort that Michelle's sister owns is Pendana Shangani. Their website is below. I can't find a phone number or an e-mail address. I will keep trying to call him every day. I am so afraid they may have run into bad weather and capsized. Please help.*

To make sense of Harrison's postings, which were in latitude and longitude, I would have to plot them to figure out where Harrison had disappeared off the radar en route to Mafia Island. Since he'd already made it more than half way round the world, I doubted he had capsized. Although there, was always the rogue wave. I clicked on the link to the Pendana Shangani.

The website touted it as a luxury eco-resort with 15 bungalows on the island of Mafia, one of the Tanzanian Spice Islands. Mafia, whose name means archipelago in Arabic and has nothing to do with organized crime, is reached by a slow ferry from mainland Tanzania or a 30-minute flight from Dar es Salaam. The website photo gallery included shots of beautiful chocolate brown faces, fishing dhows, and a thatched roof lodge located inside the Mafia Island Marine Park. The undersea dive pictures showcased a number of specimens I would prefer not to meet up with, either above or below the water.

And Luisa was right: there was no e-mail address or phone number shown. I found this peculiar. The best I could do was to submit my own contact information, requesting that they let me know if Harrison Petrovsky and crew had arrived or if they had any information as to the whereabouts of *Ocean Dancer*. After which I e-mailed Luisa and Carolyn, put Harrison's nautical posts aside for later.

I went downstairs for coffee to discover I'd forgotten to turn on the brew button. As I was cursing my stupidity, the door opened and a slight, wiry, white-haired man came in. He had a professorial stoop and wore a dark green anorak over a dark sweater and blue jeans. Wondering if he was a new client or one of Zelda's admirers, I belatedly realized this was the British scientist and photographer who had moved into the space formerly occupied by Soraya, the naturopath from Orcas.

"Good morning," he said with a smile. "You must be Scotia MacKinnon, the lady investigator." His smile was warm, his eyes were a piercing glacial blue.

I admitted my identity. "And you must be the gentleman scientist from London."

He blinked and extended a hand. "From Bristol, actually. Anthony Bolton at your service. Please call me Tony." We shook hands. I'm not one for early morning small talk, but I did my best. "What brings you all the way to Friday Harbor, Tony?"

"Abigail Leedle. I came across her book on the foxes and she friended me on Facebook. I e-mailed her. Turns out we share a number of common interests. I'm on my way to Africa."

At that point Zelda and Dakota arrived. Zelda wore a long black trench coat over a red micro-mini-skirt and black fishnet stockings with knee-high black boots. She hung the raincoat on a peg near the door. Tony's cell phone rang, and he disappeared into his office. Dumping a daypack on her desk, Zelda gave me a long inquiring look. I must have looked worse than I felt. "Bad night?" she said. "Anything you want to talk about? Man trouble? Daughter trouble? Boat problems?" She motioned to the chair beside her desk. "Sit."

I put the scones on a paper plate and sat. "Insomnia," I lied. "How was the Police Academy class?" Dakota hovered around looking hopeful. When I ignored him, he circled three times on the rug in front of the stove and lay down.

"Awesome. The topic for last night was crime scene investigation. CSI. It started out with a pep talk from the Sheriff. About sheep and sheepdogs and warriors. About how most people in our society are sheep, but the sheep are in denial about all the bad guys, the wolves, so there have to be sheepdogs to take care of them. And warriors."

"You're going to become a warrior?" The coffee maker produced a final burble and gasp. I filled my cup. She grinned, then sighed. "Probably have to settle for being a sheepdog. The CSI tech was from Oak Harbor. We spent a lot of time learning about fingerprinting. Did you know that your lifestyle can affect the ridges of your fingerprints? And that door handles are the hardest places to get prints?" She got up and filled the large blue *What Happens in Friday Harbor* mug. "The coolest thing was the shoeprinting. Next week we'll learn about wilderness tracking from T.J. Tahoma."

"Is that a name I should know?"

" T. J. is the new park ranger here. Used to work with the Alaska Coast Guard."

"I thought the Alaska Coast Guard did ocean rescues. Where did the tracking come in?"

"His grandfather was a Navajo tracker. He's going to teach me."

"Could be important when you're chasing varmints with a price on their head," I offered between bites of the scone.

"I betcha if crooks ever took a C.S.I. course, they'd change careers in a heartbeat. Between fingerprints, shoeprinting, electronic surveillance, and DNA, most don't have a chance."

"What did you learn about DNA?"

"The turnaround time on most DNA analysis is six months to a year. That would really slow down a court case, huh? Unless you send it to a private lab and then it's two to five weeks."

I thought about my far-fetched idea that if any of the evidence on the Gundersen case had been stored, it might be possible to get a DNA analysis. Although I wasn't sure what I would match it to. "What does a private lab charge for DNA analysis?"

"Between two and five thousand dollars."

"You covered a lot in one evening."

"We finished up with blood spatter and GSR."

"I think that's what convicted Hazel Gundersen."

"Gunshot residue? But there was no body."

"No, the blood spatters on the ceiling. I need to look at the actual court records, but apparently the expert testified that the pattern was consistent with a gunshot wound."

"But who did they match the blood to?"

"Exactly."

"I'm free this morning after I make a few calls. How about I trot over to the courthouse and see what I can find?"

Unless it involves technical internet research, I prefer to review records myself. Information you didn't know existed sometimes turns up and you have to follow it down unexpected paths. I still didn't have a signed contract with Tina Breckenridge, but while Zelda was talking her way into the court archives, I could pursue contact with Hazel Gunderson's defense attorney. "Good idea. Give me a few minutes and I'll make a list of the testimony and the witnesses I'm interested in." I swallowed the last of the scone and took my coffee upstairs. "I also need a complete list of the jurors, if you can get it."

Twenty minutes later I handed her my list. "If it's available, I'd like a copy of the audio recording of the testimony. If not, then paper copies."

"Will do, boss. By the way, you're invited to the next meeting of the Coronas. We're meeting out at Abby's for a special session Sunday afternoon. Abby and Lily and me and Tina and Peg."

"Peg O'Reilly? Seriously?"

"Yeah, she hates McCready"

"How's Tina doing?"

"Her wasband is back on the island."

"Paul Breckendridge? Already?"

"He found out about M's hate publicity campaign, so he came back early."

"I thought the Coronas met at George's."

"This is an executive session. Special agenda. You get three guesses. First two don't count."

"McCready."

"He was at C & S last night, huddled for over an hour with two honchos in black jackets. Wish I'd had a parabolic mike."

"A bug in his martini olive would be less noticeable."

"Has anyone ever done that? Bugged an olive?"

"According to the lore, an infamous San Francisco P.I. embedded a miniature transmitter inside a pimento inside an olive. And the toothpick in the olive housed a copper wire as an antenna."

"That is so FFO."

"Yeah. So, what am I expected to a contribute to the executive meeting on Sunday?"

"We want to put together a rebuttal to Mc-Cready's negative propaganda."

"And you want my creative input?"

"What's legal, what's not. How far we can go."

"As in the First Amendment cuts both ways?"

She smiled. "By the weekend I plan to know a lot more about M than what he's included in his cute little brochure." She waved a copy of the flyer I'd looked at yesterday. "Whatever I find out will help Tina. Just in case you can't get her aunt's conviction overturned."

"I don't think 'overturned' is precisely the right term."

"We've already got a head start."

"How so?"

"After the Black Jackets left, according to the grapevine, M was reported fondling a beautiful blonde that sounds like Elyse Montenegro."

"Are you sure it was Elyse? Maybe it was his wife." Elyse Montenegro was the stable manager at Ravenswood Stables and a former client of mine. I would have thought she had better sense than to get involved with a married politician.

"No. I found a picture of wifey. She's dark-haired. Not sure about fondable." The main office phone rang. She glanced at the buttons on the phone. "It's for you."

I headed upstairs, thinking it was probably Tina,

hoping it was Melissa. It was Carolyn Smith. When she told me why she was calling, I knew what had been nagging me about Harrison Petrovsky's postings. Carolyn's first words confirmed it.

Chapter 8

OLD GAZETTE BUILDING

Friday Harbor

"Petrovsky and his crew have been kidnapped."

"Who kidnapped them?"

"Somali pirates."

"How do you know that?"

"Luisa got a phone call from Harrison in the middle of the night."

"When did this happen?"

"Four or five days ago."

"Since he's been posting his position all the way from the Seychelles, he can't have been surprised."

"Sorry?"

"Haven't you been following the piracy in the Indian Ocean?"

"I thought it was declining. I heard all the bad stuff was further east. In the South China Sea."

"There've been fewer boardings, but posting your GPS location on line when you're sailing from the Seychelles to the east coast of Africa is tantamount to saying, hey pirate dudes, here we are, come and find us."

"So what are we talking about? Is this life threatening?"

"We're talking about a bunch of young thugs in fiberglass skiffs and rusty or not so rusty Kalishnikovs. They like to patrol the waters up to 1500 miles off the coast of East Africa, working from mother ships in the Indian Ocean."

"This is going to be nasty, isn't it?"

"If he's been kidnapped by pirates, it will be nas-ty. I hate to sound unsympathetic, but there's no way Harrison *wouldn't* have known how dangerous the Indian Ocean is. One couple from the U.K. was held for over a year while the pirates tried to extort millions from their family. It was on all the cruising websites. Last year a cruising family with children were captured. No one knows where they're being held. Or even if they're still alive. The IMB has a whole website devoted to piracy."

"IMB?"

"International Maritime Bureau. They've got a 24-four hour reporting centers somewhere in Malaysia."

Carolyn was silent for a minute. "I remember now. Those two sailors from Seattle, the pirates killed them."

"They did. What exactly did Harrison tell Luisa?"

"That they were boarded three days out of the Seychelles and their cell phones and satphone was confiscated. At first they thought they were just going to be robbed. The pirates virtually took the boat apart looking for money. When all they found were a few thousand dollars, they beat them. They're on land now, but he's not sure if it's Somalia or further south. The woman is not good shape."

"Do we know what the pirates are asking for?"

"He's not sure. The interpreter's name is Hassan. He's going to call tomorrow. Scotia, how does all this work? Will they kill Harrison and Michelle if the family can't meet their demands?"

"Kidnapping is a business with the Somali pirates. They actually have investors backing them. They try to figure out what the hostages are worth and keep asking for an outrageous ransom. The best way to deal with them is through a risk-management firm that does hostage retrieval."

"Can you recommend one?"

"The people I used to work for in San Francisco, H & W Security, have expanded. They're now H & W Risk Management. They've brought in some special force's people and intelligence analysts. They're not cheap. Probably around $3,000 a day."

"Petra is going to have a coronary."

"These dudes are perfectly serious. If the family wants to see Harrison any time soon, you may have to petition the court to distribute the money."

"How much will they ask for?"

"Depends on how much they think the family is worth. They assume anyone who can afford a sailing yacht is rich. They'll start with several million dollars. Let's hope Harrison doesn't tell them about the will."

"Luisa says she'll give up her inheritance if that's necessary. So what happens now? What's the first step?"

"If you retain H & W, the first step will be to form what they call a crisis management team."

"Which is?"

"Family members and colleagues that can look after Harrison's interests. Might be a good idea to find out something about his crew. Does her family have any money? Or influence?"

"I'll see what I can find out. Then what's nex?"

"H & W will establish contact with the kidnappers. Possibly through a local contact. Then it negotiates the ransom. The family should know this could take months, unless either Harrison or Michelle have friends in very high places."

"Please call H & W. I'll take it from there."

I hung up the phone. Harrison's stupidity was going to be costly. He and Michelle Yee would prob-ably come out of it alive if they didn't make any more stupid moves.

Falcon and I had followed the piracy updates online, hoping that the seagoing thugs didn't start marauding farther north, into the Med. Piracy was down from what it had been a few years earlier, but at last count something like 15 ships were being held, ranging from small wooden dhous to European supertankers, along with hundreds of hostages. Ransom collected was averaging several million per ship. Until the fatal incident involving the Seattle couple, the violence was minimal. Since then, a number of governments have gotten involved, pirates have been captured, tried, and sentenced in various countries. One rescue incident involved the Navy SEALS, snatching two aid workers out of a pirate compound. Now it was more like war.

I pulled out my leather address book and found the number for H & W Risk Management. Jules Du-

Pont, my former boss, was in the office and available to talk to me.

"It's about time. Thought you forgot about us. Did you ever catch up with the itinerant sailor you were chasing all over the South Pacific the last time we talked? Or was it the South China Sea?"

"Captain Petrovsky has been kidnaped."

"By landlubbers or by pirates?"

"The latter. He was headed from the Seychelles en route to some place called Mafia Island. Posting his position along the way."

"Nice place, Mafia Island."

"You've been there?"

" Myra and I spent a week there diving last year after we assisted a French TV star retrieve his yacht from the Somalis."

"Dare I ask what that cost the TV star?"

"Not quite seven million. But it was just the yacht, no hostages involved. And you'll never read about it in the news. Now tell me about Captain Petrovsky. Is he alone? Have they taken him inland? Do you want H & W to be involved?"

I told him what I knew and that Carolyn Smith was representing the family.

"It's not necessary that we meet with their negotiator and sometimes it's best not to. But I have a man in Nairobi just now. He's meeting with some U.K. people at the anti-piracy intelligence center they've established. If the family decides they're willing to ransom the hapless brother, let me know. Meanwhile, it's best that anyone who talks to the pirates not disclose anything. Although the pirates have most likely done their own search on the family. They're pretty savvy as far as the internet goes. I'm available. Just let me know."

"What are your fees these days?"

"We usually charge a percentage of the ransom, but that's negotiable."

I told him Carolyn Smith would be in touch, sent best wishes to Myra. I hung up the phone and e-mailed the H & W contact info to Carolyn, along with a link to the International Maritime Bureau's update on piracy. I also cautioned her that Luisa should be discreet in any conversation with Hassan. I thought about the ordeal the British couple had survived, and the tragic deaths of the people from Seattle. After a few months eating fried bread and spaghetti in 100-degree Somali heat, Harrison would regret not facing the wrath of the pregnant fiancée's father. With the Petrovsky matter in Jules DuPont's hands, I went back to the Gundersen file.

Chapter 9
OLD GAZETTE BUILDING

Friday Harbor

Downstairs was quiet and cozy. Zelda had built a fire before she left for the courthouse. Tony Bolton's door was closed. chitchat. I rummaged in the little fridge, wished I'd picked up a tuna sandwich at the market. The only thing I found was a carton of straw-berry yogurt whose use-by date had not expired. I took it upstairs, ate it, checked my cell phone, found a text from Callahan, my racing friend: *Foredeck is covered. Meet at the y.c. at 9 sat. rain forecast.*

No word from Melissa. No further words of congratulation from Jewel Moon. Nothing from Falcon. I leafed through the Gundersen file, thought about Falcon. Read the clippings on the ship grounding, thought about Falcon. It was something like nine p.m. in London. Ditto in Cornwall, where his sister lived. I would call him.

Three rings, then the recording, the voice calm, deep and sexy. *You've reached the mobile number for Michael Farraday. Leave a message or ring back later.*

"Michael, it's Scotia. Just checking in. I miss you."

Oh, well. Nothing ventured and so on. I texted Zelda to bring back a tuna sandwich, and began reading the voluminous clippings on the 1980 ship incident – a grounding more than a collision -- which took over an hour. I turned to my computer, opened a new sub-file, and began to summarize the situation that had cost Peder Gundersen his pilot's license.

On October 15, at 3:45 in the afternoon, the container ship Polar Sea was heading northeast in Haro Straight off the coast of San Juan Island. The vessel was headed for Boundary Pass and the Straight of Georgia, en route to Vancouver. Master of the vessel was 45 year-old Captain Dragomir Zorco, a Russian national. Piloting the vessel was 78-year old Puget Sound Pilot Peder Gundersen. To enter Boundary Pass, the vessel had to make a sharp turn to starboard at Turn Point on Stuart Island.

As confirmed later by the captain of the S.V. Four Winds, a 30-foot sailing vessel that was proceeding southeast under sail in Haro Straight just off the coast of San Juan Island, the Polar Sea drifted closer and closer to the island instead of staying within the normal northwest-bound traffic separation zone.

* *Fearful of being forced onto the rocky shore because of limited maneuverability of the vessel (the Polar Sea was over 1,000 feet long, 140 feet wide and over 80,000 gross tons) the Four Winds hailed the ship numerous times by radio, received no reply, and finally retreated into a small shallow cove from where the skipper and crew watched in amazement as the huge ship drifted so far off course that it finally grounded on the rocks on the southeast side of Stuart Island, over half a mile from where it should have been to make the turn*

into Boundary Pass. The vessel was able to unground itself after an hour, back up, and round Turn Point.

*As a result of the report made by the Four Winds skipper and photographs she supplied to the U. S. Coast Guard and to the San Juan County Commissioners, the Coast Guard, among others, investigated the incident. Captain Gundersen was unable to supply a valid reason for the deviation, except to say that the instruments had malfunctioned. The investigators were unable to confirm any malfunction had occurred, or was even likely to occur, despite the pilot's statements, nor did they find evidence of any other cause. Gundersen's pilot's license was subsequently revoked. The master of the vessel lost his job. All the local papers ran features on the incident, and published a photograph of the vessel with its bow wedged on the rocks of Stuart Island.

An experienced ship's pilot who loses his way in broad daylight and clear weather and goes aground. What a boondoggle.

Given his advanced age, Peder Gundersen must have been ready for retirement, but how would he live down the shame? As for Captain Zorco, where the hell was the captain while the ship was meandering about Haro Strait? Catching up on his sleep? Sipping an afternoon cocktail? I wondered what had happened to him and if he was able to get another job. A Google search for Dragomir Zorco turned up nothing. Perhaps he went back to Russia.

It was nearly noon. The fog had given way to blue sky and pale sunshine. As soon as Zelda returned from the courthouse, I would make a list of the jurors, find out if any were still around. Meanwhile I could track down the defense attorney. I dialed Tina's number. She picked up on the first ring and said she was just down the street.

"Have you come up with anything to stop Mc-Cready?" she wanted to know. "Stephan is having a really bad time."

"I'm working on it. Can you come to the office? I'll give you an update and we'll do the contract."

"On my way. Aunt Jeanette has a check for you."

"One more thing."

"Yes."

"Please bring me a tuna sandwich from the deli. And a ginger ale."

"Done."

She arrived twenty minutes later with two white deli bags. I attacked the sandwich while she read through my client contract, asked a couple of questions, signed it, and then handed me a check. "What do you think so far? Did you go through the stuff on the trial?"

"I'll have a more intelligent answer after I talk with the jurors, if any of them are still available. And the defense attorney."

"What about the physical evidence? Do you think it was destroyed?"

"That's next on the list. Since the appeal was rejected, I'm not optimistic."

"What do you think about the ship incident?"

"Amazing. Makes one want to stay as far away from ship traffic as possible." I finished the last of the sandwich. "Must have been awful for Peder. No wonder he was depressed."

"Aunt Hazel said he talked about just ending everything. Jumping off the ferry." She wadded up the deli bag and tossed it in the wastebasket. "I'm sorry I didn't make it in yesterday. I sorted out things with the headmaster, then Stephan said he wants to move over to his dad's place."

"What are you going to do?"

"I'm running out of energy and I'm tired of fighting with him. Let Paul deal with the homework and fights and all that crap. He blames me for everything, anyway."

"Stephan or Paul?"

"Both of them." She sighed , stood up and buttoned her coat. "Did Zelda talk to you about the Coronas meeting on Sunday? I'm working on some ads and flyers to discredit McCready's smear tactics. Can you be there?" She stood up and buttoned her coat.

"I'm racing on Saturday, but if I'm still vertical, I'll come by. Be careful what you say. McCready's not stupid. Thank you for the check."

She went downstairs. I heard the front door open and voices below. Zelda and Dakota were back. A few minutes later Zelda pounded up the stairs and handed me a big envelope and a white deli bag. "Mission accomplished, boss," she said breathlessly. "I got copies of it all. List of all the jurors, even the alternates. All the testimony. Everybody. I hope you're a speed reader. It's about two hundred pages." She stared at the crusts of bread on my desk. "I thought you wanted a tuna sandwich."

I put the white bag on my desk. No need to cook dinner.

Chapter 10

Old Gazette Building

Friday Harbor

Zelda had been unable to find any audio recordings of the trial. As I scanned the two hundred pages of trial testimony, I made a list of the fifteen jurors who were selected from the original pool of several hundred. Ultimately ten women and five men were seated. No Old Island Families among the jurors. Two of the jurors became ill during the trial and were excused. One juror vomited when Ruth's nephew testified how Ruth had allegedly cut Peder up and put him through the meat grinder.

I pulled the San Juan County phone directory from the bottom drawer. The only listings that matched the jurors' surnames were for Reeves on San Juan Island and Huerta on Lopez Island. Rather than make cold calls or spend time Googling for people who might not still be among the living, I decided to run the names past the one person who had been around long enough to recognize everybody. In addition to being a charter member of the Coronas, Abigail Leedle had taught high school biology on the island for forty years. She answered on the second ring.

"Scotia. Are you coming to the meeting on Sunday?"

"If I survive the regatta on Saturday."

"Good. We're going to silence that SOB once and for all."

"Abbey, I need your help. You know Tina Breckenridge is trying to clear her aunt's name."

"High time. That case should never have gone to trial."

"I've got a list of the jurors. I'm hoping you might know where I can locate them."

"Fire away. I'll write them down."

I read the list slowly. There was silence on the line for a few seconds when I finished.

"Okay. Five of them have passed away that I know of." She gave me the names.

"That leave ten."

"I can do math, Scotia. Melva Reeves was living on Lopez at the time of the trial. She just recently moved over here and she's living at The Village with her third husband. Her name is Wheeler now. She won't know you, so I'll call the director at The Village and see what I can set up. Pearlman lives with his son in Anacortes. Or maybe Mt. Vernon. Don Aviles met a tango instructor and moved to Buenos Aires. The Coffin woman has Alzheimers."

"What about Deborah Zito?"

"Hold on, I'm thinking. Yes. Debbie Zito went to India for an ashram. She got pregnant by her guru. I think she went back there to live after she had the baby."

Scratch Debbie Zito. "And the others?"

"The other names I don't recognize. Wait a minute. Helene Bertrand is Soraya's mother. She's a chiropractor. She used to live here, then she got divorced and remarried . Her name is Kreef. She has a clinic on Orcas." She was silent for a minute, then said, "And the Huerta name. There used to be a farrier here. Lance Huerta. His wife died and he moved. That's all I know."

"I appreciate your help."

"I'll call Melva. Be careful Saturday. There's a new storm front headed our way Friday night."

I made a mental note to watch the weather and drag out my foul weather gear. Knowing Callahan, we would be racing even with gale force winds.

There was no category for farriers in the Yellow Pages, but I found two listings for Huerta on Lopez. One for Robert, the other for Lance and Susan. I called the latter, got a recording in a woman's voice, left a message.

M. Pearlman had a listing in Mt. Vernon. A woman answered. I asked for Maurice Pearlman.

"I'm sorry, the family is at the funeral home. Would you like to leave a message?"

"This is Scotia MacKinnon in Friday Harbor. Mr. Pearlman has passed away?"

"Yes. Last night. Are you family?"

"I'm not, but please give them my condolences."

One more to check off. Next on the list was Dr. Helene Kreef. No residential listing, but I found Kreef Chiropractic in Eastsound. Helene answered the phone. She recognized my name. "Hello, Scotia. Soraya has mentioned you. What can I do for you?"

"Tell Soraya we miss her." That was true. Soraya had quietly dispatched her naturopathic remedies from the OGB for as long as I'd been there, and she would never refer to me as a lady investigator. "I'm calling because I'm researching the Gundersen murder trial. Your name came up as one of the jurors. If I come over to Orcas, do you have time to talk for a few minutes?"

"I can't imagine why anyone would want to dig up that old case," she said. "It was all so sad. Especially since she died in prison."

"I'd like to get your personal impressions, Helene."

"Yes," she said slowly. "That would be all right. I guess there's nothing to prevent me from talking about it now. It was a long time ago, but I ll never forget some of the stuff we heard. When do you want to come over?"

"Thursday or Friday?"

"I'll be here Friday afternoon. Anytime after one o'clock. I'm next to the dance studio."

I promised to reconfirm Friday morning, and searched my case notes for the name of Hazel's defense attorney. I located a Joseph & Jarvis in Tacoma on Crosswinds Drive. The woman who answered the phone informed me that Joseph Jarvis was no longer with the firm. Would I like to speak with Ms. Jarvis? I would.

Alicia Jarvis had a calm voice. "My father retired several years ago. Were you a client of his?"

"I'm a private investigator in Friday Harbor. How can I contact your father?"

"He lives in Costa Rica. Might I ask what this relates to?"

"I'm writing up an account of the Gundersen murder trial. It would be helpful to talk to your father."

"That's not possible."

"Did he ever talk about the Gundersen case?"

"My father had no desire to talk about the case. He put his heart and soul into getting that woman acquitted, and believe me, she was the client from hell."

"So I've heard."

"I was just a little girl, but I remember the night the appeal was dismissed. He came home and cried. It was a terrible time for our family." I heard her take a deep breath.

"Did your father believe Hazel Gundersen was innocent?"

"He believed that all the evidence was simply hearsay or circumstantial. That there was no way to match the physical evidence when there was no trace of a body. The problem was, Hazel Gundersen was her own worst enemy." Alicia Jarvis was speaking rapidly. "She never stopped drinking. And all those phone calls she made saying she'd killed Peder. All those D.V. calls to the sheriff. Even her girl friend testified against her. If she hadn't been so crazy, she might have gotten off." She paused, was silent for a moment. "Does this have something to do with the election that's coming up? I heard somebody in her family is running for County Commissioner or County Council, or whatever you call it."

I explained that my client was Tina Breckenridge. "Did your father ever keep any personal journals while the case was going on?"

"I have no idea, actually. If he did, I wouldn't know where to find them. No offense, Ms. MacKinnon, but I think you're spinning your wheels."

"Did your father ever talk about the missing captain?"

"He thought Peder Gundersen was as crazy as she was. The captain was quite the womanizer. Ex-wives and girl friends everywhere. Some of the women on the jury thought he got what he deserved. And I doubt that any of the prosecutors will take kindly to you trying to re-open the case. The State of Washington spent millions on the prosecution. It's all water under the bridge. I wish Tina Breckenridge the best. I really must go."

So the defense attorney had made a mistake in not getting a change of venue. Keeping it local had backfired. If the jury, all islanders, hadn't been so intimately acquainted with the couple's shenanigans, the late-night calls to the sheriff, the publicity about Peder's crazy piloting, and Hazel's alcoholism, there might have been more sympathy for an abandoned wife of a philandering sea captain, which might have led to an acquittal. A lot of 'ifs' and 'mights'. At the end of the day, a jury trial was little better than a crap shoot.

I updated the computer file on the case, noted my Friday afternoon appointment with Helene Kreef on my calendar. While I was over there, I might as well visit the house on Dolphin Bay Road. It had been inherited by Hazel's nephew after her demise in prison. Would it be best to call the nephew for an appointment or just show up on his doorstep? If I called, he might say no. I organized the papers and clippings and internet reports into three separate files and locked them in the bottom of my filing cabinet.

The day had brightened considerably and I was looking forward to the walk over to the health club. I hoped the swim would unknot the aching muscles that had been plaguing me since the long flight from Madrid to Seattle. From underneath my swim stuff in the canvas carryall my cell phone rang. I scrabbled to the bottom of the bag, praying it was Falcon, returning my call.

It wasn't Falcon. I stared in disappointment at the caller ID and phone number that had gotten transferred to the new smart phone I'd purchased in Lisbon. Nick Anastazi's ID and phone number. He was being persistent. It was rude of me not to answer, wasn't it?

"Scotia MacKinnon."

"Scottie. It's *you*. Where are you?"

"Olde Gazette Building on Guard Street."

"I just flew into Roche Harbor. Are you free for dinner *chez moi*? Some poached salmon, fresh out of the water this morning, served with sauteed baby bok choy? Maybe a chilled New Zealand Sauvignon blanc? I have lots to tell you."

Just like that. No preamble, even though we hadn't spoken for months. Not since he invited his ex-wife up to the island after Nicole's wedding last spring. Nick exits and Falcon enters. Falcon dallies and Nick lurks in the wings. Why was my life a soap opera? And who the hell was writing the script?

Then I heard myself saying, like some prime-time ingenue, "As a matter of fact, Nick, I *am* free this evening. What time is dinner?"

Chapter 11
SAN JUAN ISLAND CENTER FOR WELL BEING

Friday Harbor

The health club looked spiffy under the new ownership: new tile in the showers, designer shower curtains, comfy furniture in the women's locker room. The parched and dying plants had been replaced by tall, verdant specimens. A sign beside the stairway to the second floor announced *Massage Room and Salon*. I showered, changed into the flowered swim suit I'd bought in Lisbon, locked up my valuables, and slipped into the lane next to Angela. She finished a lap, popped her head up long enough to give me a smile, returned to the fast crawl that kept her body in what seemed perpetual youth. The afternoon had brightened and sun poured through the overhead enclosure. We were the only swimmers. Angela's quick splashes broke the watery silence. I'm a lazier swimmer, preferring a slow side or back stroke. As I swam, I mulled over my brief conversation with Nick. Why had I accepted his invitation? I'd sworn I was done with him. If I'd had any real communication from Falcon . . . would I have?

After half an hour, Angela hauled herself out of the water and perched on the end of the pool, svelte as a young seal in her red tank suit. She pulled off her swim cap and shook out her dark curls. I finished the lap and joined her.

"Shall we hit the hot tub?"

I retrieved my towel and dried my head. She gave me a once-over. "I like the new haircut. Even wet. And you've lost weight, girlfriend. In all the right places. "

"Thanks. Michael is good influence. Only eats lean meat and fish and veggies and fruit. No grains."

"It's called paleo."

"What?"

"A paleo diet. Like our Paleolithic ancestors consumed. The hunters and gatherers." She grinned. "No cinnamon buns?"

"No cinnamon buns. There was a scale in the villa where we were staying. In addition to your weight, it shows body mass index and percent of fat. It was embarrassing. Now I'm down two sizes. I plan to stay that way." *As long as I stay away from the Netshed.*

The spa room was empty and steamy. I lowered my grateful muscles into the 104-degree water and took in the newly painted mural on the wall, a cool gray and teal rendition of two great blue herons wading among spikey reeds. Angela perched on an underwater ledge beside me and stretched out her long tan legs.

"So where *is* Michael Farraday? Why didn't he come back with you? Or why aren't you with him, wherever that is?"

I took a deep breath and shifted my left shoulder into the full force of a jet. "He got a call two weeks ago from his brother. His mother died last year. Now there's argument with a sister about who gets the house in Scotland. He had to go back."

She gave me a long uncompromising look. "Is he coming here when he gets his castle sorted out?"

"I don't know. He's texted a few times, but we haven't talked since . . ." It sounded even worse when I said it aloud and my voice faded to nothing.

"Since you got back?

I nodded. "What do you think that's about?"

"The silence? Either he's really tied up in the estate stuff . . ."

"Since you got back?

I nodded. "What do you think that's about?"

"The silence? Either he's really tied up in the estate stuff or . . ."

We locked eyes. "Or it was just a summer fling. Are you in love?" She asked"

There it was again. I took a deep breath. "Yes. I'm in love. It breaks my heart that I haven't heard from him. I don't know if he's coming here. I don't know if I'll ever see him again. My life is a soap opera."

"I see," she said quietly. "Didn't you tell me he works for British Intelligence?"

"He did."

"Five or Six?"

"Six. But he retired."

"How old is he?"

"Forty-six. Why?"

"Isn't that young to retire?"

I shrugged.

"Did you ever do a background on him?"

I shook my head.

"Shouldn't you?"

I didn't answer.

"I suppose Michael is tall, dark and handsome with brown eyes."

I frowned and stared at her. "Brown eyes, not terribly tall. His mother was Italian. I think he's very handsome."

"You're smart and pretty and as long as I've known you, which is about 20 years, you've always attracted gorgeous men with brown eyes. And they never stick around. It's all totally predictable. "

"What are you saying?"

"Did you ever think of falling in love with an average looking guy? Maybe one with blue eyes and a few extra pounds? Maybe even a bald man? One that would stay around and grow old with you?"

I couldn't think of an appropriate response, so I stared into the steam. A plump young mother came in with a flaxen-haired toddler, probably three years old. The toddler reminded me of Melissa at that age. It was when her father went off to the Seychelles on a dive expedition and never returned. One of the many tall, dark and handsome loves of my life.

Angela stood up and headed for the steps. "Well, sweetie, my life is a soap opera, too, and I don't like the current episode."

"What are you talking about? Matt adores you." I'd known Angela since my law enforcement days at the San Diego P.D. when she was Dr. Angela Morales, medical examiner.

"It's October. Matt's still in Alaska. He's not re-sponding to my calls or texts. I think he's having an affair. I don't know what to do. Let's get showered."

I followed her down the hall to the locker room. We showered in adjoining stalls. I toweled off, wrapped the towel around me, and stepped out of the dressing room at the same time that Angela emerged au naturel, drying her short dark hair with a towel. Angela is Cuban, her skin is the soft brown of warm caramel, her body is slender and toned and perfectly proportioned. A short, 30-something pudgy brunette had come in while we were showering and was disrobing in front of the lockers. She turned to stare at Angela. And stared and stared. It was not a woman to woman appraisal. "Oh, my God, you're beautiful," she whispered, then shook her head, finished pulling on her suit, and ran out of the locker room.

We stared at each other and burst into laughter. "Maybe we need a third locker room," Angela said impishly as she pulled her clothes out of her locker and began to dress.

I pulled on a pair of bikini underwear and stepped into my orange lace camisole. "What makes you think Matt's having an affair?"

"When one of his crew backed out in the middle of the season, he was desperate and he hired a female."

"So?"

"I checked her out on the Internet. She's got a Facebook page. She's a knockout. Born and raised in Alaska, won a few beauty contests. And I can't think of any other reason why Matt hasn't come home."

"Matt is not going to trade you in for some north woods beauty queen."

"I'll give him one more week."

"And then?'

"Then I'm going to pay him a visit."

"Is that wise?"

"I have no idea what's wise."

"Before you leave, will you do me a favor?"

"Of course."

"Find out if the county preserves forensic evidence from a murder trial. And for how long."

"Will do. What are you doing this evening? Want to come by the house?"

I zipped up my jeans and pulled the white sweater over my head. "Can't." Without meeting her eyes, I shook out my hair. "I'm having dinner with Nick."

She burst out laughing. "Girl friend, you are out of your freaking mind."

Chapter 12
ABOARD S/V DRAGONSPRAY

Port of Friday Harbor

Wednesday morning. Sunlight slanting through the hatch. The soft pressure along my leg that told me I wasn't sleeping alone. Eyes closed, I ranted to myself. How *could you*? What were you thinking? Are you out of your *mind*? I pulled the duvet over my head and tried to go back to sleep. Maybe I was dreaming.

A few minutes later there was a tug on the duvet next to my ear. Reluctantly I opened my eyes, sat up, and started laughing. The eyes that stared into mine were not brown but green and very feline. I hadn't succumbed to Nick's brown-eyed Hungarian charms. I hadn't been seduced by the sunset over Vancouver Island. I had made it home to sleep alone.

Mazel tov, Scotia.

Calico was back. Purring loudly, she nudged her way under the duvet and snuggled against my shoulder. I hugged her, replaying pieces of the previous evening's conversation with Nick.

His living room overlooks the deep blue waters of Haro Strait and the snowy glaciers of the Olympic Mountains. The furniture is simple and masculine and expensive. It's the kind of place where you want

to spend the rest of your life. The bad weather forecast hadn't materialized. Across the water, lights were
beginning to twinkle on the hillsides in Victoria and
Sidney.

"I understand why you got angry, Scotty. About
Cathy and Nicole's wedding and not being invited.
But everything's different now."

"Different how, Nick?"

"Cathy's going to AA. And she's met someone."

"I didn't know she had a drinking problem."

"It was a closet problem. When she was drinking, she'd get depressed, and when she got depressed,
she'd call me to talk about the old times."

"Wasn't Cathy the one who initiated the divorce? She wanted to marry her tennis coach? Or her
personal trainer?"

"Our financial advisor. He bailed when he found
out she wasn't getting as much money from the divorce as he thought. "

"The new boyfriend?"

"He's an electrician."

At the end of the day, I didn't know what Nick's
ex-wife's boyfriends had to do with us. And then the
timer went off and we moved into the dining room
where candle light glimmered off the old family
sterling Nick's mother had brought all the way from
Hungary. Nick served the capered salmon. We both
raved over the bok choy and the Sauvignon blanc. He
told me he'd had the Seattle condo re-painted and he
showed me the photographs and hoped that I would
come down and see it. We lingered over coffee and
watched the moon paint a golden fairy path across

the Strait. He told me about one of his current cases involving something called Rule B attachment and garnishment and a foreign vessel that had received services while docked in Seattle and then sailed away without paying.

And then he asked about my absence from Friday Harbor. "Zelda said you were away sailing. Summer in the Med. Must've been nice."

I agreed that it was nice, and when I wasn't more forthcoming, he asked about Melissa. We laughed over her creative phone recordings and he invited me to stay over. I declined and half an hour later I departed with an open invitation to come to Seattle and check out the renovations on the condo. I drove carefully down Starflower Road to Westside Road and back into town by moonlight, wondering if Angela was right about the TDH syndrome. Was I sabotaging myself, over and over again, for a tall physique and a pair of brown eyes?

I slid out from under the duvet, careful not to disturb Calico and regarded my naked self in the mirror. Angela was right. I looked terrific. The little roll of belly fat was gone. My legs looked longer. The short tousled blond hair looked good with my golden Mallorca tan. My skin looked smooth. I smiled a silly smile. I even looked a few years younger. I brushed my teeth, washed my face, applied moisturizer and sheer make-up, donned a clean pair of blue jeans and a soft red shirt. While the coffee was brewing I searched in the locker over the sink for a can of cat food. I popped the cover and Calico flew off the bed and I watched her scarffing up the flaked tuna fish, wondered if she had escaped from Redhead or been abandoned. There might be an unfinished score there. Or had I finished it in the dream?

I poured a cup of coffee, added a few drops of milk, slid into the settee behind the table. I pulled the Gundersen file from my canvas bag, opened my laptop, and began to make notes on the trial. Two hours hour later I reviewed what I'd learned.

*It took seven days to reduce the original three hundred-plus jurors summoned to thirty, then the judge increased the pool to thirty-five.

*None of the jurors was from Orcas Island, where Hazel and Peder were living. To the dismay of Hazel's attorney, the state removed them all "for cause."

*The prosecutor's opening statement promised the jurors eye witness testimony – Hazel's brother, Fred Kortig, Jr., who had allegedly helped her dispose of the body – as well as numerous items of physical evidence to support the circumstantial evidence of premeditated murder.

*Evidence presented by the state included scrapings of dried blood from an old wooden coffee table, a 38-caliber Smith and Wesson, shell casings, chunks of blood-stained flooring, and pieces of the blood-spattered ceiling.

*Witnesses included Hazel's niece, Jeanette Gish of Seattle, and Brenda Sue Benton, Hazel's neighbor and longtime friend.

*Jeanette reported receiving numerous drunken phone calls from Hazel in the months preceding Peder's disappearance saying she was going to kill Peder or had already killed him. Absent from the witness stand was Hazel's brother Fred Jr., the only alleged eyewitness to the alleged bloodbath. By the time of the trial, Junior was no longer sentient and was living in an institution.

*Brenda Sue Benton testified that Hazel described to her how she and Junior had shot Peder, then cut him up and fed him into a large commercial meat grinder and had the remains hauled away with the manure pile. No one was able to locate either the meat grinder or the manure hauler.

Tina Breckenridge was right: Despite the prosecuting attorney's promise to provide eyewitnesses, all the testimony was hearsay.

I read and reread comments from the jurors after the trial:

"Everything was hearsay, but the state did a really good job of collecting evidence, so it must be true."

"Nobody who saw Hazel do it ever testified. No eye witnesses."

"I would have voted for acquittal if I'd known the truth about that ad in The Gazette."

"I didn't realize when I voted for conviction that she would get life."

I mulled over the jurors' second thoughts and considered the drama of a murder trial: A life and death deliberation in the hands of twelve peers of the accused. It was a concept that had long bothered me. A true peer would have to be the same sex, age, race, and socioeconomic status.

A true peer of Hazel Gundersen would have been female and over 75 years of age.

I scanned back over the proceedings. Like all juries, they would have been instructed not to talk about the case except during deliberations and to arrive at a verdict based strictly on the evidence presented. Given the rumor mill that constitutes these islands, and the lapse of time between the first investigation and the trial, there couldn't have been even one juror who hadn't spent hours if not days and weeks chatting to friends or neighbors about the notorious case. Hadn't anyone told them that if they voted for conviction life imprisonment was a possible penalty?

The phone rang. It was Jared. "You're home."

"Where else would I be?"

"I came by the boat last night about nine last night. You weren't there."

"No, I wasn't."

"Have you had breakfast?"

"Just coffee."

"I found a old file on the Gundersen trial. Meet you at the bakery? They're doing breakfast until 11:00. I'll buy."

"Deal."

Chapter 13
BAKERY CAFÉ

Friday Harbor

The café was half full, mostly strangers waiting for the ferry. None looked like locals. Jared had the front booth. The waitress followed me to my seat and poured coffee while I read the menu. I chose the Ferry Traveler special: scrambled eggs, sausage, fruit, no toast. Falcon would be proud of me. That is, if I was even on his radar any more.

Jared pushed a faded red portfolio across the table. "I'd like to have it back when you're done. Might not be anything you haven't already uncovered, but you never know."

The file was bound with a large rubber band. I opened it. A thick stack of photos lay on the top. Shots of the inside of the Gundersen house and of all the hundreds of pieces of evidence the deputies had confiscated. I studied the chronology of the case and leafed through the tear sheets from the *Gazette*, all the articles they had printed before and during the county's most infamous trial. There were also tear sheets from Seattle papers and sur-rounding communities. I scanned the old headlines.

"I knew about his affair, says Gundersen."
"Trail of blood led from living room to the porch."

98

"Deputies search stable and manure pile for evidence."

"Juror says he based his vote on a mistaken assumption."

The waitress brought our breakfasts and I tucked into the scrambled eggs. Jared watched me quizzically. "You're frowning."

"I keep reading about these jurors having second thoughts after the conviction."

"There's probably never been a capital conviction when at least one juror didn't wish their vote had been different. When you get right down to it, jurors may end up as executioners. Not everybody can live with that. "

"How the hell do you vote for a conviction when there's no body, and the alleged weapon doesn't turn up for months after the alleged crime?"

"Have you ever served on a jury?" Jared piled strawberry jam on his toast and took a huge bite.

I shook my head. "I've been called three times, always got eliminated."

We ate in silence for a few minutes. The eggs were excellent.

"My take on jury trials like the Gundersen case," Jared continued, "is that when the prosecuting attorney is really good, he or she can present a whole lot of pseudo evidence in such a way that ultimately the jury thinks it's all real."

"Like blood spatters that weren't matched to anyone?"

"Exactly."

"In fact, no one could say whether the blood was

human or animal. Any good defense counsel would have pounced on that."

"It's no accident that some of the highest-rated TV shows have been law and order dramas. Forensics and courts are sexy. All about life and death. And the Gundersen trial was CSI Miami and Law and Order and Criminal Minds all rolled into live, local theater."

"With the jury a captive audience." I nibbled on the sausage and contemplated the implications of what Jared said. "So at the end of the day, the winner is the attorney who's the best actor and has the best supporting actors and the glitziest props."

"That's about it. However, MacKinnon, if your investigation comes up with any evidence that the sea captain was not, in fact, murdered, but disappeared under his own volition, I would be happy to put out a special edition of the *Gazette*."

We finished our breakfasts and our eyes met over the rims of the coffee cups.

"I saw Nicholas at the market late yesterday afternoon," he said. "Is that where you were last night?"

Our eyes locked for a long minute. "What's with the interrogation, Jared?" I said finally. "When did you start monitoring who I have dinner with?"

"Is that what it was? Just dinner?"

I felt my face grow warm. "Just dinner. And I drove home and slept alone. Until Calico came back."

He smiled. "I was delighted when you dumped him last spring, or whenever it was. Then you take up with a smooth talking Brit who ostensibly works for Her Majesty's Secret Service. Is it Five or Six?"

Despite being my best friend, Jared's questions

were rubbing me the wrong way. "It's Six. And he *did* work for them. That's past tense. Michael retired from Six. He's going to do consulting work."

"For whom?"

I shrugged. "Interpol, perhaps. What's with the interrogation?"

"How old is Michael?"

"Forty-six."

"Isn't that a bit young for retirement. What does he live on?"

I shrugged again. "He has an inheritance from his mother. That's why he had to go back to the U.K."

Another long silence. He reached across the table with both hands and clasped both of mine. "MacKinnon, you're beautiful and smart. You deserve better than handsome scoundrels." He gave my hands a squeeze. "Or if you must pick a scoundrel, why not me?"

I tried to control my anger. "Michael Farraday is not a scoundrel. You and I have been friends for a long time and that does not give you the right to poke around in my private life. It's none of your business who I have dinner with. Or who I sleep with." I grabbed my jacket and stood up, refusing to acknowledge the shock on Jared's face. Heading for the door, I hear my cell phone chirp for a text. It was from Me-lissa: *Shaun and I are going to have a baby.*

Chapter 14

Olde Gazette Building

Friday Harbor

Reeling from Melissa's a text message and fuming at Jared's meddling, I raced back to the office, trying to remember who Shaun was. Had Melissa ever mentioned him? Or was Shaun a her? Perhaps while I was in the Med with Falcon and not paying attention? Obviously Melissa had told Jewel Moon about the pregnancy before she told me.

Zelda and Abby were holding a whispered conference and my cell phone rang as I came through the door. It was Melissa. I answered, asked her to hold, raced upstairs and closed the door. I took a deep breath, trying to control the adrenaline rush. "Melissa . . . wow, you're pregnant. Well, congratulations. That's terrific, wow!"

"Are you okay with it, mummy? I thought maybe you'd be upset with me."

"It's very exciting. Of course, it might have been better after you graduated, but, I guess it's time I was a grandmother. When is the blessed event?"

"Late May or early June, which is good, 'cause I can graduate with my class."

"So, are we going to have a wedding? Do I know the baby's . . . father?"

"Mother, I texted you all about him last summer and he's on my Facebook page. You would know if you ever went there. Even grandma's on Facebook. She posts on my timeline almost every day. "

Facebook. Freaking social media. That explained why Jewel Moon was apprised of the news before I was. Merde! Merde! A few seconds of silence passed while I concentrated on deep breathing.

"His name is Shaun," she continued. "Shaun Timmerman. He's from Chicago. He was in medical school at Northwestern, but he hated it so he dropped out and got a job at the ranch as a wrangler. That's where we met. He might take over as a foreman. He might take over as a foreman. He's really nice. You'll like him.

"Well, are you moving to Colorado?"

"I think I should finish school first, don't you?"
"Finishing school is important, yes."

"He's coming out for Thanksgiving and we're going to talk about it. Grandma's invited us to Mendocino."

"Mendocino for Thanksgiving. Finishing school is important. Very important." I couldn't stop babbling. "Uh, are you still planning to go to graduate school?"

"Absolutely. I'm going to do law. I'm applying to Harvard, Stanford and Berkeley. Is that okay?"

"Great schools, sweetie. Especially Berkeley. " I swallowed, my brain spinning in an attempt to calculate what graduate school tuition would be. My third

Sharon Duncan

husband, Albert, had set up a small trust fund for Melissa which nicely covered her undergraduate ex-penses, but I doubted it would maintain even one year of graduate study at either of the two private institu-tions. Not the time to mention it. I tried to imagine her juggling an infant and dirty diapers and waking up at night for feeding along with the demands of law school. "What about paying for your pregnancy, Me-lissa? Your school insurance won't cover it, obvious-ly."

"*Obviously,* mother." A silence. When she continued her voice was smaller. "Shaun promised he would help. He's going to talk to his dad."

"What does Shaun's dad do?"

"He's a plastic surgeon. I think he has piles of money."

"Well, that's a good thing,"

"It's not like he's running out on me or anything."

"I certainly hope not."

"What do you mean, you *hope* not? Do you have to be negative?

What I meant, Melissa, was that it would be a good idea to have your doctor give you an estimate of what the pregnancy and the delivery will cost. So there won't be any surprises."

"All you ever think about is money." Another silence. "I'll go to the women's clinic in Berkeley." More silence. "*Okay*, I'll ask them. Look, I've got to go to class, I'll call later and we can talk more."

I turned off the phone and sat back in the chair, still breathing deeply, processing the conversation.

My daughter was pregnant. With a drop-out medical student who was now a Colorado cowboy. And they weren't planning to get married, at least not now. She was going to have a baby by herself. I would go down to Berkeley, of course. Help her with the first few weeks. It would be summer. Hopefully after her graduation. Then my negative brain reverted to the thousands of dollars a pregnancy and delivery without insurance probably cost. And if the cowboy didn't help her financially, or the cowboy's father, I would have to. I was going to be a grandmother. Should I make a new will? Would Melissa end up being a single mom?

There was a knock on my door and Zelda came in. "I have some preliminary . . ." She stopped. "What's wrong, boss?"

"Melissa's pregnant."

"Congrats, granny." She gave me a big grin. "Can I be auntie?"

"She's not going to get married. At least not now."

She shrugged. "Smart woman. Marriage is so yesterday."

"I suppose."

"Who's the father?"

I told her what I knew of Shaun Timmerman. "A wrangler from Chicago. I don't even know if she *should* marry him."

"Hey, cheer up. Over 50% of all babies being born are to single women. Melissa won't have to argue about child rearing with anyone. Anyway, I printed out the DataTech report on McCready." She handed me a file folder. "Some of it might help Tina. I have

105

to leave for a while. Lily MacGregor called. Sage and a friend of hers are missing."

"Lily's niece?"

"Yeah. She keeps a horse at Ravenwood Stables. Elyse Montenegro says the two girls took the horses out for a ride and they're three hours overdue. I'm going to help look for them."

Lily McGregor was a Corona and Tina Breckenridge's best friend. "Shouldn't they be in school?"

"International School holiday. They had a sleepover at the McGregor's. Lily dropped them at the stables this morning. They left half an hour later, headed for Cady Mountain. Lily's been trying to call them for two hours."

"No cell reception in that area. It's pretty dense and rocky. Be careful."

"We'll take Dakota. Lily's been working on passage cairns up there. I just hope one of the horses hasn't gone lame."

I started to inquire about passage cairns, but she had bolted down the stairs. I heard toenails on the floor, then the door slamming. My phone rang. It was Helene Kreef, the Gundersen juror on Orcas.

"Scotia, my Friday schedule is all bolloxed up. Could we meet tomorrow instead?"

The Thursday square on my calendar was blank. I agreed to be at Helene's office at 11:00. I made the change on my calendar and looked up the information on Hazel Gundersen's nephew who had inherited the Orcas property. His name was Rudy Kortig, son of Fred Kortig, Jr. I was under no illusion that I would learn anything from visiting a 20-year-old crime scene, even if I could persuade the nephew to let me on the property. Since Rudy was living in Wisconsin at the time of the murder, there would be little he could tell me. But at least I could drive by the property. Maybe some intergalactic time-lapse telepathy would provide insight into what actually transpired the cold January day Captain Peder Gundersen disappeared from the face of the earth.

I opened the DataTech report on McCready. The more I read, the more puzzled I became as to why such a high-powered individual had zeroed in on the tiny, remote village of Friday Harbor to carry out his political aspirations.

DataTech   Confidential   report   #25983226

Lochlan Ayden McCready
DOB: 11/18/1955
Place of Birth: Los Angeles, California
Parents: Roberta L. Ayden and Jock J. McCready
Wife: (1) Celeste Rossingnol, a French national, married Nice, France, 1984, deceased

(2) Patricia Correia, nationality unknown, married Washington, D. C. 1995

No children.
Education: St. Joseph's Military Academy, San Bernadino, CA;

B. S. In Mechanical Engineering, Univ. Of Michigan (summa cum laude)

M. S. in Aeronautical Engr., M. I. T.,

Master's Thesis: *Use of Biological and Chemical Sensors in Unmanned Aerial Vehicles*

Languages: Spanish, Arabic, Russian, Swahili

Military: U. S. Air Force , Special Tactics Squadron (no dates available)

Career: Recruited into the CIA 1990 - ?. Assignments included Alexandria, Va., Panama City, Panama; Caracas, Venezuela; Paris, France; Tegucigalpa, Honduras; Chad, West Africa. Transferred to National Clandestine Services (NCS) 2005.

Consultancies: DARPA, 2010-2011. No details available.

Politics: Independent. Supporter of Libertarian Independents and the Reagan Society.

Club Memberships: Seattle Yacht Club, San Juan Island Golf & Country Club; Bay Area Vintners Club

Professional Organizations: International Society of Biological Engineers; Institut de la Technologie Future.

Police record: None

F. B. I. Record: None

FIT **Due**: None

Childhood hobby: Model airplanes

Childhood pet: Turtle named Wilbur

Credit Rating: Top 1%

Whatever I expected to find that would explain McCready's dirty tricks campaign, it wasn't in the report. No criminal record. No sinister associations. Under the Daniel Craig tough-guy exterior, Lochlan McCready was a pretty interesting dude. Smart, too. Maybe Tina had to accept that his only motivation in getting elected was to turn his back on all the clandestine folderol and settle for being a big fish in a small pond. Other newcomers had done it.

It was nearly three o'clock. Nothing from Zelda on the whereabouts of the missing horseback riders. Carolyn Smith said Hassan, the Somali interpreter, was going to call today. I thought that the time differ-ence was about ten hours, which meant it was already 1:00 a.m. tomorrow in Somalia.

The phone rang. It was Abigail Leedle. "Melva Wheeler will see you today. Her husband doesn't want her talking to you about the trial, but she's going to do it anyway. You better get over there before he changes her mind. She'll meet you in the Great Room in half an hour. I told her you were researching a novel about the trial. She thinks you'll put her in it. Don't tell her you're a P.I."

"I'm on my way."

I did another quick check on my email, found messages from Carolyn Smith and my mother. I opened Carolyn's. *Luisa had a call from Hassan. He told her they will kill Harrison and Michelle if the family doesn't come up with the money this week. He wants five million. She's falling apart. She gave him your telephone number. He'll call later today.*

I muttered an expletive. Why the hell hadn't Luisa given him DuPont's name and number? I had neither the training nor the desire to play head games with a Somali pirate. I messaged back: *The p irates won't kill the hostages unless they decide they aren't worth any money. I will direct Hassan to Jules DuPont at H & W. Have you filed petition to get the court to release the inheritance?*

Jewel Moon's message was less dramatic. *You must be so excited. We're doing Thanksgiving here in Mendocino with Melissa and Shaun. Please come down and bring your British friend. I'd like to do pumpkin pies. Do you have your grandmother's old recipe?*

Jewel Moon and Giovanni and Shaun and Melissa and Michael Farraday and me. Free range roast turkey with chestnut stuffing, garlic mashed potatoes and organic pumpkin pie in the old dining room overlooking the deep blue Pacific Ocean. All in some parallel universe.

Chapter 15
THE VILLAGE

Friday Harbor

I power walked along Blair Street and up the hill on Spring Street and found my way into the Great Room at The Village by 3:30. Bent over the keyboard of the grand piano at the far end of the room, a white-haired man softly played *Smoke Gets in Your Eyes*. Through the window beyond the piano I glimpsed winding paths of the landscaped garden. At the reception desk I asked for Melva Wheeler. The receptionist nodded toward the scarlet suede sofas behind me. "That's Mrs. Wheeler, in the pink cardigan."

As I approached, the woman put aside her book and inched her way off the sofa. Her handshake was warm and firm. " You're t he a uthor. Th e on e wh o's writing about the Gundersen trial."

"Scotia MacKinnon. It's a pleasure to meet you."

She waved toward the piano. "That's my husband, Maury. I have to go with him to the doctor in about half an hour." She lowered her voice, still keeping her eye on the piano player. "Let's go into the library. There's no one in there right now." She led the way into a book-lined room with an old oak library table in the center. We settled ourselves at the table. I pulled my notebook from my bag as Melva began talking.

"I don't want Maury to hear us. He was a bailiff during the trial. He says the Gundersen trial was shameful. Pathetic defense counsel and just a media circus." She glanced at my notebook. "It's been over twenty years, but I remember it like it was yesterday."

"You were living on Lopez then?"

She nodded. "I was still married to Gordon. I was teaching at the Middle School. There were so many of us that were called up. And they eliminated all of the ones from Orcas. For causing . . . for, what do you call it?"

"The term is 'for cause'."

"Yes. I suppose they thought Hazel's neighbors knew too much about her. " Her eyes went far away for a few seconds. She shook her head. "And they told us not to watch TV or read any newspapers."

"Did you follow directions?"

She laughed. "It was pretty dumb, don't you think?"

"What do you mean?"

"The case and the arrest, it was in the newspapers and even the Seattle news stations, for almost *five years* before the trial. That's all everybody talked about at the Grange. Did they think we were *hermits?*"

"Mrs. Wheeler, what part do you remember most about the trial?"

"Call me Melva, please." She smiled, smoothed her black skirt. Her eyes went away again. She took a deep breath. "It was so dramatic, like a Hollywood movie. Or like Perry Mason. There were TV reporters, even helicopters. I had to pinch myself to believe

I was really a part of it. And of course we women loved watching Aaron."

"The prosecuting attorney? Aaron Stout?"

"He was so handsome and so smart. He told us from the beginning that Hazel and Peder had a bad marriage. He called it 'vicious and destructive.' Then he told us that Hazel's niece, the one that lived in Seattle, and Hazel's brother Junior, would tell us exactly what happened the last day of Peder's life." She paused, smiled. "He had such an honest face, it was easy to believe what he said. I had to remind myself that it was his job to convince us to convict Hazel. That I had to keep an open mind."

"Did you feel the same about Mr. Jarvis, the defense attorney?"

"Joe Jarvis." She looked uncomfortable and pressed her lips together. "I don't think Hazel should have picked him. She knew him because he helped her when she bought the stable on Orcas, but I don't think he knew anything about criminal law. And he dressed funny." She paused, then added, "He cried when we convicted her."

From the other room, Melva's husband segued into September Song.

"I heard the trial took a long time. It must have been tiring."

"Over four weeks. We were exhausted. It was hard for some people, being away from their work and families every day. Part of the jury had to take the interisland ferry every morning from Lopez. And there were so many pieces of evidence. I don't know how they expected us to keep track of everything."

"What do you think was the most important physical evidence?"

"You mean like the gun?" She shivered. "I suppose it was the blood," she said doubtfully. "The blood stains on the floor and on the ceiling. And the expert testified that the spatters on the ceiling had to come from a gunshot wound."

"Is that what convinced the jury, do you think? The blood spatters?"

She frowned. "The problem was, one of the experts said there was nothing to prove it came from a person. It could have even come from an animal."

"Who do you think was the most convincing witness?"

"Well, it wasn't the niece. All she talked about was all the times Hazel called to say she'd killed the captain. Or was going to kill him. So I suppose it was Brenda Sue."

"Hazel's neighbor?"

"And her very best friend. They came to Orcas together, from Wisconsin. She couldn't have had any reason to lie."

"Do you remember what she testified?"

"I'll never forget it. Never. She was this little person, with beautiful eyes. " She folded her hands over her chest and was silent for a minute. " She said it was a really cold night, snowing and windy. Hazel called her and invited her over for a glass of wine with her and Junior. A nice Cabernet, it was. From California. They were sitting there by the fire as cozy as could be and then Brenda Sue asked where Peder was and Hazel just told her straight out that they'd had a big fight and she'd shot him and Junior had helped her dispose of him. Ground him up in the meat grinder." She shivered. "Brenda Sue said Junior just sat there shaking his head and smiling."

"What did the jury think of Brenda Sue's testimony?"

"Brenda Sue was just repeating what someone told her. I can't remember what you call that?"

"It's called hearsay. When a witness reports what someone else told her rather than testifying to what actually happened."

She thought about that. "No one who actually saw Hazel kill him ever testified," she said slowly. "Even though Aaron promised they would."

"Did Hazel's attorney call Hazel for a rebuttal?" I asked, "To deny Brenda Sue's testimony?"

"Oh, yes, Hazel said Brenda Sue was making it all up because she was jealous. We didn't know what there was to be jealous of and Brenda Sue didn't look like the jealous type. I think testifying was really hard for her."

"What did you think of Mr. Jarvis' final argument to the jury?"

She pressed her lips together. "You mean when he said Junior was a drunk and all we had was Brenda Sue's testimony about what Hazel told her? And that there was a really good chance Peder committed suicide?" She shrugged. "He really did try to make out that Hazel was just a poor old woman whose husband had gone off and left her. The problem was, by then everybody knew that Hazel had a terrible temper, and every time they got drunk and had a fight, she told everybody and their cousin that she was going to shoot the SOB. You know about all the domestic violence calls to the Orcas deputies, don't you?"

"What was your impression of the deliberations? Was it hard to get consensus?"

"It seemed like it took forever." In the Great Room the piano went quiet. Melva darted a glance over her shoulder and spoke quickly. "There were two jurors that wanted an acquittal."

"Do you remember who they were?"

"Pearlman. Ben Pearlman. He said there'd never been a conviction in the state without a body. That all the testimony was hearsay. Nobody ever saw Hazel kill Peder and that most likely Peder would come strolling up Spring Street someday and walk into George's and order a beer and then wouldn't we all look like fools."

"And the other juror?"

"The Bertrand woman," she said in a whisper. "She agreed with Pearlman, but she changed her vote when she found out about the ad in the *Gazette*."

Chapter 16

OLDE GAZETTE BUILDING

Friday Harbor

Before I could ask for an explanation of the *Gazette* ad, the white-haired piano player – Melva's husband and former bailiff – came into the library and stood beside the table. He didn't say anything. He didn't look at me and Melva didn't introduce him. She stood up immediately.

"I hope I was of help to you," she murmured and took hold of Maury's arm. "Good luck with the book." I followed them outside where a minivan was waiting. As I was about to head back for the office, Melva turned away from the van and bustled back to hand me a small white card. "So you know how to spell my name when you publish the book. That other crime writer spelled it wrong. She spelled it like toast."

I tucked her card into my carryall, got in the car and checked my phone. There was a text message from Carolyn Smith. *Hassan called u, had a hissy fit when u didn't answer. Call me.* I pressed the Call Back button.

"Carolyn, I thought we agreed I wasn't going to talk to the pirates. That's Jules job. What's going on?"

A long sigh. "Sorry, Scotia. I relayed that to

Luisa, but she'd already given him your number. He thinks you're part of the family. He insists on talking to the family first, probably put the fear of God into you, before he talks with a negotiator. Would you please talk to him?"

"It's about two a.m. in Somalia. He's probably not going to call until tomorrow, but I'll be at the office until five."

Back at the OGB, Zelda was on the phone, Dakota resting on his haunches nearby, watching her. Tony Bolton's door was open and I glimpsed a denim-clad female derriere that looked familiar. The derriere turned around. It was Abigail. She kicked the door shut with her foot. Zelda hung up the phone. "You are so not going to believe what happened to Sage and Leslie."

"Lily's niece and her friend. The horseback riders."

"Yeah. We hiked all over Cady Mountain and the DNR land, never found them, then they turned up at the stables half an hour ago."

"So what happened? Did they take a detour?"

"That's the weird part. At first they both refused to talk about why they were late. Then Sage started crying and said that she'd lost her phone and they rode around in circles for a while looking for it and they took a short cut across a pasture and two vampires told them they weren't supposed to talk about it or bad things would happen."

"Two vampires."

"Yeah, I know. But that's all they would say."

"Are the horses okay?"

"Apparently. Lily thinks the girls must have wandered onto somebody's private property where they weren't supposed to be."

"A reasonable supposition. People who live on Cady Mountain cherish their privacy."

"There's another thing."

"Which is?"

"Lily's cairns. They've been destroyed."

"Okay. So what exactly is a cairn?"

"Gee, boss, you being a Scot and all. A cairn is a pile of stones. Or a column of stones, like the tall stone pillar out at American Camp that marks the trail."

"Lily's been building cairns on Cady Mountain for what reason?"

"Not really building them. She found two disintegrating ones and she was reconstructing them. One cairn is a huge flat piece of rock over a cave. She thinks they're very old and that the cave used to be a grave. Everybody that hiked up there was adding a stone. It was really cool."

"And somebody destroyed them?"

"Yeah. Probably the same somebody that put a big ugly fence around the area. With an even uglier 'no trespassing' sign. She's furious."

"Maybe the Department of Natural Resources doesn't like cairns."

"Abby is going to take it up with the County Council. By the way, what did you think of the background on M?"

"Smart dude."

"Is that all you have to say? What about the CIA

assignments? DARPA and Africa, etc."

"The CIA is a legal U. S. entity. So is DARPA. I once considered working for the Company myself."

"You *didn't!*"

"I did, but then I met Melissa's father and got married and got pregnant. So . . . I've only got one more Gundersen juror to interview. Unless you dig up something more interesting on M, I may have to return a large portion of Tina Breckenridge's retainer."

"You can't. We've got to stop him. Did you know he actually has a super-Pac? And that it has collected over fifty thousand dollars in donations. Is that legal?"

"Super-Pac's are legal as long as the candidate is not managing them."

"I'll dig up something, I promise."

I left her glowering at her monitor and went upstairs. Exactly ten minutes later the phone rang. The caller spoke in heavily accented but intelligible English.

"You Mack Kinnon?"

"Yes, Scotia MacKinnon."

"You Michelle sister?"

Here we go. "I'm a family friend of Harrison's."

"You Harrison sister."

"No, I'm a friend of Harrison's family."

"Harrison need help friend."

"How can I help Harrison?"

"You talk DuPont. Crazy man. Liar. DuPont send five million now. No money we sell Harrison and woman Al Shabaab." The connection was cut.

I stared at my buzzing phone. The request for five million was no surprise. It was about where a number of civilian hostage discussions had begun. But the threat to sell hostages to Al-Shabaab was a new twist. The Somali-based cell of Al-Qaeda had carried out their own hostage taking of foreigners along the Kenyan coast and had taken credit for the vicious attack on a mall in Nairobi that killed 72 people. If Harrison's family didn't come up with a figure, the pirates were happy with, Hassan's threat might not be an idle one.

I e-mailed Jules DuPont and Carolyn Smith a report of my chat with Hassan and asked for guidance on future calls. As in how to avoid them. A minute later a message came back from Carolyn. *I'll talk to DuPont. I checked the IMF statistics for this year. Incidents are way down.*

The light on my cell phone was blinking. A text message from Melissa. *Please get a FB page. Luv u.*

"A Facebook page?" Zelda responded to my request with a half-hidden smile. "Sure, boss, no problem. I'll work on it tomorrow. Is the page for you personally or for SJM Investigations?"

I considered the question. "The only reason I'm doing an FB page is so I'm not the last one to find out what's going on in Melissa's life. I guess it will be personal. After that we can talk about one for SJM."

"I'll need at least one photo of you, unless you just want an avatar, and I'll make up the rest." She chewed on her lower lip, then announced, "But I think you need a business page as well. I haven't seen a lot of clients knocking down your door lately."

"What do I have to do for that?"

"Oh, gruesome gumshoe photos, testimonials, wanted dead or alive posters, and so on." She glanced at my face and burst out laughing. "Just joking. I'll create a personal page for you tomorrow with all the firewalls and privacy levels, and so on. Then we'll talk about one for the business."

Chapter 17
THE HOUSE ON FRANCK STREET

Friday Harbor

I left the office wondering what sort of tangled web I was creating by dabbling in the social media. Speculating that my grandparents had felt the same sort of disconnect with the invention of the telephone, I wandered into the market and filled a pint carton with chicken curry soup and found a loaf of kalamata olive bread to go with it. A glass of Zin and *The Lonely Silver Rain* and I'd make it through the evening without spending too much time on Hassan's threat. Or obsessing about a dark-haired scoundrel with high cheekbones and a Roman nose.

"I have some jasmine rice that would go really well with that soup. And an unopened bottle of Menage a Trois Silk. Supper at my place? " It was Jared Saperstein, his basket overflowing with soft green bags of produce. His eyes searched my face. "I'm sorry about this morning. Really sorry. You're right. I have no business poking around in your personal life. Forgive me?"

I stared at him. "Of course I forgive you. Was that only this morning?"

"It was. You look tired and harassed. You're frowning. Bad day?"

A pregnant daughter.

A non-communicative lover.

A nasty Somali pirate.

I didn't know whether to laugh or cry. I shrugged. "The usual. I'm frowning because I'm caving in on social media just to keep up with my daughter and having mixed feelings about it."

He chuckled. "So you're going on Facebook. And how is Melissa these days? Any exotic new boyfriends? Brazilian soccer players? Sky divers?"

I hesitated, considering whether the term exotic could be applied to a medical student turned Colorado wrangler, and finally said, "It's complicated. I'll accept your invitation and we can catch up"

"Excellent. I'd like you to see my kitchen remodel."

Half an hour later, wine glass in hand, I wandered around Jared's new kitchen in the house on Franck Street, took in the espresso cabinets and white granite counters, the new stainless appliances.

"The granite is called White River," he said proudly.

"It's luscious. I totally approve. The cook top is amazing. But why the upgrade? The last I heard, you thought the house had character and you liked it that way."

He hesitated, and I felt a small frisson of fear. "You're going to sell it," I said quietly. "Where are you moving to?"

"Don't jump to conclusions. While you were away the refrigerator died and all the new units were stainless and then the range and the dishwasher looked shabby".

"And that led to new cabinets and White River granite and chic new bar stools."

"More or less. Also, I received a, um, small inheritance from a great-aunt."

"The one in New York?"

"No. The one in Tel Aviv."

"Are you going to sell the house?"

"Maybe. Maybe not. There's a place on North Bay Lane that might be coming up for sale. Great water view all the way to Cattle Pass. You'd love it." He refilled my glass. "Don't fret. I'm not going anywhere. At least for now. Have a seat on the chic new barstool while I assemble the rice and tell me why you were looking so harassed. Is it the Tina Breckenridge case or the missing sailor? If it's something personal, I won't meddle. Promise."

I pulled out one of the wood and steel bar stools and settled in at the island counter. "I'm not getting anywhere on the Gundersen murder trial. All I've found out about McCready is that he's smart and has spent a lot of time on military and intelligence pursuits. No scandals, no dirt. Nothing Tina could use against him."

"Does it bother you that he's so lily white?"

"A bit. It means I have to focus on clearing Tina's name of her aunt's murder charges so he has no ammunition. I'm going to Orcas tomorrow to talk with another juror. As for Harrison Petrovsky, I did have a short and unpleasant conversation with a Somali pirate this afternoon."

"That must have been a barrel of laughs. How much does he want?"

"Five million dollars or they will sell Harrison and his girlfriend to Al Shabaab." I gave him the details of my short conversation with Hassan.

"Has that ever happened before?" he asked. "That hostages were sold?"

"Not that I've heard of, but Al Qaeda-spinoff groups are getting stronger in Africa. If the pirates could turn a quick one or two million, they'd be crazy not to grab it."

"I imagine guarding hostages gets expensive after a few months. How do you see this ending?"

"I wish you hadn't asked."

"You've been following this case a long time. You must feel some ownership in getting the sailor out alive."

"I was hoping to get through the evening without thinking about it. At the end of the day, it depends on how much the family can come up with and how good a negotiator DuPont is."

"DuPont?"

"My old boss at H & W." I stared into the wine, wishing I had better answers. "It also depends on the whims of the pirates, how much khat they're chewing, what the weather is, how many hostile tribes are about, which of the pirates has had a fight with his girlfriend. From all reports, they're extremely volatile. It's like dealing with a gang of drugged up juveniles who are about to break down your door. Or worse."

Jared came around the island and put his arms

around me. "Enough. There's nothing you can do tonight. While the rice cooks, let me show you my new bedroom furniture. All recycled wood."

"I think the term is repurposed."

The bureau and headboard were reclaimed saal wood. "It used to be railroad trestles in India," Jared said. "They also used mango and acacia wood." The carpet was an old faded red oriental. We paused beside the French doors that led out onto a trellised back deck where wisteria vines draped over a railing. The room was masculine and comfortable and safe. A room with character. I didn't know whether it was the terrible day or the wine, but suddenly the big pillows and the patchwork quilt on the bed in shades of what I could only think of as squash and pumpkin was way too inviting. I wanted to curl up there and forget about Melissa's pregnancy and an old woman who died in prison and a sailor and his first mate being held by a band of pirates. Something in the air changed and we both knew it. Jared smiled, put one arm around my waist and drew me close. I took in the spicy scent of his skin and I felt a warmth that started in my throat and spread downward.

"Nothing is as it seems," he murmured, pulling me easily into his arms. We kissed, and then kissed again, and when the lingering embrace ended I buried my head in his neck. We stood that way for a bit as I pondered whether my longing to extend the embrace was for the right reasons. Without finding the answer, I detached myself and used my empty wine glass as an excuse to move back to the kitchen.

The jasmine rice was steamed to perfection.

Jared added crystalized ginger to the chicken curry concoction – more thick sauce than soup – and we ladled it over the rice and carried the steaming bowls into the dining room. Jared refilled our wine glasses and we chatted about the deteriorating state of national politics where lies seemed to be the playbook of the year. He talked at length about the house on North Bay Lane and said he'd like me to see it. As we moved on to family, I evaded any discussion of Melissa except to share that she was planning to go to law school.

Besides being smart, Jared is highly perceptive. He's been my friend for long enough to know that I wasn't telling him everything, but all he did while I babbled on about Melissa's trust fund and the astronomical cost of tuition at various institutions of higher learning was to lean over and kiss me on the cheek. "My dear friend," he murmured, "I think there's more bothering you than pirates and cold case murders. I'm here when you want to talk about it."

I sat quietly for several minutes, sipped the rest of my wine. The silence continued while he removed the dinner plates and brought coffee and we ate our way through the amazingly sweet strawberries that must have come from South America. I finally broke the silence, fingering the cutlery. "You've known me for a long time, Jared. You know how hard it is for me to share . . . deep things in my life. Negative stuff. And you're right. It was a terrible day in almost every aspect possible."

"Does one of those aspects involve the Brit?"

I didn't want our evening to be about Michael

Farraday and whether or not I was ever going to see him again. Or to get into my anxiety about Melissa's relationship with an absent university drop out who was the father of her unborn child. "Yes, one of the aspects is about Michael. But I'm not quite ready to talk about it."

"You know I wish you only happiness, Scotia darling," he said quietly. "If that Limey isn't smart enough to appreciate what a treasure you are, please know that I do. Always have. Always will."

I left a little after nine, muzzy from the wine and a last embrace. The night was cloudy and damp. A light breeze out of the southwest, a creamy half moon struggling to light up the earth from behind roiling clouds. I made my way down the hill, cut over to Harrison above the harbor. One of the ferries – it looked like the *Elwa*, but I couldn't be sure – was tied up for the night, dark except for a few dim lights on the bridge. At the bottom of the hill in the loading zone two vehicles were parked in lane one. They would be the first to board the 6:00 a.m. "red eye" to Anacortes the next morning. I didn't have to be in Eastsound to meet with Helene Kreef until 11:00, so I could take a later ferry.

A sudden cold breeze swept up off the water. I buttoned my jacket closer around my neck and hurried past the Bistro. A familiar voice hailed me. "Hey, boss, hold up a minute." It was Zelda. She and another woman moved out of the lighted entryway and made their way to the sidewalk. The woman was Lily Mac-Gregor whose niece had been missing that afternoon.

"How's Sage?" I asked.

"Watching a movie with my neighbor. Very chastened and unlikely to wander around on Cady Mountain again," Lily said.

"Any further information on the two vampires who accosted them?"

Lily smiled. " ere are no vampires on San Juan Island. I think what happened is, they got lost and made up the vampire story so they wouldn't get punished for being late." Her phone rang. She answered it and moved away to talk.

"McCready's at it again," Zelda said in a low voice. "He's just mailed out a campaign yer linking Tina to drug runners. We're stopping at the C & S for a brandy. Join us?"

"I'm going over to Orcas tomorrow. Need a clear head."

"Visiting the scene of the crime?"

"At least driving by."

Lights from the liveaboard boats were scattered across the marina. I met nobody on "G" dock. There was a light behind the curtains on *Pumpkinseed*. I considered stopping and sharing the news of Calico's return with Henry, then thought better of it. As I stepped onto *Dragonspray's* deck, I heard a small "meow." She was curled up on the lazarette. She stood, stretched, rubbed against my ankles to be petted, meowed again. I unlocked the hatch covers and paused for a minute before going below, listening to the horn on Reid Rock buoy. Its familiar tolling in the fog was both eerie and comforting.

Chapter 18
FRIDAY HARBOR TO DOLPHIN BAY STABLES

Orcas Island

All places have a rhythm and ritual. On San Juan Island, a large part of daily life revolves around the ferry schedule. Island business hours are dictated by arrivals and departures of the huge white vessels. A trip to the mainland – "over to America" – to the big box stores or a medical specialist requires hour-by-hour planning worthy of an efficiency expert. Inter-island transit is somewhat easier, at least in the off season.

On Thursday morning, only six other cars were lined up for the 8:30 sailing to Orcas Island. We boarded the *Klahowya* on time and I left the Alfa Berlina on the lower deck, climbed up the steep stairs to the cafeteria. Tightly buttoned in my blue wool cape, coffee container in hand, I went to stand on the outside deck in the fog as we made our way up San Juan Channel, through Wasp passage between Crane and Shaw Islands, and on to the terminal at Harney Point. There were no other vessels on the water. At this time of year and this time of morning the mist and forests obscure any waterfront structures, and I could almost convince myself that we were passing undiscovered, uninhabited islands. Islands that Captain

George Vancouver and his crew charted back in the 1790's on their voyage from Puget Sound to Queen Charlotte Sound on the Inland Sea.

Cruising the Inside Passage to Alaska was something Falcon and I had talked about. Now, as I stared at the hillsides dark with tall Douglas fir, I considered that Angela and Jared were right: My choice of male companions was so shallow that I couldn't see beyond brown eyes and broad shoulders. From tall, lean Simon with golden brown eyes, to tall, dark and handsome Nicholas Anastazi and the dark fringed brown eyes and olive skin of Michael Farraday.

I didn't like seeing myself that way. I felt a slight chill that was more fear than temperature. Fear that my inability to relate to an 'ordinary man', in Angela's words, would doom me to forever waiting for a text message from some handsome adventurer who had already moved on.

By the time we docked at the terminal on Harney Point at 9:15, the fog was thinning. I wasn't due in Eastsound until 11:30. There was time to check out the property where the whole sorry Gundersen saga had taken place. I stopped for another coffee in Westsound, then followed the road north and east, winding through heavily wooded countryside. I found the address on Old Orchard Lane at the end of a cul-de-sac, past two other houses. On the property nearest to the Gundersen place, a man in brown coveralls was repairing a railing on his porch. He waved as I passed and I waved back.

What was once Dolphin Bay Stables was now a dilapidated brown house screaming for TLC and a large red barn and weathered sheds begging for paint. I spied an ancient green John Deere tractor inside one of the sheds, several runs where horses could be put out for exercise, but no sign of any livestock. Two fenced pastures lay to the right of the barn. A driveway curved to the left around the house, past a yard that was mostly tall weeds. The other fork of the driveway led to a large metal gate with a dent in the center. A sign on the gate entreated visitors to "Close the Gate." But they hadn't.

I followed the left fork around to the back, parked on the strip of cracked concrete in front of the garage door. The siding on the house was covered with green mold as was the roof. The entry door to the house had once been painted blue, but most of the paint had flaked off. I rang the doorbell, waited, rang again.

"Rudy's off island, ma'am. Gone to Bellingham."

It was the neighbor in the brown coveralls. He was medium height and extremely thin. Early 40's. There was something lissome about his figure, more than just the long softly curling brown hair that tumbled over his shoulders. He leaned against my car, arms folded over his chest, a brown beer bottle in his left hand.

"I'm Scotia MacKinnon." I came down the steps and extended my hand. "Do you have any idea when Rudy might be back?"

"Will Benton," he responded, shaking my hand. He looked me over from head to toe. "I recognize you from the photos that were online. After you captured that sweetheart swindler. That was very cool."

He took a swig of beer, glanced at the house and then back at me. "Rudy's got a girlfriend in Bellingham. Probably be back tomorrow." He glanced back at the house. "Anything I can tell you about the house? That's what you're here for, isn't it? That's what people always come for. The old Gundersen place where that crazy bitch murdered her no-good philandering husband."

"You're Brenda Sue Benton's son."

"Yes, ma'am." He looked back at the house. "If you're interested in the history, you might as well walk around the place. Can't go inside, of course. Even if Rudy was here. He took the whole thing down to the 2 x 4's after his aunt died. Stable's pretty much the same." There was a slight slur to his voice.

"Did your mother ever talk to you about the trial?"

"Goodness gracious, Miz MacKinnon. That's all everybody talked about for years. It got so bad, after Hazel was arrested, my mom took me to live with my aunt in Sacramento."

"But she came back for the trial. Your mother."

"Yes, ma'am."

"Brenda Sue and Hazel were best friends?" He smiled a lazy smile. "They were very best friends. They lived together in Wisconsin for ten years before they came out here. It broke my mom's heart when Hazel took up with the sea captain."

Will watched for my reaction with a lazy smile and I stared back at Will for a long time while I tried on a new way of looking at Brenda Sue Benton's testimony. A new way of looking at the friendship between the two women, remembering that Melva Reeves had mentioned that Brenda Sue was jealous of Hazel. Then I finally got it. "Brenda Sue and Hazel were lovers."

"Yes, ma'am. Lovers, partners, a couple, whatever. My mom fell in love with Hazel when she was only nineteen years old. Hazel promised her if she left me and my dad they would stay together forever and ever. After they moved here, my dad got married again and moved to Tennessee. His new wife had four miserable rug rats, so I came out and we all lived here and we raised the horses and trained then. Fresians, they were. " He raised the bottle and took a long swig. "We didn't have hardly any money, but life was good."

"So what happened?"

"Hazel met the sea captain, is what happened. The whore-mongering, skirt chasing sea captain."

"You and your mom moved out?"

"Hazel told us we had to move next door. She swore she was only marrying Peder for his money, that there wasn't nothing else between them, and her and my mom would be together again one day. All fucking lies. My mom told Hazel the captain was a scumbag, but that went in one ear and out the other. Hazel had her eye on the captain's pension from day one." He took another swig of the beer. "What goes around comes around, if you get my drift."

"Brenda Sue testified that Hazel told her she murdered Peder."

"Yes, ma'am."

"Cut him up and ground him up and burned his remains in a burn barrel. Is that correct?"

"Yes, ma'am. Ol' Hazel Gundersen got what she deserved."

"Is your mother still alive?"

He shook his head. "She had a stroke, died seven years ago."

"Was your mother telling the truth when she testified?"

A lazy shrug as he emptied the bottle. "The jury believed it, didn't they."

Chapter 19
FISHERMAN'S BAY, ORCAS ISLAND TO FRIDAY HARBOR

San Juan Island

The village of Eastsound nestles above Fishing Bay and is a mecca for summertime bikers and kayakers. Many of its buildings date from the 1880's and one travel writer labeled it a 'Cape Cod village at the end of a Norwegian fjord.' It was 10:25 when I parked the car in the lot between Eastsound Dance Studio and the blue frame building that housed Kreef Chiropractic. The village lay in pale yellow sun. To the east, low clouds wrapped around Mt. Constitution. There were no kayakers nor any other vessels on the choppy dark blue waters of the bay.

An OPEN sign was displayed on the glass door of the clinic. Inside I found a spartan office space of pale wood and glass. Two chairs sat against a wall in front of a tall counter. The woman standing behind the counter had a cloud of curly dark hair lightly threaded with gray. Helene Kreef's face was smooth and devoid of makeup and she appeared to be in her late 40's, but would have to be older if she had been a juror thirty ago. She came around the counter and turned the sign to CLOSED. "I don't have another appointment for an hour. Let's go in the back."

I followed her into a back room with a small

desk, two chairs and a padded examining table. She sank into one of the chairs and gestured me to the other. I pulled my notebook and a pen from the carryall. She began talking almost immediately.

"I've been thinking a lot about the trial since you called. I don't like to think about it. It's been keeping me awake again."

"Had you ever served on a jury before?"

"Never. And never have since."

"When you think about the trial, what comes up?"

"That I was a coward."

"Why do you say that?"

"Because I should have held out for acquittal even if it would have meant a mistrial."

"There were two of you who originally voted for acquittal?"

"Yes. Ben Pearlman was the other. A smart man. A writer. I think he used to teach philosophy or something. He argued that all the pieces of a murder were there except one."

"And that was?"

"The body, of course."

"Why do you suppose that missing piece of the puzzle didn't bother the other jurors?"

She knitted her brow, tapping her fingers on the desk. "I think they – I think there was just so much evidence . . . the carpet, the pieces of concrete from the living room, the gun they found, the shell casings in the living room." She shook her head. "It was all the people saying Hazel had told them she had done it. Her niece, even her neighbor and best friend, the

Benton woman. And everyone started believing it."

"Tell me whatever you remember about the Benton woman's testimony."

"Ah, Brenda Sue Benton." Helene took a deep breath and leaned back in her chair, arms folded across her chest, as if for comfort. Or courage. "It was right after the defense attorney made his statement. Everything he said about Peder just giving up after the boat collision and losing his license and going back to Norway made a lot of sense. Or even committing suicide. Then Hazel testified."

"Tell me about Brenda Sue Benton."

"Right. I think Brenda Sue talked to the police before the trial, but I was a little confused about that. She acted like she was scared half to death. She was a little thing. She wore a blue wool dress that made her look really young. Waifish, actually. She must've been a size zero. She had a perfectly innocent face with long hair pulled back in a ponytail. I'll never forgot her eyes. They were this shade of dark blue and she looked right at us and told how Hazel had called her and said she was in real trouble and would Brenda Sue come over. She lived right next door. So Brenda Sue went next door and Hazel was there with her brother." Helene stopped talking. Her eyes glazed over and I knew she was back in the courtroom listening to Brenda Sue.

"Hazel's brother?" I prompted.

She nodded. "It was Junior, the one that got dementia."

"What did Brenda Sue say happened then?"

"I'll never forget it. She said Hazel just poured

them a glass of Cabernet sauvingnon that she said
was from the Anderson Valley in California and told
her that she had finally decided enough was enough
and she had shot Peder and her brother had helped
her cut him up and they ground him up into sausage
and buried it in the manure pile."

"In the manure? Not in the burn barrel?"

"Yes."

"What did the stables do with the manure? Did
it get spread on the fields?"

"I've no idea. But I remember when Aaron made
his opening statement he talked about checking the
manure pile and they didn't find anything."

"Did Jarvis, the defense attorney, cross exam-
ine Brenda Sue?"

"Yes. He tried to make out that she was a liar
because she had originally tried to protect Hazel, but
she started crying and said she had a change of heart
or found God or something and just had to do the
right thing. She had to tell the truth. Even about her
best friend."

A change of heart, indeed. "But you and Pearlman didn't believe her."

She shrugged. "Pearlman kept hammering on
the fact that you can't convict someone without a
body and there was nothing to tie any of the physical
evidence to Peder. I went along with that."

"Eventually both of you changed your minds."

"One of the jurors was engaged to a man in Seattle. She hadn't seen him in three weeks and she was
going crazy to get the whole thing over. She reminded
us about the ad that ran in the *Gazette* just a few weeks

after Peder disappeared. It was an ad for men's clothes and some tools with Hazel's phone number. She said that if Hazel was expecting the Captain to come back, why was she advertising his clothes? I guess it was the last straw, so Pearlman and I just gave up." She shook her head in disbelief. "Hell, if I had a husband that was as big a philanderer as Peder Gundersen, I'd have thrown his clothes out the window long before he disappeared."

"That's the issue on which the conviction rested? The ad in the *Gazette*?"

She stared at me for several seconds, then nodded. "At the end of the day, that was it. The twist is, though, a few months or so after the trial, I heard that the ad had been placed by a friend of Hazel's who'd been living with her boyfriend while her husband was in Alaska and she needed to get rid of the stuff without her husband finding out. Apparently Hazel was just helping her sell them."

"So on that tiny piece of pseudo-evidence, a woman was given life in prison?"

Chapter 20
ORCAS ISLAND TO SAN JUAN ISLAND

Friday Harbor

I got back to the Orcas ferry landing in time to board the 12:35 sailing for Friday Harbor. I locked the car and climbed up to the lounge area and thought about my visit to Orcas. Had I learned anything that would help Tina Breckenridge clear her family name? Did it make any difference that Brenda Sue Benton was the odd woman out in the triangle? Was there any way to short circuit McCready's dirty tricks?

The two pieces of information I'd picked up from Will Benton and Helene Kreef née Bertrand – that Brenda Sue Benton and Hazel Kortig were lovers before Hazel met the sea captain, and that Hazel's first degree murder conviction had turned on a misleading ad in the local newspaper – were startling. But what could I do with them now? The bit about the ad in the must have come up in the appeal. Even if Jared Saperstein were to publish a feature article in the Gazette on Brenda Sue and Hazel's relationship and how Brenda Sue's testimony had affected the jurors' decision, what would it produce except endless snickers over drinks at George's Tavern?

As the ferry rounded the corner into San Juan Channel I decided there was only one thing that might cast reasonable doubt on Peder being murdered in the house on Old Orchard Road: that the blood on the ceiling and the carpet did not belong to him. And even that wouldn't exclude the possibility that Hazel had murdered him somewhere else.

I pulled my phone from my carryall, called Tina Brreckenridge, told her I'd talked to Will Benton.

"Brenda Sue's son is *here*?"

"He's living next door to Hazel's old place on Orcas."

"What did he say?"

"What he said was, your great aunt and Brenda Sue were lovers and Brenda Sue never got over Hazel marrying the captain."

"*Lovers*?! Aunt Hazel and Brenda Sue. Oh, my God." She stared at me for a minute, one hand over her mouth. "That would explain why she changed her story."

"Very possibly. Nothing like a woman scorned."

"Do you think she lied?"

"Her report of being invited over for a glass of wine so Hazel could confess to the murder goes along with all the drunken phone calls. Who knows? You were right that all the evidence was circumstantial and it's possible Brenda Sue flat out lied. But there's no way to attack the conviction. The prosecution dotted their I's and crossed their t's. The jury convicted her. The judge turned down the appeal."

"What about the DNA? You said there might be a chance . . . " Her voice trailed off.

"It's a long shot. If the evidence hasn't been destroyed we can get the DNA, but then it's a matter of finding a sample of Peder's DNA to either match or eliminate. That would take six months unless we go to a private lab."

"I don't have six months. And I can't find Stephan."

"Was he staying with you or Paul?"

"With Paul. Stephan told him he had a tutorial after school yesterday and that he'd get a ride home with a friend. The school secretary thinks she saw him outside about four o'clock talking with another student. A girl. Paul was out late and doesn't know if Stephan ever came home, but he wasn't around this morning. He's not in school today. Paul says it's my fault, because of the election."

"Has Stephan done this before, stayed away from home?"

A long sigh. "Yeah, back when he was using drugs. He used to hang out at Lime Kiln and smoke weed. I thought that was all behind us. "

"Stephan has a cell phone?"

"He's not answering it. I know he'll turn up, but it's just one more thing I don't need right now."

"Have you checked with parents of his friends?"

"He hates it when I do that."

"My daughter hated it, too, but that didn't keep me from doing it."

"I hate to make things even worse . . . " Her voice trailed off.

"Have you thought about a tracker? I can get a small one for you. You could attach it to his backpack. He'd never know and you'd have peace of mind."

"*A tracker*? How do they work?"

"Do you have a smart phone? An iPhone or an Android?"

"It's an Android."

"You insert your GPS SIMM card and use the phone to send a message to the tracker. You'll get the tracker position in coordinates. Degrees and minutes. Or you can view the location on the map on your cell phone or your computer."

"If he found out, he'd never forgive me."

"Better than the alternative."

"I have to think about it. Where would I get one?"

"I ordered two for a client last year. She only took one."

There were a few seconds of silence, then "Okay. Zelda is meeting me this afternoon. Would you send it with her?"

"I will. Meanwhile, call the sheriff's office. Tell them what's going on."

"If I call the sheriff, everybody on the island is going to know I can't control my son. McCready will be all over that in a heartbeat. And I just heard the sheriff's sister held a private fund raiser for Mc-Cready last night. Grapevine has it that they collected over twenty thousand dollars."

She agreed to keep me posted on Stephan and I put the phone down. Twenty thousand dollars was a lot of money for an island with a population of seven thousand. Where was it coming from? Or maybe the question was, where was it all going? Unless I came up with something to clear her name, Tina Breckenridge was going to lose the election.

We docked in Friday Harbor on schedule at 2:05. The weather was deteriorating, marine strato-cumulus creeping in from the northwest. An early winter in the making. I drove the Alfa Berlina up to the Port lot and parked, then detoured down the hill to the Drydock where I ordered a bowl of clam chowder to go. I wandered into the bar. It was empty except for the bartender who was chatting on his cell phone and polishing a wine glass into oblivion. I took a seat at the table in the corner by the window and checked e-mail. I found messages from Deputy Angela Petersen and attorney Carolyn Smith. Angela's was the good news.

I talked to Keith Duffy, manager in charge of the evidence locker for SJ Cnty. The good news: evidence collected in felony violent offense cases is kept forever post conviction. The bad news: storage space is limited , some of the evidence from the Gundersen case may have been sent down to Island County for safekeeping. Call Duffy, make an appmt to check out what's there. I'm thinking of taking a short leave, heading north. A.

Heading north meant leaving for Alaska to check on Matt. I wondered if she would let him know she was coming or was planning to surprise him. Was that what I should do with Farraday? Hop on a plane to London and tool down to Cornwall and knock on his door? Or was it Devon? I couldn't remember.

I dialed the Sheriff's Office, got connected to Keith Duffy. He was assembling evidence for an upcoming trial, but he could see me in the morning, at 8:30. I hung up the phone and thought about the bulging files and envelopes of information on the

Gundersen case. The relationships were as byzantine as the press had hyped them. Hazel and Peder's, Hazel and Brenda Sue, Hazel and her brothers. In fact, the reality was more bizarre than the journalists might have guessed.

There was no sign of my chowder. I pulled a paper napkin from the dispenser and began to doodle, started drawing circles, connecting them. Ten minutes later I stared at the character web I'd drawn. Hazel Gundersen (HKG) in the center circle with lines connecting her to the supporting cast:

. . .To brother, Fred Jr., to niece Jeanette, great-niece Tina Breckenridge; best friend Brenda Sue Benton and Brenda Sue's son Will.

. . .To Captain Peder who was connected to his former Norwegian fiancée B rette, t o h is s hip p ilot friend Arne Ormdahl who reported Peder missing.

Finally, the network spokes connected HKG with the attorneys, Aaron Stout and Joseph Jarvis; with San Juan island deputies Lion and Vidrine, and to the criminalist whose name I'd forgotten. And most importantly, to the 12 jurors who sealed her fate, and the judge who pronounced the sentence and rejected the appeal.

A network worthy of Facebook. If there had been a body, it would have been an open and shut case. End of story. But if, in fact, Brenda Sue Benton lied on the witness stand and Hazel was wrongly convicted solely on hearsay, if, in fact, Hazel had been planning to murder Peder and he had escaped from Hazel's clutches, then what characters were missing from the web? If Peder wasn't murdered, where did he go? Who were his close friends? Did he have any, besides Arne Ormdahl?

He might have hid out with Arne for a while, for weeks or even months. But not for years. The Prosecuting Attorney, Aaron Stout, hired a P. I. in Oslo who found no trace of Peder. I didn't remember seeing any mention of the P.I. talking to Brette, the ex-wife or fiancée.

Peder's family testified that he was worried for his life, but he didn't show up on their doorstep. No money was missing from Peder's checking account. If he wasn't murdered and didn't commit suicide but simply ran away, what did he live on? Where were the missing puzzle pieces? If I couldn't find them my client would have to live with the conclusion that Hazel Gundersen's conviction was a just one.

Chapter 21
OLDE GAZETTE BUILDING

Friday Harbor

I stopped by the Post Office for my personal mail on my way back to the OGB. Bills from Orcas Power and Light and the Port of Friday Harbor, five handbills and numerous pieces of junk mail. I stood at the counter near the door, sorted, discarded the junk mail and almost threw the post card away. It was from London, a photograph of a flaming sunset behind the Tower Bridge. I turned it over. *I miss you. M.* The postmark was ten days ago. Did Michael Farraday a.k.a. Falcon still miss me or had out of sight become out of mind? Was it true when he wrote it? Was there now another truth?

Back at the OGB I found Zelda and Tony Bolton deep into a discussion of the concept of time. Something about neutrinos and six-sigma levels. That the laws of physics were not the same for all observers and time depended on who was experiencing it. My world was shaky enough as it was, my cubby was empty, and I went upstairs.

I powered up my computer, waited for Windows Mail to deliver two new messages from Carolyn Smith. I read the one sent at 8:30 a.m. Subject: Michelle Yee.

Michelle Yee is a stock trader in Shanghai, or was, before she quit her job to crew for Harrison. Her father is with the Bank of Shanghai, a manager or something. Her uncle is an inspector with the Shanghai municipal police. Apparently papa Yee was not happy when his daughter sailed away with a laowai sailor. Luisa doesn't know if Michelle's family knows she's been kidnapped. She doesn't know how to contact them. Can you help? They might be able to provide some of the ransom.

The second message sent at 11:38 a.m. was not good news.

Harrison just called Luisa. He and Michelle were beaten this morning when Michelle tried to escape and got feisty with one of the guards. They have been separated. He thinks Michelle has been taken inland. He thinks she has broken ribs. Hassan told him he would never see her again. Harrison is only allowed to use his phone sporadically.

Damaging a hostage on which they expected to collect ransom or sell to another tribe wasn't logical, but pirates high on khat aren't geniuses. I picked up the phone and called Carolyn's office, just as my second line rang and the green button lit up. It rang again, then the light stopped blinking. Carolyn answered with a question. "What are we going to do, Scotia?"

"If Michelle's causing trouble, Hassan may be making good on his threat to sell her to al-Shabaab. Have you talked to DuPont?"

"I've left umpteen messages. The woman on the switchboard said he's in South America. What are we going to do?"

"I'll follow up." I thought for a few seconds. "The only thing that will get the pirates' attention is money.

Or the promise thereof. Any luck in getting the estate funds released?"

"Petra refuses to sign off. She doesn't care if she never sees Harrison again. I'm going to meet with the judge privately."

"We have to bring Michelle's family into this. I'll try to track Jules down."

I heard Zelda's footsteps on the stairs. A pink message slip was thrust through the half-open door.

"That Hassan is a nasty piece of work."

"He called again?"

"Yeah. He said, and I quote, 'Tell Mack Kinnon no four million dollar today we sell Michelle al Shabaab tomorrow.'"

"*Merde.* I'm not a hostage negotiator."

"You're not."

"Michelle Yee should have stayed at home in Shanghai."

"Yup."

"I want to go back to the boat and have a tall, very tall, vermouth and soda. I want to forget Harrison Petrovsky ever existed."

"I'll bring the vermouth."

"I doubt very much that al Shabaab is going to pay anywhere near four million dollars for a Chinese female. Unless they know something we don't." The phone rang and the green button lit up once again. "Please, God, not Hassan."

Zelda raised an eyebrow at me and moved toward the door. "Good luck, boss."

It wasn't Hassan, it was Harrison Petrovsky. "Carolyn Smith told me to call DuPont," he began, "but he's not available, so I called you. It's about Michelle. We have to talk fast. They'll only let me have the phone for five minutes."

"They've taken her away?"

"Yes. She's in really bad shape."

"Do you know where they've taken her?"

"No. Hassan just says, 'far away.' He says they'll bring her back when we raise four million dollars. There's a new guy here, sort of a pirates' lawyer or negotiator or something.

"Do you have a name?"

"It's Sharif. He says he wants to help us and he's trying to persuade the pirates to accept less money. He asked how much money Michelle and I have. He thinks she's my wife."

"What did you tell him?"

"That we're just poor sailors and all we have between us is ten thousand dollars, but he doesn't believe me. Carolyn Smith promised DuPont would call Hassan."

"DuPont may be in South America."

"Oh, my God. And Petra hates me so much she'll never agree to a distribution of my mom's money. We are so up shit creek. Please help us."

"Do Michelle's parents know about the kidnapping? That you two are being held hostage?"

"Michelle was trying to get a call through to her father yesterday when one of the pirates grabbed her phone and smashed it. She went ballistic and tried some black belt moves and that's when they started beating her."

"Tell me what you know about her parents."

"Her dad's a bank manager. Bank of Shanghai or

Bank of Hong Kong. She's got an uncle that's a police inspector or a detective or some shit."

"Did you meet them when you were in Shanghai?"

"We met her parents and her uncle at this really posh golf club. They treated me like something the cat dragged in. Not up to their expectations for their darling daughter."

"Can you give me any names?"

"Her dad's name is Bao. Bao Yee or Yee Bao. I never got it right."

"What about the uncle, the detective?"

"Reggie or Reginald Archer."

"He's not Chinese?"

"Michelle's mother's family is English. Been in Hong Kong and Shanghai for a hundred years. All in banking."

"Any idea how we might find Reginald Archer"

"I think he—oh, shit, here comes Hassan. He's going to take the phone. I'll . . . "

The connection was gone and I sat listening to dead air, trying and then trying not to imagine what might be taking place in a gangster's hideout in a lawless country on the edge of the Indian Ocean.

It wasn't like Jules DuPont to drop the ball on anything. I dialed his direct number, got the switchboard, asked to speak to his P.A. Her name is Portia Madrid and before she started working for Jules she was an F.B.I. profiler. She's half Jewish, half Spanish. I used to crew on her Pearson 385 for Sunday sails on San Francisco Bay and I knew she would be straight with me. She came on the line and I explained what I knew about Harrison and his crew.

"Scotia, Jules had to fly to Peru last night. The president's daughter is being held by some terrorist group. I expect to hear from him this afternoon. Is there anything I can help you with?"

"The Petrovsky case. I think it's escalating. I need to know if Jules arranged for a Somali negotiator. If Jules isn't going to be available, I need help tracking down a Shanghai banker. And a police inspector." I passed on the information on Michelle's family, suggested that a dossier on both Yee Bao and Reginald Archer would be helpful.

"I'll get right on it. Expect a call or an email tomorrow latest."

I sent off an email to Carolyn Smith summarizing my aborted phone call with Harrison Petrovsky and updated her on Jules DuPont: *If we're going to keep the ball rolling until Jules returns, I see no other option except to bring Michelle's parents into it. Let's hope that after a hundred years in banking, they can afford a few million dollars.*

My clock had long ago chimed five bells. Outside my window, early darkness shrouded the village. A good night to curl up on *Dragonspray's* settee with Travis McGee. I wondered what Falcon was doing and who he was doing it with. I stared out the window into the dark and wondered if his mother's country house had a big fireplace and was he there alone. I locked up the files, shut down the computer, and wrapped myself in my wool cape, then remembered I'd promised to send a tracker to Tina.

Downstairs Zelda was also closing up, Dakota panting impatiently beside her desk. I handed Zelda the manila envelope that contained the mini-tracker for Tina. I glanced at the big white board where she'd drawn a simple sociogram that more or less resembled the doodling I'd done on the napkin at the Drydock. With one difference: she had added a circle I had omitted: Lochlan McCready.

"Take a look at this, boss." She handed me a set of stapled pages. The first page was titled "Cyborg Moths and Mosquitos: Science fiction or reality?" I speed-read through the article. " . . . *university researchers have teamed with DARPA, U. S. Air Force, and two private contractors to develop a micro aerial vehicle (MAV) about the size of a bug. intended to be used for reconnaissance operations in both urban and rural areas . . .*"

"Science fiction, indeed. What's it got to do with the price of tea in China? "

"It's off the internet, but what's interesting is that guess who, our own Colonel Lochlan McCready is a major player in a company called BioIntel Systems."

"So?"

"So BioIntel Systems has a contract with DARPA and the U. S. Air Force to develop and produce micro UAV's specifically described as, and I quote, "Cyborg insects whose purpose is to provide miniaturized surveillance and to deliver biological weapons."

"Drones, in other words."

"Itsy bitsy baby drones."

"How do you know this?"

"I had breakfast at the Doctor's Office. So did McCready. He was waiting for the ferry, which was late. He was online using the unsecured network.

Again. I just happened to peek over his shoulder, in a manner of speaking. I was getting to the interesting stuff when the ferry came in."

"You hacked him again."

"Yep."

I scowled at her. "I think you should cease and desist."

"Why?"

"You did his background. You know who we're dealing with here. Engineering plus military career plus intelligence. "

She scowled back. "I won't get caught. I went to Defcon last summer while you were swilling Italian wine with your handsome beau."

"The hackers' conference." I gave her a long speculative look. "Are you thinking of giving up your amateur status?"

"Defcon has some of the smartest people on the planet. I have a new friend. Her name is Cee Gee."

"Cee Gee?"

"Cyber goddess. She writes visionary fiction and teaches at U-Dub *and* consults with some really big companies to test their security systems. Her dad worked on the database that the CIA uses and she has a gorgeous older brother named T.J."

"That would be T.J. Tahoma, the tracker."

"Yes."

"Cee Gee's background is impressive. But she's still a hacker."

"A white hat hacker."

"I think you should stay out of McCready's computer.

"We've got to find out more about BioIntel."

"There are other channels. Legitimate channels."

"If it will make you feel better, I'll order a second level dossier on McCready and BioIntel from DataTech. Can Tina afford it?"

"It will make me feel better. Her Aunt Jeanette can afford it."

"By the way, I set up a Facebook Timeline for you. The password is Dragonspray initial cap plus your birth year. You can change it. You can add pho-tos."

"Is it secure? Can just anybody see what I post?"
"I set the privacy settings at Friends only. You can link a separate business page to it."

"Thank you. I think."

She glanced at the web on the white board. "Uh, boss, with all due respect, it strikes me that you're moving in the wrong direction on the Gundersen case. Maybe you need to work forward rather than backward."

"Say more."

"McCready's definitely going to determine the outcome of the Gundersen murder case."

"The Gundersen murder case was decided several decades ago."

She traced a circle around the HKG box with one finger. "Didn't somebody famous say that a murder case isn't over until the murderer says it is?"

Chapter 22

ABOARD S/V DRAGONSPRAY

Port of Friday Harbor

I thought about Zelda's question all the way down the hill and out to "G" dock. For all intents and purposes, the Gundersen murder case was concluded when Hazel Gundersen died in prison. But if Mc-Cready was still able to use it as a dirty trick to defeat Tina Breckenridge's run for County Council, then it wasn't over. No matter whether Hazel killed Peder or not.

I'd left the forward hatch open for Calico that morning and I found her curled up on the settee in the main salon. The diesel furnace was doing its job and the cabin was cozy. Calico stretched, leaped to the floor, and did figure eights around my ankles while I refreshed her dish of dry food and poured dry vermouth over ice. I added soda and a wedge of lime, put some kalamata olives in a small dish, and we both returned to the settee. She's not a lap cat and she stretched out along my leg, purring passionately. I told her about my day and how I was about to give up on the Gundersen case and that I dreaded the thought of negotiating with Hassan the Pirate or Sharif the Pirate Negotiator and why did she think Falcon hadn't called. She gave me a long slant-eyed stare accompanied by several backward curls of her tail, repositioned herself, and went to sleep. I watched her for a few minutes, marveling that a cat's life had no past, no future. Only the present.

I put on KING 5 evening news. There had been three flu deaths in Western Washington. A bicyclist was killed on Highway 2 near the town of Monroe. There was a Chance of Rain in the next 24 hours, with Rain predicted beginning on Friday afternoon and extending through Saturday evening. A high of 58 degrees was predicted for Friday and 56 for Saturday. Just as I was deciding that it would be a good weekend to stay in, do the laundry, and clean out *Dragon-Spray*'s lockers, my phone chirped with an incoming text from Callahan, my racing friend. *Skippers mtg tmorow 6 pm @ Griffin Bay y.c. Free beer. C u there?*

I'd forgotten I'd promised to crew for the race on Saturday and I'm not a big beer drinker. Some racing crew never attend skippers' meetings, which are traditionally held the night before a race, but it's a good opportunity to find out what the possible courses will be, discuss the weather, and get acquainted or reacquainted with the rest of the crew. I texted back a confirmation.

When the KING 5 anchor segued into a special segment on the employment situation in Spain, I turned off the TV and put on the CD player. Calico disappeared into the aft cabin. Piano by David Lanz accompanied dinner from the freezer, orange chicken with almonds. It was edible, but just barely, and I'd rinsed off my dishes when another text message came in. It was from Melissa. *Mummy, I haven't heard from Shawn for 5 days. I invited him 2 Mendocino 4 Thnxsgiving. I've texted and called.*

I texted back. *Has this happened b4? Unexplained silences?*

Her answer came twenty minutes later. *Yeah, coupl of times. Always has a gd xcuse. Food poisoning, one of the horses is sick, cell discharging.*

A male friend once told me that when men have unexplained disappearances, it's usually connected to alcohol, drugs, or a woman. Or all three. I considered calling her, but people choose to text rather than call for a reason.

I collected my towel, shampoo, and PJ's, reluctantly let Calico out, and trudged up to the shower room at the Port administration building. *DragonSpray* does have a shower, of sorts, but I use it only when I'm out cruising. The temperature was dropping and the wind was rising. I had the shower room to myself and I dried my hair before scurrying back to the boat. Calico was not around. I heard a few drops of rain on the hatch covers. I hoped that the Redhead wasn't in the vicinity, hoped Calico would find her way back to the boat. Despite the rain, I propped open the small porthole in the aft cabin for her.

I tucked myself into bed, ready to read myself to sleep with Travis McGee. *The Lonely Silver Rain* was MacDonald's last novel. Despite it being my third reading, I quickly lost myself in Travis' efforts to locate a missing yacht for a friend, a search that evolved into a nasty triple murder and a game of cat and mouse with international cocaine smugglers.

An hour later, a dripping wet feline slithered through the open porthole. I closed up and toweled her down, wondering how Melissa's relationship with

Shaun was going to play out. She was probably posting blow by blow updates on Facebook. Probably updates on the pregnancy. I was seriously out of touch
with the world.

I pulled my tablet from the bedside locker. On
the Facebook website I was prompted for my e-mail
and password. I dutifully entered them and up popped
S.J. MacKinnon's Timeline. I found a photo from Porto Sollér of me on Aphrodite and downloaded it. I entered the town I was born in (St. Ann's Bay, Nova Scotia) And my highschool (St. Ann's Bay H.S.). For the
Status Box I checked "It's complicated," and passed
over the possibilities of notes, gifts, trends, etc. Then
I took the big step of inviting both Melissa and Jewel
Moon to Friend me. And I was done.

I sat staring at the screen for several minutes,
speculating on the probability that Somali pirates had
web pages, wondering where Michelle Yee was being
held and if she was still alive. Speculating on what, if
anything, Jules DuPont's P.A. had discovered about
the Shanghai banker and Shanghai police inspector.

The tablet doesn't have the same Spam filter as
my office computer and I had to wade through twenty
or so junk mails before I found, not a message from
Portia Madrid at H & W, but a message from Michael
Farraday a.k.a. Agent Falcon.

Nothing warned me not to open it. Nothing
alerted me not to read it, not even the subject line
– *Please understand* – which should have given me
goose bumps. *Dear Scotia. I hope you will not hate me
for what I have to tell you.*

I stared at the words and for several long seconds, fixated on the tiny fluttering black bird that has always been an icon of his messages. Then I took a deep breath and read on as something inside me began to unravel. *I am married, Scotia. My wife has an incurable brain disease which has erased all her memory and has been institutionalized for several years. She has recently been receiving new medication. I visit her periodically. Sometimes she recognizes me and is quite lucid. Other times, not at all. When you and I met I was dazzled by you. It was easy to simply pretend what I wished. I know that does not excuse my misleading you. I cannot leave the U.K. at this time. Would you consider moving to the U.K.? To the house in Scotland? All my love, Michael.*

Chapter 23

ABOARD S/V DRAGONSPRAY

Port of Friday Harbor

Friday morning dawned appropriately overcast with heavy gray clouds the color of what I imagined a Russian battleship to be. If I were a romantic heroine, I would have spent the day sequestered under my white duvet in the aft cabin, sobbing my way through a large box of tissues, cataloging *ad nauseam* the inti-mate embraces shared with Falcon, the long nights of soul-scorching kisses.

But I'm not and I didn't. Not because I wasn't deeply saddened. I was, but what added insult to injury or salt to the wound was slightly different: After the fifteenth or twentieth reading of Falcon's epistle, I turned to my internet search engine. And by 4:00 a.m, I'd come up with nothing. No Farraday family in Port Isaacs or any other place in Cornwall or the U.K. No Farraday siblings named Donald or Talia. No public records on any of the names. No London stockbroker named Donald Farraday. No registration on a Nautor Swan 42 named *Aphrodite*, no Civil Aviation record of the Learjet that had flown me and Michael from Seattle to Lisbon. No trace of a house in the highlands called Invergary House where Michael had spent his boyhood summers, devouring hot scones with fresh strawberry jam. . . . stomping around the hills and fishing in the loch . . .

Nada, rien, niente.

I gave myself half an hour to absorb the possibility that the man I knew as Michael Farraday did not exist. Then, in the event that he and the rest of the Farraday clan took extra precautions to protect their privacy, I logged on to the DataTech website and submitted a request for a full-scale report. If he existed, DataTech would find him.

It would be at least 24 hours before I had a response, so I consoled myself briefly with the thought that through no fault of his own Michael Farraday found himself in an impossible situation and had fallen in love with a gorgeous private investigator while enmeshed in a marital nightmare.

And denial is not a river in Egypt.

I hauled myself out of bed around seven o'clock. I had no scheduled meetings with clients, new or otherwise, and no court appearances, so I pulled on my favorite pair of soft faded blue jeans and a sweater the color of ripe blueberries. Attire that would take me all the way through the Harvest Regatta skippers meeting that evening.

Blocking out any and all thoughts of Falcon, I stirred up an omelette with tomatoes and bok choi, filled Calico's food bowl, and arranged the hatch cover so that she could come and go without the aft cabin getting flooded should the promised rain arrive. I took my coffee into the salon and put on CNN where the morning anchorman was describing the latest drone strike over the tribal lands of Afghanistan. Apparently the local population – sheepherders and the like – had been seduced into betraying the hideouts of their terrorist countrymen to the CIA for three hundred pieces of silver. Whereupon said terrorists hunted down the sheepherders and tortured and executed them in creative ways.

What was intriguing about the expanded use of drone warfare was that if the U. S. could hire "pilots" to sit at their computer consoles at a National Guard Base in the state of New York or Nevada or Texas – where a pilot could manipulate his joy stick to take out a house in a rural area in Pakistan, then surely said terrorists are training their own pilots and acquired knock-off drones to target their own idea of bad guys . . . in New York or Dallas or Seattle. How hard would it be to target the President in the Rose Garden? Or an oil refinery in West Texas? Is the next step anti-drone drones? Drone raid shelters? Did drones have anything to do with Tina Breckenridge?

I turned off the TV after the newscaster con-firmed the forecast of rain for the next three days and I rummaged in the hanging locker in the aft cabin for the foul weather gear I'd need on Saturday. I found the jacket and my sailing boots, but couldn't locate the waterproof pants and hat. I gathered up my per-sonal effects, spent five minutes searching for my cell phone and found it inside my shoe under the table . . . where is was in a state of discharge. I pulled on my winter boots, grabbed my warmest parka, and locked up the boat.

Chapter 24
OLDE GAZETTE BUILDING

Friday Harbor

Heavy dark stratus hovered over the village. People plodded along Spring Street, heads down, huddled in parkas and hoods. I nodded to those I knew and hurried uphill, avoiding small talk, trying to pretend it was a day like any other. I got to the OGB a little after 8:30. The fragrant fire in the wood stove provided welcome warmth, but neither the fire nor the smell of freshly brewed Kenyan Dark Roast did anything to lift my spirits. I barely had the door closed before Zelda thrust two sheets of paper into my hands. "It's all here."

"*What* is all here?"

"The lowdown on BioIntel. A press release. It explains everything."

"Nothing explains everything, especially press releases."

She gave me a long speculative look. "Bad night?"

"Ungodly bad night." I retrieved a pink message slip from my mailbox. It was from Portia Madrid at H & W. Check your e-mail, it said. *Tried to call you early this morning.*

There was a second message slip, this one from Carolyn Smith. *Need to talk asap. Nothing good. Did your phone die?*

I filled one of the Meh coffee mugs – Zelda had found a set of four at a garage sale – and headed upstairs thinking about Harrison Petrovsky. While I waited for Windows Mail to load, I connected my cell phone to the charger and called Carolyn Smith, explained that I wasn't trying to avoid her.

"Harrison called me this morning," she said. "Hassan told him they will only wait one more day before they dispose of Michelle. That's the word he used, 'dispose.'"

"Carolyn, they won't kill her as long as there is the faintest possibility of money. We need to keep that possibility alive, even if it's a fiction. What's the story on getting the inheritance released?"

"Petra still won't sign o . Her words were, 'I never want to see the bastard again and if they kill him, there will be more money for the rest of us.'"

"I'm working with H & W and we may have a lead on getting in touch with Michelle's parents. I'll keep you posted."

The e-message from Portia was brief. *See attached info on Yee Bao from H & W Hong Kong office. Not much on Reginald Archer. Call me to discuss how you want to proceed.*

I downloaded the attachment. Yee Bao was not a bank manager. He was a Second Vice President of the bank's cybersecurity division at the bank's corporate office. He had an MBA from Stanford University and had worked for five years at the San Francisco headquarters of Bank of America before returning to Shanghai. In banking terms, cybersecurity usually refers to surveillance of cyber-laundering: where bank accounts are opened for legitimate- looking businesses to serve as fronts to money-laundering rings. Six months previously, Yee Bao had been in the news for tracing nearly a trillion dollars that had been routed through the bank, funds that came from a Mexican drug cartel. Mr. Yee's leisure activity was golf. He was a member of the Shanghai 18 Golf Course and Spa and owned a villa there with his wife, Isabelle Archer Yee, whose name had appeared a month earlier as co-ordinator of Shanghai 18's mah jongg tournament.

In the same vein, Yee Bao's name was mentioned in press coverage of a recent international golf tournament hosted by Shanghai 18, which, according to a quote from one reviewer, was "one of the 50 best golf courses in Asia." It didn't appear that the Yee family was living a hardship life. They should be able to contribute to ransoming their daughter and her sailor consort. Mr. Yee should have no trouble figuring out how to route the money to the Somali gangsters. The question was, would he? Or were Chinese daughters disposable? Mr. Yee's business e-mail address was shown, as was his business phone at the bank.

As for Reginald Archer, he was 42 years of age, had been born in Shanghai, and was connected to both the Shanghai Public Security Bureau and the

Ministry of Public Safety. There was no contact information.

I re-read the background on Michelle's family, pondering the best approach . I recalled Harrison's comment about meeting the parents at a posh golf club and his sister Louisa's note that papa was not happy with his daughter's choice of companions. I clicked up the Petrovsky file, found the original message from Carolyn. Luisa had used the term *laowai*, which according to one of numerous Google sources, was a Chinese mandarin word meaning foreigner or alien. The challenge would be to persuade Papa Bao to come up with sufficient U.S. dollars in exchange for both Michelle *and* the *laowai* sailor. And the money would have to be paid in such a way that the hostages actually got released. In the case of the couple from the U.K. who were held for over a year, the first delivery of ransom was stolen by a rival tribe before it reached the pirates holding the couple. I was way out of my comfort zone. Jules DuPont had to handle this.

"Jules is still in Lima," Portia informed me when I got through to her. "I spoke with him this morning and sent him the same information that you got. He thinks the best way to go is through a private negotiator in Nairobi."

"Portia, there's nothing to negotiate without money to negotiate with."

"I thought Harrison had an inheritance."

I explained the will's stipulations. Petra muttered a rude expletive.

"Exactly. The only hope is Michelle's parents." There was silence for a minute, then she asked, "How do you feel about calling her father?"

I sighed. "I would prefer that Jules do it, but we don't want him leaving the Peruvian president in the lurch."

I put down the phone and watched the big fat raindrops spattering my window. Somehow I had gotten trapped into doing what I most dread: tackling a task for which I have no expertise or experience. While it was unlikely the pirates would kill the hostages as long as there was hope of ransom, I abhorred the thought that two lives might depend on my stringing Hassan along until one of the families raised enough money. I found Yee Bao's phone number, then consulted my online time/date calculator: It was midnight in Shanghai. I would have to wait until later in the day. I was only slightly ashamed of the relief I felt.

My cell phone had regained its charge. I had missed three texts from Melissa. *Shawn is going to ND 2 work in fraking. I think he's lying.* The second text was briefer: *WTF. In the third one she got serious. Cn u do a bckground search on Shaun? I don't trust him.*

I texted back a request for an address and/ or social security number, then went downstairs for a refill on my coffee where I found Tina Breckenridge. They handed me The first one was a color photo of Tina at at a lectern. The balloon coming out of her mouth said, "WTF." The second one was a take off on the one she had shown me at our first meeting: A mug shot of Tina with a *Wanted For Murder* line, followed by *Don't Waste Your Vote*. The last one simply said, "*Tina Breckenridge? What a joke!*"

I shrugged. "What can I say? They're nasty. Obviously Lochlan McCready really, really, really wants to win this election. Where did you get these?"

"Lily MacGregor was at the print shop. They were printing up a huge stack of each one. She sorta borrowed a few."

"I don't know who's managing McCready's campaign," I offered, "but propaganda this negative usually backfires. Did Stephan show up?"

"Yes. He was out geocaching. Couldn't find what he was looking for, and decided to sleep over with a friend in town. Sorry, I should have told you."

"Are you going to use the tracker I sent with Zelda?"

"Not yet." She avoided my eyes. "Anything new with the trial?"

Merde! I checked my watch. "Sorry. Don't get your hopes up, but I'm due over at the Evidence Storage Locker an hour ago."

I raced back upstairs, grabbed my parka, speed walked down the hill and over to the old building across from the post office. Reviewing physical evidence collected over 30 years ago might prove to be another dead end, but I was chagrined that I'd dropped the ball. I knocked briskly on Room #3. No one answered the door and I remembered Duffy said he was preparing evidence for trial. Which might also mean he would be called upon to testify as to its chain of custody and might not be back for hours. The rain was pouring off the hood of my rain jacket and dripping on my nose.

"Another bad day, MacKinnon?"

It was Jared Saperstein, face mostly hidden behind his own parka hood, a big plastic bag under his arm.

"Bad day, bad night, bad life. Forgot an appointment with Keith Duffy."

He gave me a sharp look. "I met Duffy heading over to the Courthouse half an hour ago. Anything I can help with?"

I shook my head. "Just following up the last lead in the Gundersen file. Speaking of which, have you seen McCready's latest propaganda efforts?"

He smiled. "Ah, yes. Negative campaigning. It just so happens that's the topic of my editorial tomorrow. " He tilted his head to one side and gave me a searching look. "You look like you need some TLC. What are you doing tonight?"

"Promised to attend the skippers meeting at the yacht club tonight. I'm racing tomorrow."

"Griffin Bay?"

"Uh-huh."

"How about I materialize around six-fifteen or so and spirit you away to our favorite waterside bistro. One of my stringers is the new chef."

"I'm wearing grubby clothes."

"You never look grubby. And this is Friday Harbor."

I thought about what had and had not transpired the night before. And that for all intents and purposes, my relationship with Falcon was ashes. "I'll see you at the yacht club."

I stared after his retreating back, then sprinted back to the OGB. Tina was gone. Zelda eyed me warily as I refilled the Meh cup. "Any calls from the African continent?" I asked. I shook out my parka and hung it on the clothes tree in the corner.

She shook her head. "All quiet. Is that good or bad?"

"God only knows. I need to track down Hassan."

"Don't forget to read the BioIntel press release," she called as I headed for the stairs. "And we're still on for Sunday. At Abby's." Before I could get to the top of the stairs, my phone announced an incoming text. It was Carolyn Smith. *Luisa hs coordinates on Harrison's location! Ck yr email.*

And there it was in the message from Luisa. 6 degrees, 08' 24"N, 46 degrees 37"32"E. *I figured this out*, she explained, because *I arranged for Harrison to have a Satphone before he left Shanghai. The SIM card is on a contract, direct debit from my bank acct. This last week I noticed an increase in volume to an 0025 number, and I got the provider to give me coordinates.*

I Googled the coordinates and located the town of Adaddo. Wikipedia confirmed that Adaddo was a town in the central Galguduud region, 475 kilometers inland from the coast, largely inhabited by members of the Saleeban sub clan of the Habar Gidir. And coincidentally, just 12 miles from where an American and a Dane, both aid workers, were rescued a year or so ago in a raid by Seal Team Six. It was not likely that either Harrison or Michelle were important enough to draw the attention of the CIA or the U.S. Navy.

It was currently 21:15 hours in Adaddo, still a respectful hour to call a pirate. Or should I call Harrison? I opted for the latter. To my surprise he answered.

"Scotia, thank God. Are you going to get us out?"

"We're doing everything we can. How are you?"

"Terrible. I have a horrible intestinal thing. Did Petra sign off on the money?"

"Carolyn Smith is working on it," I lied. "Are you and Michelle still separated?"

"They brought her back this morning. Everybody's armed to the teeth and they look scared shitless. I think they got into an altercation with al-Shabaab or some other tribe. When are you going to get us out of here?"

"Jules DuPont is working with a negotiator in Nairobi." Another lie. "Hang in there. What is Michelle's condition?"

"She's got a broken ankle. Probably some broken ribs. Her whole face is purple from the beating. They're cruel bastards. This afternoon they brought in some dude named Mohammed, a local witch doctor, I guess. He put a splint on her ankle, but she can't walk. And she won't eat. Mohammed said something about 'hospital Mogadishu.' The heat is awful. I . . ." There was a silence, then a dear familiar voice. "Who this?"

"This is Scotia MacKinnon, Hassan."

"Mack Kinnon. You have money? Three and half million dollar? Michelle sick, soon die. "

"Jules DuPont is arranging a payment through Nairobi."

"DuPont big fat liar."

"Are you going to take Michelle to a hospital?"

"No hospital. Much money. Adaddo one hundred dollars every day. *Every day*. Somali poor people."

"We are grateful that you're taking good care of them, Hassan."

"Money this week, three and half million." The connection went dead.

I tried to find hope in the fact that Hassan had not made any further threat of selling Michelle. Perhaps they had tried and the negotiations fell apart, hence a jungle skirmish. And with his last demand, the ransom had come down from the initial five million to three and a half million. A reasonable sum for a Shanghai banker to pay for the return of his daughter. With Jules in Peru, the ball was in my court.

I could either wait until eight a.m. Shanghai time to call Yee Bao or I could send him an e-mail. I rejected the e-mail. How do you tell a parent in an e-mail message that their child is being held captive in a pirate stronghold in East Africa and it's going to take three and a half million dollars to get her back?

Zelda had ventured out into the downpour, brought back chicken noodle soup for both of us. After programming Greek flute music into the sound system, she disappeared with Dakota for another session of her Police Academy adventure. I left my door open, enjoying the pan pipes version of Unchained Melody and dialed Keith Duffy's number at the Evidence Locker. I got his voice recording, apologized for missing our meeting, and asked to reschedule.

There were a number of e-mails reminding me of bills to be paid. I had just clicked up my bank's website when a new text came in from Melissa: Shawn's social security number, date of birth, and two addresses: One in Loveland, Colorado, the other in Elgin, Illinois. I finished my bill paying, reviewed the diminishing balance on my checking account and tried not to think about what Shaun Timmerman's peripatetic existence might mean when it came to financing Melissa's pregnancy. There was nothing to keep Shaun from sending money from North Dakota. The question was, was the move to South Dakota motivated by a desire to provide for his incipient family? Or was he pulling a Harrison Petrovsky? I clicked up the website for DataTech. As I entered Shawn's DOB I noted that he was over ten years older than Melissa. I used to brag about my daughter's common sense. When had she started making bad decisions?

The strains of I Dreamed a Dream drifted up the stairs. Were Melissa's dreams starting to drift away? Did she have any idea how hard it would be to continue on to law school with an infant? As an only child, she had no experience with younger siblings. With diapers and bottles every four hours and diapers and colic and teething and diapers. With the incessant 24/7 responsibility.

I checked on the search I'd requested on Michael Farraday and found only an "in progress" on the status line. I hit the Submit button, and logged off the site.

Tidying up my desk, I found the BioIntel press release Zelda had mentioned earlier and retrieved from who knew what illicit address in the cybersphere.

BioIntel's Flying Insects Eyed for Cyber Defense

BELLEVUE, WA - September 15 – BioIntel Systems, Inc. (BSI), a designer and developer of next generation micro aerial vehicles (MAV's), announced today it has received a fifty million-dollar grant for the purpose of test piloting a 'microaviary' of miniature drones. The drones will replicate the flight patterns of flying creatures of the natural world, and will be equipped with micro cameras and sensors to detect various types of weapons.

These insect MAV's, which have been under development by U. S. Government agencies for over 20 years, will be used for military reconnaissance operations in urban areas. According to Lochlan McCready, BSI's Vice President of Engineering, the microaviary – moths, butterflies, dragonflies, and hawks, -- will play a significant role in data collection and environmental monitoring as well as for civilian surveillance and Search and Rescue (SAR). An earlier generation of MAV's (2G) is already being used in various areas of Florida for anti-crime surveillance.

The pilot testing will be jointly funded by the U. S. Office of Defense Research (ODR) and the Cyborg Division of Astronautical Engineering at the Massachusetts Institute of Technology (MIT).

Whatever connection there might be between baby drones and Lochlan McCready's maniacal efforts to get elected to the San Juan County Council remained elusive. It wasn't anything that would help Tina win the election. I slipped the press release into the Breckenridge file, put the Petrovsky file into my carryall and locked up everything else.

Downstairs I turned off Zelda's sound system. Ready to head over to the GBYC for the race meeting, I read Zelda's whiteboard aphorism for the day: *Enter any 11-digit prime number to continue.*

Chapter 25

GRIFFIN BAY YACHT CLUB

San Juan Island

I have a love-hate relationship with racing.

On the positive side, there's nothing to compare with the euphoria generated by sailing a perfectly trimmed vessel in a 15-knot wind when you're leading all the boats in your class. On the negative side, it's a rare skipper that doesn't metamorphose into Captain Bligh at the veminute starting signal.

One of the challenges of managing a racing crew is that it's very hard to do every race with the same crew. Someone's mate wants him or her to do the gardening, or there's a major sports event scheduled, or whatever. And even the most anal-retentive boat owner forgets or ignores when a traveler needs a new jam cleat or the foredeck crew neglects to repack the spinnaker a er the last take-down.

My skipper friend Ron Callahan was no exception. e last time I crewed for him was on a windless day, he refused to even consider a Did Not Finish, so we sat becalmed out in San Juan Channel for five hours until an incoming tide propelled us to the finish line.

The Griffin Bay Yacht Club is a floating,

free-wheeling yacht club, its clubhouse permanently moored, naturall, along the shore of Griffin Bay,
just north of the shipyard. Skipper Ron was already
there with the rest of the crew. I turned down the
free beer and Ron got me a vermouth and soda at
the bar. I nodded to the skippers I knew as well as
the ones I didn't. Then my eye fell on a big man with
sandy gray thinning hair standing at the bar in a yellow foul weather jacket who seemed to be watching
me intently. I made eye contact and he looked away.
A potential client? A newcomer dazzled by my Shag
Chic tousled beauty?

Captain Ron handed me a copy of the race instructions. The start time was ten a.m. Three possible
race courses were listed; we wouldn't know until just
before the race which one we would sail. I kibitzed
with two crew members from an Etchells 22 and was
about to ask Ron if he'd checked the latest forecast,
when I felt a hand on my arm. It was the man in
the yellow jacket. Up close he was even bigger than
I thought. Wide shoulders, big open face, pale blue
eyes, fifty or sixty years old.

"You're Scotia Mac Kinnon," he said tentatively.

"Yes. Have we met?"

"I'm Duane Ormdahl."

I hid my surprise and shook his extended hand.
"You must be Arne's son. Are you racing tomorrow.

He shook his head. "I'm not a racer. I was wondering, could we have a word when the meeting is
over? It's about Tina Breckenridge."

I glanced around the room. The fleet captain was felding questions on the race instructions. Most of the skippers were conferring with their crew or trading sea stories and guzzling the free beer. "I'm leaving right a er the meeting. What about now? It's a little quieter over there." I nodded to a table in the back corner.

"Perfect." He glanced at my nearly empty glass. "Get you another drink?"

"Club soda, please." I waited for him at a table in front of the big windows. He brought my drink and a cup of coffee and sat across from me. "Sheldon told me about your case. at you're trying to help Tina Breckenridge."

"Sheldon Wainwright?" Sheldon is Zelda's long-standing boyfriend, a ship's pilot who lives in his aunt's house at Cape San Juan.

"I ran into him and Zelda at George's last night. She said you and her were trying to keep that badass McCready from sabotaging Tina's election chances. They suggested I talk to you."

Since by now half the population of San Juan Island knew I'd taken Tina Breckenridge as a client, I didn't waste time pleading client condentiality. "Tina would like to clear her family name. I don't know if I can help her."

"I might know something." He shrugged and wrapped his hands around the white mug. "Or maybe not."

"Your father was the one who first reported Captain Gunderson missing," I prompted.

He nodded. "Peder was my dad's mentor, way

181

back when he was learning to be a ship pilot. He hated to see Peder so depressed after the *Polar Sea* incident and he lost his pilot's license." Duane took a sip of coffee and stared into his cup. "Everybody knew about Peder's home situation. My mom and dad talked about it a lot, about what a dumbass Peder had been to marry Hazel. When dad didn't hear from him for months, he was afraid, you know, that he might have ended it all."

"Is that what your dad thought happened? That Peder committed suicide?"

"Either that or he just ran away." "Because he was afraid of Hazel?" Another head shake.

"No, because he was afraid of Zorco." "Who's Zorco?"

"Dragomir Zorco, captain of the Polar Sea." "Why Zorco?"

"After the grounding and the investigation Zorco lost his job and his wife divorced him. He blamed Peder for it."

"Isn't the ship under full command of the pilot when he has the helm?"

"Yes, but the master of a vessel is supposed to know what's going on at all times. I heard my dad say, the scuttlebutt was Zorco had a woman on board. Not his wife. They were having a little lay-down while Peder was piloting the ship. Dad said Peder must have been drinking. Nothing else to explain why they were that far o -course on a bright sunny day."

"How did your dad know Peder was afraid of Zorco?"

"Peder told him he had a run-in with Zorco. In a

bar in Ballard. Zorco told Peder he'd lost his kids and his wife and he was going to kill him."

"Did your father tell the sheri that?"

Duane sighed into his coffee. "No, he didn't." "For God's sake, why not?"

He gave a long sigh. "I remember my mother begged him to, but he said the last thing Peder ever asked him was not to tell anyone about the threat."

"When was the last time your dad talked to Peder?"

"You're going to think this is weird, but Peder left a message on my folks' answering machine. My dad kept it for a long time. Even afer the trial."

"Did you ever hear it? Do you know what it said?"

"Real short. Just said he'd gotten in a spot of trouble and please don't tell anyone about Zorco."

"Do you remember when that was?"

Duane sighed and sipped his coffee. "I know it was in the winter," he said carefully. "Probably early 1982. I got married right after that and moved out."

"When Peder disappeared, didn't your dad think maybe Zorco had carried out his threat? at he should report it?"

"I don't know what he thought. He was stubborn as a mule. If Peder asked him not to say anything, nobody could've dragged it out of him." "A loyal friend."

"To the grave."

"Both your parents have passed away?"

"My dad did. Mom's in a care facility in Ballard." Dragomir Zorco certainly had motive to kill the man he saw as having cost him his job and ruined his marriage. Even more motive than Hazel. If the prosecutors had known about Zorco's threat, the trial might have gone differently. But I couldn't see how another suspect was going to help Tina Breckenridge shut down McCready. Too little, too late. Way too late.

"What happened to Zorco?" I asked. Across the room I saw Jared Saperstein come in, greet several people, then scan the room for me.

He shrugged. "Dunno. Probably drank himself to death."

I waved to Jared and stood up. I pulled a business card from my pocket and was about to thank Duane and make an exit, when he began speaking again.

"There's something my Mom said when I told her I was going to talk to you. She said, "Tell her to talk to Erika.""

"Who is Erika?"

"Erika Frederiksen. She was Peder's cousin. She was a lot younger than Peder, but they grew up together in Oslo. And a er she came over here, she was his girlfriend."

"You mean before he met Hazel?"

He smiled. "Before he met Hazel and a er he met Hazel. Way a er he and Hazel got married."

"I thought the 'other woman' was somebody named Brette. Somebody in Norway he was engaged to or used to be married to."

"She was the other one."

"Two girlfriends?"

"At least. Erika was married."

"How old is Erika?" Across the room Jared

picked up a drink from the bar and headed for our table.

"Eight-five, ninety, maybe older."

"Does your mother know where I can find Erika?"

"She lived in Ballard for a long time." He pulled a small piece of paper from an overall pocket and laid it on the table. " is was where she lived before my dad died. Maybe you could track her down."

I studied the paper with the scribbled address. "Did your father think Zorco killed Peder?"

He shrugged. "If he did, Erika would know."

Chapter 26

WATERSIDE BISTRO

Friday Harbor

It was 6:30 when Jared and I got to the Bis-tro. The rain had diminished to a light drizzle and an early dark settled in. Quiet music, Vivaldi maybe, drifted from small wireless speakers above the win-dows. From the waterside table Jared had reserved we watched the lights of the ferry loading for the eve-ning departure to Anacortes. He ordered a bottle of an Oregon white wine and the Waterside's signature appetizer, a wild mushroom sampler with sun-dried tomatoes.

"New wine?" I inquired.

"Sokol Blosser. A blend of nine grapes."

"The nine grapes are?"

"Pinot gris, Reisling, Gewurtztraminer, Char-donnay and I forget the rest."

Falcon had introduced me to an Italian white blended wine, something with malvasia grapes --but I thought this one better. I didn't want to think about Falcon, so I said, "I had an interesting conversation with Duane Ormdahl."

"The dude you were talking to when I came in. Should I know who Duane Ormdahl is?"

"Arne Orhdahl's son. Peder Gundersen's friend who first reported him missing."

"You learn anything that might help your client?"

"He said Peder was afraid of a man named Dragomir Zorco, who ostensibly threatened to kill him."

"If I remember correctly, Zorco was the master of the vessel that went aground."

"Good memory. Duane said Zorco lost his job, started drinking to excess, his wife left him." I lifted my glass for another sip as the entrance door opened and a tall couple came into the room. It was Elyse Montenegro with Lochlan McCready. Elyse glanced across the room, saw me, and gave a wave. McCready followed her gaze, his eyes moving from me to Jared and back to me. He did not wave.

"Your former client," Jared murmured, studying the menu.

"Uh-huh." Elyse had come to me after her husband, a Bay Area civil rights attorney, was murdered. She'd ended up moving permanently to the island.

"She still managing Ravenswood Stables?"

"As far as I know."

"They make a handsome couple."

I watched McCready take Elyse's coat and pull out a chair for her. Both were tall and blond and exuded privilege and good health. "A perfect Aryan couple. I wonder if she knows he's married."

Jared smiled. "Friday Harbor creates strange bedfellows."

The waitress returned to the table, recited the evening specials, and we both ordered the Westcott Bay mussels with linguine.

"You mentioned you were writing an editorial about McCready," I said.

"I didn't say it's about McCready. It's about the blowback that can result from negative campaigning. A brief history. You'll find it interesting."

"Are you trying to influence the election?"

"There are probably people more qualified than Tina Breckenridge to run for County Council," he said with a quick glance across the room. "But I detest fascism in all its forms. It's an element I've been watching seep into the islands the last few years. It's troubling."

We sipped our wine in comfortable silence for several minutes "McCready is vice president of a high-tech company called BSI," I said. "BioIntel Systems, Inc. According to a press release out of Bellevue, they've received fifty million dollars to pilot something called MAV's that look like insects. Or birds."

Jared smiled. "Ah, yes, MAV's. They're like baby drones. Remote controlled. State of the art surveillance."

"Are they as sinister as they sound?"

"Depends on whose side you're on. There's something called a Sand Flea that can leap through a window. There's a six-legged robo-cockroach that climbs walls. There are foraging robots and aquatic robots and there's one called the SUGV might be helpful for private investigators."

"Dare I ask what a SUGV might be?"

"A briefcase-sized robot. It can identify a man in a crowd and follow him."

"Will it make me redundant?"

"You will never be redundant, MacKinnon. But like it or not, robots, UAV's and MAV's are no longer the future of surveillance and warfare. They're now. No more boots on foreign soil."

"With that kind of high tech stuff, what's Mc-Cready doing playing at politics in Friday Harbor? What's he going to do, pilot test the baby drones here?"

"Might be. Nice clean rural environment. Enough open space so nobody will complain if one goes astray. We've had high tech companies here before. Might even create some jobs, which we could definitely use."

"How can he have time to administer a multi-million dollar grant and be a County Commissioner in San Juan County?"

"He probably has People. " Jared chuckled. "And his own plane. Have you checked?"

I hadn't. I glanced at the Aryan couple again and met Elyse's eyes. This time she didn't smile and she looked away quickly. Our mussels arrived at that moment and it didn't take a lot of brainpower to figure out that Lochlan McCready was updating Elyse on my client. And probably me. The sauce on the linguine had a lot of garlic and oregano and thyme and I remembered Falcon had said that wheat, the genetically modified kind, was casing the world's epidemic of obesity.

"Why are you staring at the linguine?"

"Wondering if it's organic."

"I'm told everything here is organic. They get the pasta from Italy, where GMO's are not allowed."

"I'm impressed."

"Getting back to the Gundersen case: did anyone

talk to Peder's family in Norway? Or to that woman he was supposedly sending money to?"

"Peder's siblings gave a deposition. Said they hadn't seen him and they swore he was scared to death of Hazel. And they didn't know anything about the whereabouts of the Norwegian woman. Brette, I think her name was. I don't recall that anyone talked to her. His brother said he was trying to get Peder to return to Norway when he disappeared."

"What's your next move?"

"The only thing I've got left is a mystery woman named Erika, who was ostensibly Peder's girlfriend all the time he was married to Hazel."

"No slacker, our Captain Gundersen. Did you connect with Duffy at the Evidence Locker?"

"Left him a message. Haven't heard back. Actually, the case I'm worried about is the other sea captain. The Petrovsky fiasco in Somalia."

"Speaking of fiascos, did you hear about the aborted French attempt to rescue an intelligence agent in Somalia this week?"

I hadn't.

"The agent was kidnaped from a hotel in Mogadishu four years ago. Ostensibly working as a security consultant for the Somali provisional government. Last week the French went in with five helicopters in the middle of the night. An Al Shabaab stronghold. They lost a commando and one or two soldiers and failed to get the hostage out. He's presumed dead. Bad scene." He skewered a mussel and popped in is mouth. "Any contact with Petrovsky or his crew?"

"Michelle got feisty with her captors. They beat her up and took her away for a few days. Today they're back together. We're trying to get in contact with Michelle's father. He's a banker in Shanghai."

"Bankers can be helpful."

"Maybe. Maybe not. Apparently he wasn't happy to have her sail off with a foreigner." I checked the time on my phone. 7:36.

"Do you have to be somewhere?"

I explained Jules DuPont's challenges in Peru and my promise to call Yee Bao.

"I'm not looking forward to the call. He doesn't even know she's been kidnapped."

"Better you than me."

Jared offered coffee and tiramisu at his place and I asked for a raincheck. Neither Elyse nor Mc-Cready looked up as we left the restaurant. Jared gave me a long hug. I inhaled again the scent of spice and almost reconsidered the invitation.

Chapter 27

ABOARD S/V DRAGONSPRAY

Port of Friday Harbor

I got back to *DragonSpray* around 8:30, spent half an hour searching the various lockers and finally located the missing foul weather pants and hat in the locker under my mattress. By then it was nine o'clock and there was no call or text from H & W telling me I was off the hook for calling Shanghai.

I opened the Petrovsky file, found Yee Bao's office phone number. The phone was answered by a distinctly British female voice. "Security Section 5. How may I direct your call?"

"Yee Bao, please."

"One moment, please."

I was connected with another female voice that also spoke impeccable British English. "Mr. Yee's office, Mei Ling speaking. May I help you?"

"This is Scotia MacKinnon. I'm a private investigator calling from Washington State. I would like to speak to Mr. Yee about his daughter, Michelle."

"One moment, please."

There was a silence that lasted over three minutes, then the voice was back.

"Ms. MacKinnon, Mr. Yee does not wish to speak of his daughter. He thanks you for calling."

Merde! I took a deep breath and plunged in. "Mei Ling, please tell Mr. Yee that his daughter Michelle has been kidnapped and she needs his help."

"*Kidnapped*?" It was between a whisper and a gasp and then there was another silence, longer this time.

"Ms. MacKinnon, Mr. Yee will ring you back."

I supplied my cell phone number and the main office number. I gave her Carolyn Smith's number as well as the San Francisco office of H & W Security. She thanked me and I thanked her and pressed the End Call button.

Okay, I'd done my part. The ball was in Yee's court. I hoped his filial feelings for his daughter would overrule his aggravation at her sailing away with a lowly *laowai*. I also hoped that ransoming Harrison and Michelle would not be determined by Yee Bao losing face or saving face. It was ten o'clock and I needed to get to bed. I heated milk for a cup of Ibarra chocolate, took it back to the cabin where Calico was curled at the foot of the bed. As I crawled under the duvet, I momentarily wished I'd accepted the tiramisu that Jared had offered. And yes, whatever endearments accompanied it.

Chapter 28
GRIFFIN BAY YACHT CLUB

Port of Friday Harbor

There was no call back from Yee Bao on Saturday morning when I left the boat at eight-thirty. I hauled my gear up to the parking lot and drove the Alfa out to the GBYC. The Harvest Moon race will not go down in nautical history as a particularly challenging one. After a light morning drizzle, the skies were heavy and overcast. Following a slow start in barely a zephyr, the winds built to a reasonable 10 knots with gusts to 14 and 15. I managed to keep all the spinnaker lines straight, Ron only yelled at me four times, and we were the second boat to cross the finish line. The crew was happy, Ron was ecstatic. After the obligatory high fives and beer at the clubhouse where they had run out of vermouth, I packed my gear in the Alfa, drove back to the Port parking lot, transferred the gear to a dock cart. As I turned to head down to the main dock dragging the cart behind me, I collided with Elyse Montenegro, head down, phone to her ear.

I produced a quick apology, expecting the same from her. That wasn't what I got. "I can't believe you're working for Tina Breckenridge," she said with narrowed eyes. "What's she doing, paying you to invent dirt about Loch?"

"I don't invent, Elyse," I said evenly. "I research and investigate. As you well know."

"You're wasting your time investigating Lochlan McCready. He's squeaky clean. This island should be *honored* to have him on the Council. Too bad we can't say the same about your client." She pocketed her phone, whirled around and headed for the upper parking lot.

I watched her go, wondering if the rest of the San Juan Island electorate would be equally taken in by the man from Santa Barbara. Aching in every muscle, I grabbed the handle on the dock cart and headed down to "G" Dock. Despite my gloves, I had two broken fingernails. My neck was stiff from watching the trim on the spinnaker. I longed for a hot shower and fantasized a soak in a five-star spa. And the nasty little voice in my head insisted on noting how different life would be if I had stayed on with Falcon in the Med. I reminded the little voice the choice hadn't been mine. The option to stay in Porto Sollér was not only a road not taken, it was a road blockaded. Then an ever nastier little voice asked, but why didn't you see the blockade? Did you ever ask him if he was married? Did you even consider doing a background check?

Merde. Merde encore. Merde a la troisième.

Muttering expletives in French that I learned a long time ago playing with offspring of a French fisherman sometimes keeps me from crying, and in that frame of mind, I rounded the corner on "G" dock. There were two people standing on the dock beside *Pumpkinseed*. Henry and Lindsey the Redhead. They

195

were arguing. I knew that even from a distance, because their voices were raised and their faces did not look happy. Both turned as I approached. Henry stared down at his feet. The Redhead was not so shy.

"You bitch. You stole my cat."

"What are you talking about?" I heaved my gear bag onto *DragonSpray*'s deck and prepared to climb aboard.

Redhead yelled the "B" word again. "You stole her."

I turned to face her, thinking that I could handle this so much easier in a dream. "Calico belongs to Henry and me," I said evenly. "I. Did. Not. Steal. Her. "

"Henry gave her to me."

"Henry had no right to give her to you."

"Like hell he didn't. You abandoned her."

"I did not abandon her. I took a vacation. I trusted Henry to take care of her." I glared at Henry who was still studying the boards on the dock. "I trusted you." Henry continued with his study.

"Where is she? I want her back. Did you lock her up?"

"I have no idea," I lied, flashing on the part of the dream where I'd pushed Lindsey off the cliff. I glanced down at the choppy waters of the harbor and smiled.

"Henry, make her give Calico back," she stormed. "She thinks this is a joke."

Henry's response was, "I'm going up to the Legion for a drink."

"Henry, I want the fucking cat back." She strode after him, giving me a "F.U." farewell.

I unlocked the hatch covers and lowered the gear bag into the main salon. Calico raised herself from the cushions on the settee, yawned, stretched, and leaped to the cabin floor to twine around my ankles. While I extricated myself from the foul weather pants and shed my sweater, she went to sit pointedly beside her empty food dish. I refilled it, wondering whether or not I'd seen the last of the Redhead. Her tantrum would have been funny, except that it wasn't, and I didn't like Calico being tossed around like a pawn in a bad chess game. I poured a vermouth and soda over ice, stowed my sailing gear, and collapsed onto the settee behind the table.

I'd emptied my pockets last night, including the scrap of paper Duane Ormdahl had given me at the yacht club. I unfolded the paper and sipped my drink and studied the last known address of Erika Fredericksen, former girlfriend of Captain Peder Gundersen. Thirty years after the trial and conviction the case had more tentacles than a deep sea monster.

I'd given my full attention during the race to the trim of the sails and hadn't checked my phone. I'd had two incoming calls. One was from out of the country, with no number displayed. The second was from H & W Security. There was one VM. "*Ms. MacKinnon, this is Yee Bao. I am returning your call about my daughter Michelle. Please call me at your earliest convenience.*"

I didn't know what time it was in Shanghai, but right now was my earliest convenience. The number Yee Bao had left was different than the one I'd used the night before, so I imagined he was at the villa. A woman answered on the fourth ring. Again, perfect

English. The kind of English I might have learned if I'd stayed with Falcon and gone to live in Cornwall and spent weekends at the Scottish house. Or castle.

Only a minute passed before Yee answered. "I understand you are a Washington private detective, Ms. MacKinnon. And that you have information that my daughter has been kidnapped. Can you tell me how you know that?"

"I was called in to assist Captain Harrison Petrovsky after his sailing vessel was hijacked by Somali pirates somewhere west of the Seychelles. Your daughter was on board and they both have been taken to Somalia."

"Pirates?!" he said hoarsely. He uttered what I imagined to be a Shanghainese curse, there was a long minute of silence, then, "Good God, Petrovsky's a bigger idiot than I realized." In the background I heard a woman's questioning voice.

"I and the attorney have had several conversations with Captain Petrovsky," I said. "And we've contacted a hostage retrieval firm I've worked with. I believe your daughter tried to call you but her phone was confiscated."

"Yes. Last week. All my calls are going to her voice mail. " Another expressive expletive, then he asked, "Do you have any idea where they're being held?"

I pulled the Petrovsky file from my carryall. "According to Petrovsky's cell phone, they're being held near the town of Adaddo. It's in central West part of the country." I started to give him the coordinates, but he interrupted.

"I can find it, for God's sake," he exploded. "And I don't want any amateurs involved in this."

"Jules DuPont at H & W Security is not an amateur. He has an excellent record of successful hostage negotiations all over the world."

"Who exactly have you talked to?"

"I've had several conversations with one of the pirates by the name of Hassan."

"As of right now, I don't want *anyone* doing *anything*, is that clear, Ms. MacKinnon? Nothing. No more phone calls. No attempts to communicate with the pirates, no negotiations. You are off the case. Jules DuPont is off the case. "

I refrained from reminding him that he wasn't the one who hired us. "Your daughter is not in good shape. She needs medical attention."

"I will handle it. Do nothing."

The connection went dead. I pressed End Call and wondered if Yee Bao was as familiar with hostage negotiation as he was with cybersecurity. Or if he had People who were.

Chapter 29

PORT OF FRIDAY HARBOR TO VICTORIA DRIVE

San Juan Island

I should have felt a sense of relief at having been red from the Petrovsky-Yee kidnapping-hostage retrieval morass. In fact, I felt deep frustration and a sense of impending doom. Given Yee Bao's lack of a affection for his daughter's sailing companion, there was nothing to guarantee or even suggest that he would be willing to ransom both of them. There was also the possibility Hassan and his cohorts might decide to separate and/or relocate them. Without the coordinates from Harrison's phone, it would be a Somali needle in a haystack. And at the end of the day, I was working for Carolyn Smith, not Yee Bao. The one positive in the whole sorry Petrovsky quagmire was that it mostly took my mind off of the Michael Farraday quagmire.

I was due at the Corona's special Sunday lunch session at Abigail Leedle's house on the West Side at noon. I'd planned to sleep in until at least eight o'clock, take a run out to the University labs, and then do some general nautical housekeeping. Everything below decks needed a good scrub down.

I could only guess at what Zelda et al had in mind as a rebuttal to McCready's nasty propaganda. Whatever it was, I viewed my role as keeping my client from doing anything that would make her more vulnerable to McCready's attacks. As it turned out, after three sleepless hours between 3:00 a.m. and 6:00 a..m., I was awakened by the sound of tapping on the hull. The clock said 9:35. I pulled on a pair of sweats and a fleece hoodie and went topside. No rain, just a heavy overcast sky and a light wind blowing from the southeast. Duane Ormdahl stood on the dock. He was holding a brown manila envelope.

He took in my bleary eyes and disheveled hair and began a lengthy apology which I cut short. "Not a problem. I was supposed to be up at eight."

"After we talked on Friday, I called my mom. She said Fredericksen was Erika's maiden name. Her husband's name was Gus. Erika has a grandson who's in that virtual TV show. The one about crab fishing in the Bering Sea. Mom and her friends watch it all the time.

Before marrying Paul Breckenridge, Tina worked as crew on a crab boat out of Dutch Harbor on Kodiak Island. This was beginning to feel circular. "You mean *Most Dangerous Catch*?"

"Yeah. Ronstad is first mate on *Lady in Red*. According to his personal Facebook page, he gets lots of marriage proposals." Duane grinned and handed me the envelope. "There is some stuff on the captains of the boats. Thought it might help you find Erika. I wrote down my phone number. Sorry about waking you up. I'll be going now."

After Duane left, I fed Calico, brewed a cup of coffee, decided I didn't have time for a run before heading out to the West Side. I scrambled up some eggs with the leftover baby bok choi and jarlsberg cheese. While I ate I browsed the contents of Duane's envelope, which included description and photos of all the captains of the boats featured in the TV series.

It was eleven o'clock and I did a quick Google search on *F/V Lady in Red*. All I got was a lot of information about the vessel and the two skippers. Phil Ronstad was listed as a first mate, but no personal information. A search for a phone number for Philip Ronstad was equally unsuccessful. Possibly the Ronstads only used cell phones. Maybe telephone directories, online or otherwise, as we know them will be obsolete in five years and the entire planet will be wireless.

After tidying the galley and removing a package of Alaskan sablefish from the freezer to thaw for dinner, I opened up Calico's porthole in the aft cabin and wondered how long I would have to worry about her being kidnapped. There was no sign of life aboard *Pumpkinseed* and I assumed Henry was sleeping o his hangover. I made it all the way up to the Port parking lot without meeting anyone I knew. I drove out of the parking lot and up Spring Street and out of town to Douglas Road where half a dozen shaggy horses of various breeds paced in their runs. Across the road, a herd of Black Angus grazed on the hillside. Heavy dark clouds hung over the snowy peaks of the Olympic Mountains. I was feeling sun-deprived.

Abby's house is a modest gray shingle, two-story dwelling on Victoria Drive with a view of Haro Strait that is anything but modest. She'd lived there alone a er her husband died until she met the second love of her life a few years ago. But fate was not smiling on her; Zelda told me that Abby's boyfriend had died while I was away. Abby was taking it hard and had become reclusive, interested only in her wildlife photography and whatever activist causes the Coronas deemed worthy of their attention.

Zelda's Morris Minor and two other cars were parked in the driveway. Inside I found Abby, Zelda, Lily McGregor, and a short, chunky, brown-eyed woman with a stylish haircut I didn't know. The newcomer wore blue jeans and a thick black sweater and so brown leather boots. They were all gathered around Abby's old round oak table amid coffee cups and stacks of papers and a large decanter of red wine.

Zelda introduced me to the unknown woman, whose name was Patricia Correia. Patricia had creamy skin and dark silky straight hair. She also had an extraordinarily firm handshake and an accent I couldn't place. Her name was familiar but I couldn't place that either, until Zelda supplied the link. "Patricia is McCready's wife." I tried to process why the wife of my client's nemesis was invited to a Corona meeting and asked where Tina was.

"Tina couldn't make it," Zelda explained. "She got into a fight with Paul on Friday night at George's. That's where she met Patricia." She nodded at the woman in the black sweater. "They discovered they had a lot in common. Besides both having hangovers on Saturday morning, that is," she added with a smirk.

Abby muttered something unintelligible and disappeared into the kitchen. Still wondering why McCready's wife was being helpful to her husband's political opponent, I joined the group at the table, realizing that the stacks of papers were Wanted posters worthy of a posse of Old West Outlaws. Zelda handed me one. "I found the templates on the bounty hunters website. Whadya think?"

I scanned the large poster.

WANTED
Lochlan MCCREADY,
PUBLIC ENEMY #1.

Front and center below the headings was the photo from McCready's own brochure, followed by such vital statistics as birthplace, date of birth, height, weight, hair and eye color.

Under **Remarks**, I read the following: *Alias: Condor. Identifying marks: condor tattoo on right buttock.*

I wondered if all clandestine operatives preferred avian aliases. "Where'd you get this stuff?"

Zelda smirked. "CeeGee found some of it. The rest we got from Patricia."

Patricia Correia was perched on one of Abby's tall bar stools, holding a balloon glass of red wine.

"Should I assume that you and Lochlan are not on the best of terms, Patricia?"

"He's a cheating SOB and I hate his guts."

"Does he really have a condor tattoo?"

Patricia nodded. "Acquired in Chad."

Zelda said, "Patricia did a bit of her own surveillance work on Friday night. The Condor spent the night at the ranch with Elyse Montenegro."

It figured. I returned to the Wanted poster, where the **Caution** section got even more interesting: *Lochlan McCready has been associated with the CIA, DARPA, National Clandestine Services (NCS) and KU-FIRE. He is credited with at least ten "wet operations," a.k.a. assassinations, in Africa, Central America, and South America.* **Is this the individual you want sitting on the County Council, making decisions about your money and your quality of island life? Is San Juan Island ready for cyborg surveillance?**

Below the final question was a line drawing of a butterfly with a hand holding a scalpel above its thorax.

"What's with the butterfly and the scalpel?" I asked.

"You didn't read that press release very closely, didya, boss?"

"What did I miss?"

"The baby drones, the MAV's, are *cyborgs*." At my blank look, she explained further. "Cyborg. As in cybernetic organism. As in, a creature with both natural and cybernetic parts."

I stared at the drawing, feeling stupid. "You mean the baby drones, the MAV's, are actually real *creatures*?"

205

Zelda glanced at Patricia, who nodded. "We started out designing tiny, ultra lightweight re-mote-controlled MAV's that resembled small birds, like a hummingbird." Patricia paused, stared at the poster for a minute. "The MAV's were designed to allow troops in urban combat to peer around corners and inside buildings. It was a technology that significantly decreased military and civilian casualties. The 2G MAV was a cyberbug constructed of carbon fiber and fiberglass that could fly for more than an hour."

"Who is we?" I asked.

"I was with DARPA," she said. "That's where I met Lochlan. He was consulting, on loan from NCS."

"And both of you worked on these cyberbugs?"

She nodded. "Lochlan had consulted with an R & D firm in the Netherlands that created a tiny cyber dragonfly. It weighed only three grams and carried a camera that broadcast real-time wireless video." She took a deep breath and chewed on her lower lip. "About two years ago, the R & D focus changed at DARPA. Or you might say, it expanded."

"Expanded how?"

"The focus changed to surgically inserting computer chips into the larvae of moths and dragonflies. That's when I quit."

It took me a few seconds to process what she said. "You mean the insects that are hatched can be electronically controlled? Like a model airplane?"

"Exactly. The pilot can fly it wherever he or she wants. Remotely."

From the kitchen came the sound of clattering

dishes, then Abby reappeared with a basket of bread. "It's the ultimate violation," she spat out. "Helpless moths and dragonflies. I'd like to draw and quarter the idiots behind this. And one idiot specifically."

I took a deep breath, my head spinning. "That's what the multi-million dollar grant to BSI is about? Creating baby flying cyborgs?"

"Piloting them, actually," Patricia confirmed. "The micro-mechanical systems, they're called MEMS, are placed inside the insects. The ultimate goal is to control the insect with GPS nav systems. Each insect can be equipped with a camera, a microphone, or some other type of sensor. They'll be able to sniff out explosives plus transmit conversations."

"I'm feeling slightly ill." I reread the Wanted poster, wondering how much was actionable.

"Everything on it is true," Patricia offered. "I devoutly hope Lochlan has a coronary when he sees it."

"If he doesn't we can arrange one," Abby muttered, returning with a soup tureen.

"In some communities this would guarantee him a lot more votes," I said. "On San Juan Island, not so much."

"So we can post them around town?" This from Zelda.

I shrugged. "Truth in advertising, no? Let's have lunch."

The soup was lobster bisque, the bread warm and crusty, with a salad of apples and walnuts. The wine was Seven Deadly Zins. The sun appeared. Zelda suggested a hike and Lily departed to pick up Sage at the stables. Abby said she was going to take a nap. Zelda gave her a worried look and we waited outside on the weathered deck while Patricia used the bathroom. A large raven swooped by the house, circled once, and returned to make a dramatic spread-wing landing on the railing about ten feet away. It was immediately joined by another raven, slightly larger. Both birds alternated between long glances at the empty black rubber bowl on the railing and the door of the house.

"New pets?" I inquired.

"That's Edgar and Lenore. Abby's been feeding them since they were chicks. She found them on the ground one morning, no trace of mama raven. One of the butchers in town gives her meat scraps. They visit at least once a day."

Edgar produced what sounded like "quark," to which I would swear Lenore replied, "meat." "Did I hear what I thought I heard?"

"Yup. They've got a vocabulary of about ten words. Abby's started a new photo-essay collection. She's calling it The Raven Chronicles."

"What's going on with her and the Brit?"

"Tony Bolton. He's a vulpophile."

"Translation?"

"In addition to being a physicist, he's studied foxes for decades. Turns out London and its suburbs are being overrun with foxes. Or so the tabloids say. So people are hiring snipers to take out the little devils. Tony started an offshoot of the Royal SPCA. Calls it the SPCF."

Several seasons ago, Abigail had created a brouhaha about the little foxes of American Camp, got herself arrested, and published a prizewinning photo chronicle of the saga. "So what brings him to Friday Harbor?"

"Abby discovered the SPCF Facebook page, started messaging him. And voila, Tony the Vulpophile."

"On his way to Africa."

"Yeah. He's got a photography project he wants her to collaborate on. Vanishing wildlife in Tanzania." She zipped up her jacket. "What d'ya think of Patricia?"

"What's she doing in Friday Harbor?" I asked. "Stalking a cheating husband seems a bit beneath someone with her background."

"She wants a divorce and she wants the winery in Santa Barbara. Says McCready been cheating on her for years. He doesn't want a divorce and refused to sign any papers or talk to her attorney so she decided on some face time."

"There must be money involved."

"Quite a bit, I think, and he doesn't want to divide it. Or has none to divide. According to Patricia, he put a second mortgage on the vineyard at the height of the last bubble."

"Did they buy a house here on the island?"

"Yeah, it's out beyond Davison Head, part of the old Pearl Little property. Fifteen or twenty acres. But Patricia refused to move up here. She arrived unannounced at the house Friday night, got inside, waited for him until nearly midnight, then started poking around. She found some of Elyse's stuff and it didn't take her long to find the stables."

At this point Patricia rejoined us and we made our way down to the beach. A brisk wind was blowing out of the northwest, the dark clouds were piling up over Victoria. I pulled my parka hood over my head. "How long are you going to be on the island, Patricia?"

"As long as it takes to get the divorce papers signed. I may need a local attorney to help with that. And probably a process server."

"I can give you a reference. Were you and Lochlan married for long?"

"Four hundred years," she replied with a mirthless laugh. "Actually, just a little over seven."

"You know that Tina Breckenridge is my client."

"Tina told me. She also told me the lies Lochlan's been spreading about her."

"If you're comfortable talking about it, why did Lochlan decide to move up here?"

Several minutes passed before she answered. We scrambled over piles of bleached driftwood to the water. "I don't know if there's a simple answer," Patricia said. "When Loch came to work with us at DARPA, I thought it was because of some kind of logistics screw up in Venezuela that they pulled him out of the field. Somebody got wiped that shouldn't have or maybe several somebodies. He loves to talk about the assignments in Africa and Syria, but he won't talk about Venezuela."

"When did you move to Santa Barbara?"

"Lochlan already owned the vineyard. It belonged to his previous wife's family. They were French.

She died and her parents died. When I resigned from DARPA, Lochlan said, Let's go raise grapes and make wine and forget about the clandestine world. I thought it was a fantastic idea."

"That didn't happen?"

"Everything was okay for about a year. I took over the management, hired a winemaker from Sonoma." She smiled. "Should have known it was too good to last. One day friends came to visit Loch. Two men who'd worked with him in Damascus. Loch took off with them for a couple weeks, off hunting wild boar somewhere, and when they came back, Loch told me he was tired of raising grapes and he and the two friends were going to put together a start-up to do R & D on MAV's that would ultimately be marketed to municipal police."

"In California?"

"That was the idea. They formed a California LLC and were going to open a plant in Sacramento."

"That didn't fly? Pardon the pun."

"The office manager they hired discovered the product was going to be cyborgs. She freaked and made phone calls to local environmental groups and there was a big brouhaha at the Capitol. That's when they decided to move to Bellevue and work for the government instead of trying to market directly to municipalities."

"BSI is operating in Bellevue?"

"Actually just outside the city of Redmond."

"None of this explains why your husband wants to run for San Juan County Council."

There was a long silence. We reached the end of

the beach trail and turned back. The wind was cold and directly in our faces and I imagined Patricia was wishing she were back in the Santa Inez Valley. Zelda was unusually quiet. I was about to conclude my question would go unanswered, when she began to speak in careful measured tones.

"Lochlan McCready is a complicated animal. Very smart. Very well trained in a military sense. Composed of one third hunter, one third mercenary. And the last third is a dark element that I've avoided examining too closely. I can tell you he thinks whatever happened in Venezuela was not his fault and that he was set up and one day he'll get revenge. I can tell you he ran for City Council in Sonoma and was defeated by a woman not too different from Tina Breckenridge. He went around in a black rage for days. After the election, the woman had a serious accident. Single vehicle that went off the road. She survived, but the police are still investigating."

"Are you saying what I think you're saying?"

She shrugged. "Nothing was ever proved."

"Seems like a good reason to relocate."

"His finances are a mess. He never should have bought the house up here and he really needs the DARPA contract. Beyond that, as far as the San Juan Council is concerned. Your guess is as good as mine."

We hiked in silence for five minutes or so, picking our way around toe-stubbing rocks, avoiding slippery spots. Despite the cold temperature, I was enjoying the clean salt smell of wind off the ocean, the sheer remoteness of the area. We reached a fork in the trail and Zelda led on back toward Abby's.

Patricia spoke again. "I probably would've hung in with Loch, stayed with him till the end of time despite all the bad stuff. Just because he has a beautiful body and I really dig smart men. And I know intelligence scenarios can be brutal. But the last straw was the day a woman showed up at the winery saying she was Loch's girl friend from Caracas and she was going to have his baby."

We all stopped walking. Patricia leaned back against a huge bolder, smiled, and folded her arms across her chest. "Smashing news, right?"

Zelda jaw dropped, then she burst out laughing. "I know it's not funny, but I can't help it. Oh, my god, what the hell did you do?"

"My neighbor was there. We were making pasta. It was quite a scene." She laughed. "Too bad there wasn't a camera crew around. The Real Housewives of Santa Inez. It was so outrageous all I could think of was to offer her a glass of wine and listen to her story."

"Did she know Lochlan was married?"

"He told her he was separated and getting a divorce. She's the daughter of the Prime Minister or Minister of Defense or something. The more she talked, the more I became convinced that what got Loch thrown out of Venezuela was about her and didn't have anything have to do with trade craft."

"So what happened when he showed up?"

"He was in the City. She left before he got back."

"End of story?"

"More or less. I gave her his cell phone number and I spent the night at the neighbor's. When I got back the next morning, there was a note saying he was flying to Seattle and then up here. I have no idea whether they met up, whether he took her with him to Seattle, or whether she went back to Caracas. Nor do I care. Water under the bridge."

Back at the house, the ravens Edgar and Lenore were finishing what looked like scraps of a pot roast, both casting long glances in my direction. Abby was watching the birds from inside the sliding glass door and came out to see us off. Zelda left with Patricia to post the Wanted posters around the island. I was about to follow them when a third raven swooped over the deck and came to land on the railing six feet or so beyond where Edgar and Lenore were dining.

"That's Annabel," Abby threw over her shoulder as she headed back into the house. "They'll let her eat if I bring a separate bowl. Be right back."

Edgar and Lenore made no move to threaten the newcomer and Annabel seemed to know the rules, pacing up and down the railing, keeping her distance from the other two ravens. Two minutes later Abby returned, this time with a small wooden bowl that she placed on the very end of the deck railing. Annabel fell upon the pieces of meat. Edgar and Lenore finished their portion, then began a low voiced dialog, both of them watching me and Abby.

"They recognize faces, you know. Just like crows and magpies. They can remember faces up to five years. And they'll tell their friends They're memorizing your face."

"You mean if we meet up someplace else they'll recognize me?" I stifled a laugh.

"Don't laugh. And if you're abusive, they'll tell their friends."

I was back on board *DragonSpray* by six o'clock to find Calico napping on the settee in the main cabin. I turned up the heat and changed into flan-nel P.J.'s, the ones with giraffes on them. The sablefish was thawed. While I sauteed it and wrapped it in parchment paper with capers and garlic and wine, I pondered the questions of the hour: Why was Lochlan McCready so intent on winning the election? Was it about money? Power? Time was running out. Would he come up with something meaner against my client? Or, to use Patricia's term, something darker?

Chapter 30
OLDE GAZETTE BUILDING TO COUNTY EVIDENCE LOCKER

San Juan Island

Monday morning dawned cool and crisp with blue sky and big cumulonimbus clouds hovering over the Cascades. After an early morning run, a shower, and a strawberry banana smoothie, I arrived at the OGB at eight-thirty. There was no sign of Zelda or Dakota. Tony Bolton's office door was closed. The office was dampish. I turned up the electric heat, set up the coffee maker, briefly considered building a fire, then abandoned the idea as being too labor-intensive, and went upstairs.

I was feeling control slipping away on the Petrovsky case, so my first task was to type up a detailed report of my last communications with Harrison Petrovsky, Portia Madrid, Hassan the Pirate, and Yee Bao. It went on for nearly seven pages, and I transmitted it by e-mail to Carolyn Smith with a copy to H & W. Five minutes later Carolyn called.

"I think it's egregious that DuPont has disappeared on us."

I sighed. "I agree, Carolyn. I guess we can't compete with the president of Peru. He'll arrange for a negotiator in Nairobi as soon as we tell him how much money is available. Although in light of my conversation with Yee Bao, maybe it's academic."

"It is *not* academic. Neither of us works for Yee Bao. *My* responsibility is to do everything I can to facilitate extricating Harrison from the clutches of those S o m a l i thugs. I hope you feel the same. From your report and what Luisa told me, Yee Bao sounds perfectly capable of ransoming his daughter and leaving Harrison to shift for himself."

"How are we going to fund Harrison's extrication?"

"Your report said they've come down to three and a half million. I'm filing a petition with the court on behalf of Luisa Petrovsky requesting monies in the estate be distributed without Harrison being present and without approval of the other beneficiaries because of extraordinary and mit-igating circumstances. And then I need to find a way to give power of attorney to Luisa to disburse Harri-son's funds."

"How much money are we talking about?"

"About five million total, give or take a few thousand. One point six million each."
"So it would take Harrison's *and* Luisa's share to fund the ransom. And it would still be short."

"You've got to get it down to two million. Or lower."

"*I* have to get it down?"

"Who else is going to do it?" She cut the con-nection and I sat staring at the phone until it rang again. It was Keith Duffy over at the Sheriff's Office Evidence Locker. He would be there for an hour. Did I want to come over?

Twenty minutes later I listened to Duffy explain

the procedure for logging in and tracking of evidence. Duffy was a nice looking man of average height, sandy hair turning gray, intense blue eyes be-hind wireless glasses. Since I had envisioned some sort of high-tech scheme for managing forensic ev-idence, everything digitally categorized and hermet-ically sealed, I was in for a surprise. This Evidence Locker comprised an L-shaped room about ten feet by twelve feet. There were open shelves and cup-boards and a locked area at the end of the "L."

"We track everything on computer now, but back when the Gundersen case was prosecuted, we used these ledger books." He walked his fingers along several shelves where ledgers were numbered by year, then pulled down a faded book labeled *1980 - 1990.* The same kind of tall green ledger book with a weave on the cover and lined pages with columns inside that my grandmother had used to keep track of her household accounts back in St. Ann's Bay.

"At the time of the Gundersen trial," Duffy ex-plained, "it was logged it in by date and descrip-tion and stored by corresponding number on these shelves and in the closets." He opened the book, leafed through the pages, began running his index finger down the columns. "It's all here," he mur-mured, turning a page, then another. "Four hundred fifty-three items. Carpet, pieces of concrete, pieces of the ceiling, towels. The weapon they said she used, a .38. A wooden table. You wanna look at of the items?"

I told him I was interested in was anything that might carry the captain's DNA.

"The stuff with blood would be the pieces of concrete flooring and carpet. The .38 had both their fingerprints."

"There were blood spatters on the ceiling."

He nodded. "Thing is, we didn't have room for all the stuff here. The rest is in the big storage locker out on Roche Harbor Road." He looked up from the book. "You have a sample of the captain's DNA to match it to?"

"I'm working on it."

He scratched his head doubtfully. "That was over thirty years ago."

"I know. I'd like samples of the blood on the carpet and the ceiling. Can you arrange that?"

"I'll have to check with the Sheriff. We usually only do this with ongoing trials. Or when there's an appeal. Are you in a hurry?"

I thought simultaneously about my less than felicitous relationship with Sheriff Nigel Bishop and about the upcoming election. "Actually, yes." I explained about Tina Breckenridge's desire to clear her family name.

"Because of McCready's smear campaign?"

"Because of that, yes."

Duffy gave a snort and sat down at his metal desk and punched in seven numbers on the phone. I stood to one side of the desk with my fingers crossed on both hands. This was the last possibility of exonerating Hazel Gundersen. It took several minutes before he was connected with the Sheriff.

"She's a private investigator, Nigel. She's reviewing the old Gundersen case and would like to do some DNA matches with the evidence we have stored." There were several minutes of silence, then, "I know that, Nigel. I'm just passing on the request." Another pause. "Yes, MacKinnon. That's her name." A few more seconds of silence, then, "I see. Very good, Nigel, I'll tell her."

He hung up the phone and swivelled around to face me. "I'm sorry, Scotia. The Sheriff says the only way he's letting that evidence out of the locker is with a court order." He regarded me for several seconds. "You and Sheriff Bishop have some bad blood between you?"

I could have named at least six prior bad blood conflicts. At the same time I recalled something Zelda had said about the Sheriff contributing to McCready's super-Pac. "Sheriff Bishop and I don't always see eye to eye. Nothing serious."

Duffy stood up, massaged his left shoulder with his right hand, and went to lean against a counter, arms folded across his chest. "Will you be able to get a court order?"

"Probably not." *But that didn't mean I was going to give up.*

Duffy regarded me for several minutes. "Too bad about that dirt bag McCready. I hear he was involved in assassinations. And torturing butterflies."

"Something like that, yes," I murmured.

Chapter 31
OLDE GAZETTE BUILDING

Friday Harbor

Zelda and Dakota were still missing when I got back to the OGB, but there was a fire crackling in the wood stove. The door to the Kiwi's office was open. He came to stand in the doorway, a *Meh* cup in his hand. "Morning, Scotia." His greeting was accompanied by a smile that went all the way up to his sparkling blue eyes.

"Morning, Tony. Did you make the fire?"

"I did. Seemed like the right kind of morning for it. There was a chap here half an hour ago looking for you."

"Did he leave a name?"

"Nope. Just said he'd be back."

"Have you seen Zelda?"

He shook his head. "Not a trace. Nor the pup either. But Abigail was here. We had a nice chat." He smiled.

I asked about the African photography assignment. His smile broadened. "Tanzania. Dream of a lifetime. I'd love for Abigail to join me. Please put in a kind word for me."

"I'll do my best." I headed upstairs as my cell phone rang. It was Angela Petersen. "What the hell did you do to stir up such a hornet's nest, girlfriend?

The sheriff is apoplectic."

"I asked Keith Duffy if I could send some of the Gundersen evidence for DNA analysis."

"You'd think someone had threatened to demolish his favorite hunting preserve."

"Can't imagine why testing samples of evidence from a 30-year-old murder case should bother him. Must be having a bad morning."

"You wouldn't know anything about the Wanted posters that are hanging all over the island, would you?"

"If you mean, did I design, print or post them, the answer is a firm 'no,'"

"That's what I thought. I have an idea. You have time for a swim this afternoon?"

"I thought you were leaving for Alaska."

"I decided that wasn't such a good idea. Ignorance being bliss, what I don't know can't hurt me, and all that."

"Smart move." I glanced at my calendar. Today's square was blank. "See you at the pool at four."

I don't give up easily. I would persist in the assumption that there had to be some way to get my hands on pieces of the blood-spattered carpet and ceiling and spent several minutes considering how hard it might be to breach whatever security was in place at the county's 'big storage locker' on Roche Harbor Road. Even if that were accomplished, I still needed something to match the DNA to. The only possibility of that meant locating Erika Ronstad.

In the next hour I used every resource available to a private investigator to find a telephone number for Erika Ronstad or Erika Frederiksen or Phil Ronstad, Erika's grandson, in Seattle and surrounding communities. I found nothing. Phil Ronstad was apparently guarding his privacy against unwanted marriage proposals and either Erika had gone back to Norway or had passed on to the same afterlife as the captain. It was nearly one' o'clock when I gave up the search and checked my e-mail, where I found two reports from DataTech. The first was a report on the father of my unborn grandchild.

Shaun Timmerman was born 32 years ago to Dr. Douglas and Mary Beth Timmerman of Oak Brook, Illinois. Shaun was schooled at St. Francis Academy and St. John's Preparatory, followed by a B.S. degree at Northwestern. Six years ago he enrolled at the Feinberg School of Medicine at the Northwestern Chicago campus. So far so good. There was no mention of his employment at the Sweet Grass Guest Ranch in Steamboat Springs, where he and Melissa had met. What wmentioned was two arrests.

The first was for disorderly conduct at a bar in Evanston, Illinois three years ago. There was no information on how the incident was resolved. The second was for domestic violence against Tiffany Robinson of Evanston, Illinois. The couple was living in campus housing. A neighbor had called 911 when he saw Mr. Timmerman push Tiffany, and she fell down the stairs.

Shaun was arrested, but Ms. Robinson said she slipped on the stairway and declined to press charges. Shaun was given probation with 50 hours of community service. Melissa said he'd dropped out of med school. Did he complete his community service before heading West? If not, there would be an active arrest warrant, at least in Illinois.

Unsettled by the report, I stared out the window, thinking of grim situations I'd witnessed in D.V. cases at the San Diego P.D. Wondering how to tell my daughter she was worth way too much to spend her life with an abuser, even if he was the father of her unborn child. I forwarded the report to Melissa without a comment and texted her to check her e-mail. I stared through the window and tried to feel righteous that I'd resisted the urge to tell her to dump her boyfriend while she still could.

The last rainstorm had defoliated the maple tree outside my window. I had a clear view of the high school. Students were returning from lunch break, hanging about outside the back door, a small minority likely weighing the consequences of an af-ternoon truancy. As I stared absentmindedly at the street corner, Zelda's rain-spattered Morris Minor came to a stop on Blair, made a left turn onto Guard Street, and another turn into the driveway of the OGB. She got out of the car, followed by Dakota and Abigail Leedle. Only the dog looked happy.

I thumbed through an old Rolodex and found a number for Bernie Morgan, a Seattle P.D detective who I'd assisted in tracking down a ring of identity thieves hiding out on Lopez Island. Bernie answered on the second ring.

"Morgan here."

"It's Scotia MacKinnon, Bernie."

"What a nice surprise. Didn't expect to hear from you ever again."

"Why ever not?"

"Deputy Petersen told me you were sailing in the Mediterranean or the Greek Islands, or some exotic locale. What happened? You didn't like the climate?"

"It's complicated, Bernie. I'm working on an old murder case and I need to find someone in Seattle."

"How can I help?"

"A woman named Erika Fredericksen or Erika Ronstad. According to public records, she's joint owner of a house in Magnolia with her grandson, who is a cast member of *Most Dangerous Catch*."

"That would be Phil Ronstad, the first mate on *Lady in Red*."

"I'm impressed."

"My nephew worked on the *Lady* last year. You need an address for Ronstad?"

"An address and a phone number, if available. Possibly in Ballard. The number must be unlisted."

He chuckled. "Probably with reason. Even as a greenhorn, my nephew acquired quite a bevy of groupies. We have a brainy new IT clerk in the department. Shouldn't take her more than five minutes to find what you need. I'll be in touch."

The yellow message light on my cell phone was

blinking. It was a text from Melissa: *The DV stuf is B S. Shaun wanted 2 end the relationship & she freakd, neighbor calld 911. Hes coming here so we cn talk.*

I texted back a noncommital *Keep me posted.*

It was nearly noon and I was hungry. At some point I would have to go back to the boat to get my swim gear. I mentally inventoried the contents of the fridge on *DragonSpray*. Nothing that would provide lunch. I was at a standstill on both current cases. I hadn't done any cleaning on the boat since my return and I couldn't think of any excuse not to get to it.

Chapter 32

CENTER FOR WELL BEING

San Juan Island

I got over to the CWB a little before four o'clock after spending the previous three hours scrubbing, brush-ing, mopping, and vacuuming my way through the salon, the aft cabin and the head. I had no energy left for the forward cabin and the topsides would be a major weekend project. The bright work would have to wait until spring.

The club was mostly deserted. I showered, donned the orange and blue flowered Lisbon swimsuit, and completed three laps before Angela appeared. She slipped into the lane next to mine with a quick flip of her hand. Thirty minutes later I hauled myself out of the pool and sat on the end, my legs dangling in the water. I watched Angela execute her tireless crawl stroke and remembered it was at the pool in San Diego where we'd first met. She was a medical examiner then, before taking a position teaching forensic medicine at U.C.L.A. Dr. Angela Morales, who in her wildest dreams never imag-ined marrying an Alaska fisherman.

She finished her last lap and crawled up beside me, taking long deep breaths. "I need to do this more often. I didn't swim very much while you were away." She pulled off her swim cap, turned to face me. "I missed you," she said, throwing an arm around my shoulder.

"I missed you, too," I said. "It's really good to be back." For the first time, I meant it.

"What do you hear from the love of your life? Tall, Dark and Handsome. Is his arrival imminent?"

I shook my head. "No. Not now. Maybe not ever. I had an e-mail." Her eyes widened as I recited the contents of the message that I'd read and reread in my head *ad nauseam*.

"Oh, my God."

"Yup."

"What are you going to do? Are you going over there?"

"I honestly don't know."

"Do you love him?"

I could still feel the long, long embrace we'd shared at the airport, the depth of the brown eyes. "I love him terrible. Or I did before I got the e-mail." I hesitated and then told her the rest: "I did a background search. No Michael Farraday in Cornwall. No brother Donald, no sister Talia."

She gave a little whistle, shook her head, stood up in one smooth movement. "Right. I may be able to help with the Gundersen evidence you want. Can you come out to the house for dinner? I made spaghetti sauce last night. It's always better the second day."

On the way back to the boat, I stopped at the market for a bottle of red wine to take to Angela's and replenished the supply of cat food and Paleo breakfast items. A light drizzle had begun by the time I got back to "G" dock. Calico gave no indication of wanting to spend the evening out. After locking down all the hatches and making the litter box accessible, I changed into a clean pair of blue jeans and an old black turtleneck from my San Francisco days. I pulled on a pair of slouchy black boots with rubber soles and headed up to the parking lot.

It was dark by the time I got to the Petersen house. Through the big kitchen window I saw Angela moving around the lighted kitchen, phone to one ear. I closed the door behind me and hung my parka in the hall closet. The house smelled of garlic and onions and rosemary and thyme. I pulled off my boots and headed into the kitchen.

"That was Matt." Angela laid the phone on the island counter top, filled the pasta pot with water, and put it on the cook top to boil. "He still won't tell me why he's not home and I've never heard so many wimpy excuses in my entire life. What do you think I should do?"

"What are the excuses?"

"First he sprained his ankle. Then one of his crew was getting married in Sitka and wanted Matt to be his best man. The last one was that he needs to get some engine work done before he brings the *Princess* back here for the winter."

"Could all be true. It's a long way from Bristol Bay to Friday Harbor if the engine is sick."

"I s'pose." She frowned and pulled the bottle of wine from the sack, examined the label and smiled. "Matt told me about this wine. Thanks." She took two wine glasses from a cabinet and opened the wine. "I miss him so much. It was okay when the days were long and daylight until ten or so and I could read or work in the garden, but now it's dark when I get home. Or I'm getting up in the dark early in the morning and there's no one to warm up the house. I feel like crying and I don't like to cry."

"At least your time is your own. When he's home, you have to cook three meals a day and keep the house clean." I took a sip of the wine. "I recall he wasn't particularly happy about your becoming a deputy."

"Don't remind me." She idly swirled the wine in her glass and watched it form legs on the sides. "Please don't ask me if I ever regret leaving San Diego."

"Wouldn't think of it." Angela and Matt had a whirlwind courtship that began at a yacht club wedding after I moved to the island. The courtship was followed by a Mexican wedding and honeymoon. Angela had gone with Matt to Alaska the first year they were married, but not after that. Then, to Matt's chagrin, she'd taken a job as a sheriff's dispatcher, and finally applied for and obtained a deputy sheriff position. Women in Matt's family – an old island Norwegian line of Alaska fisherman – didn't work, and there had been some tense months. Had Matt found someone who better fit his idea of a fisherman's wife? The bubbling pasta water interrupted any further dark thoughts. "What can I do? Set the table? Make the salad?"

"The salad, please. Fixings are in the fridge. I got

some bread at the bakery. Rosemary and Parmesan cheese. We're eating beside the fire."

I found the romaine, tomatoes and carrots, tore and chopped and mixed up olive oil and balsamic vinegar and minced garlic. Angela sliced the bread, put the pasta in the pot, set the table in the bay window by the fireplace where madrona logs were crackling and throwing up red sparks. Ten minutes later the pasta was drained and on our plates. I watched Angela ladle a large dollop of the sauce on top of each. She brought her phone with her and we had just settled into our chairs when the phone rang. She answered, glanced at me, listened, nodded, and said, "See you there."

She turned off the phone and gave me a smug smile. "That was Keith Duffy. We're meeting him the storage locker at nine o'clock. You're going to have your DNA samples." She raised her glass. "*Salud*, girl friend."

Chapter 33

SAN JUAN COUNTY EVIDENCE LOCKER

Roche Harbor Road

The drizzle had turned to rain by the time we left the house at 8:15. Angela loaned me a rain jacket with a hood and insisted on driving her black SUV that she said would be less easily identified than my Alfa Berlina. We dropped the Alfa at the Port parking lot and Angela monitored her police radio all the way out Roche Harbor Road. Except for a car prowl on Argyle near the fairgrounds, the island was quiet. Fifteen minutes later, we left the SUV at the trail head on Roche Harbor and West Valley Roads. Angela grabbed several canvas bags from the back of the car, handed me a pair of gloves, and we walked back along the road half a mile or so without meeting any cars to an innocuous looking windowless shed I'd passed by countless times.

The driveway was narrow and surrounded by Douglas fir and thick bushes. There was the smallest of signs along the side of the driveway that said *San Juan County Sheriff's Office*. We stood beside the sign for several minutes, the rain falling steadily on our heads. A fat raccoon ambled past, stopped to give us a once-over and scurried into the wet bushes. Angela nodded toward the building and I saw a shadow move around the corner. As we approached, Duffy moved over to a rolling door and lifted it slowly. It slid up with way too much grinding noise and I wondered nervously how much trouble Angela and Duffy would get into if we were caught.

If there was an alarm, Duffy must have turned it off. He moved inside the cavernous warehouse and we followed. After a minute, Duffy switched on a flashlight and began moving it up and down the shelves that lined the walls. There appeared to be many, many years' accumulation of evidence. After a few minutes, he gave a soft curse, pulled a ledger book out of his jacket, and checked it with his flashlight, then disappeared into the gloom at the back of the building. A few minutes later, we heard something large dragged across on the concrete floor and saw a hand beckoning.

"The pieces of the ceiling and the carpet are in this box," he whispered. "The stuff with the blood stains and spatters. How much do you need?"

I peered into the open wooden crate, extracted a piece of each and put them into the two bags Angela had waiting. Duffy closed the cover on the box, pushed it back under a shelf. He consulted the ledger again with the flashlight, moved further back into the shed, and pulled a plastic bag off one of the upper shelves. "Some towels from the house. Blood on them."

I nodded, pulled one towel from the bag. Duffy looked at me and raised his eyebrows. I nodded my head. I had enough.

We filed out of the building silently. Duffy pulled the door down while Angela and I hurried back to the road in the pouring rain. Just before we reached the trail head where we'd left the SUV, car lights bore down on us. The car slowed. We kept on walking briskly, heads down. The car sped up, and turned onto West Valley Road.

"No alarm on the building?" I asked as we headed back into town.

"Duffy had the code."

"How did you get him to help?"

"His daughter ran a stop sign in town a few weeks ago. I let her go with a warning, but I let him know about it. He's not a fan of McCready, so he wasn't too hard to persuade."

When we got back to town, Angela dropped me at the Port parking lot, helped me put the two canvas bags into the trunk of the Alfa. "I know a private lab that will expedite the analysis for a fat fee," she said. "I'll e-mail you the contact info."

I locked the trunk, gave her a quick hug, and she was gone. Now all I had to do was find Erika Ronstad née Fredericksen.

Chapter 34
OLDE GAZETTE BUILDING

Friday Harbor

On Tuesday morning the weather had seriously deteriorated to sheeting rain and gusty winds. I ate a hurried breakfast of rye toast and poached egg and grapefruit sections, made it up to the OGB at 8:15, whereupon I noticed two things. The first was that the downstairs was cold and silent : no Verdi or Puccini, no soaring tenors or crystal-shattering sopranos. The second thing was that Zelda was seated at her computer and did not look up from her monitor when I came in. No finger action on her keyboard. No pithy comments. Her hair could best be described as 'bedhead.' She appeared to be meditating on the flat screen monitor, which was displaying the New York Times morning headlines.

Dakota lay sprawled on his red futon beside the cold wood stove, regarding Zelda from between his two front paws. Tony Bolton's door was closed. The coffee had been brewed, but a stack of unsorted mail lay on the table in front of our three cubbies. The white board was blank.

"Good morning," I said, hanging up my dripping rain jacket. "Everything okay?"

"I'm in love. Totally, completely, madly in love." She continued staring at the screen.

I began to sort through the mail. "Might I know the object of your affections?"

She swivelled around on her chair, folded her arms across her chest. Her face was pale, no mascara, no lipstick. She was wearing dark washed blue jeans and a sweatshirt that said *Zombie Apocalypse Survivor.*

"It's T.J. Tahoma."

"Cee Gee's gorgeous older brother."

"Yeah."

"When did all this happen?"

"We had a brief fling when I met him at Defcon."

"T.J.'s a hacker, too?"

"No, no, no. He was just hanging out with Cee Gee before he started the job up here."

"Maybe T.J. is the love of your life."

"He wants us to be together. Like live together. I have to make a decision."

"You mean about whether you want an actual, long-term, forever and ever relationship."

"There's no such thing."

"What's T.J.'s real name?"

"Tahoma Jason Pulos."

"Greek?"

"Greek father, Navajo mother. Super smart, great in bed."

"Might be a keeper."

"He is."

"So what's the problem."

"I don't know what to do about Shel."

"Shel's always been there for you."

"He has."

"He took you back after your fling with Boris."

"He did."

"And your fling with Jean Pierre."

"Yes."

"Has the playbook changed?"

"I spent most of the night with T.J. When I got home, Shel was waiting up for me. He said I have to decide: it's him or T.J."

"And T.J. said the same thing."

"Yeah."

I repressed a smile. "Shel ever given you an ultimatum before?"

"No. Usually just sulks for a few weeks."

"I had a stock broker friend in San Francisco who was trying to decide between two boy friends. She put together a rating sheet and rated each of them on the characteristics she thought most important."

"Such as?"

"Usual stuff: education, their politics, how much money they made, could they afford the life style she was accustomed to, did they like cats."

"She did the ratings, didn't like the results, and married the one who liked cats and could dance Argentine tango."

Zelda smiled. "T.J. doesn't tango, but he loves Dakota."

"It's all a matter of priorities." I pulled one message slip from the cubby. The caller was Seattle P.D. detective Bernie Morgan.

"We had an early morning visitor," she said.

"We?" I read Bernie's message that provided the address and phone number for Philip Ronstad and Erika F. Ronstad.

"He said if we didn't take down every single eff-ing Wanted poster on the island Tina would regret it for the rest of her life."

"Lochlan McCready was here?"

"Yep. The Condor in person."

"One of the ways you know if your advertising is successful," I said, "is when your competitor gets nervous enough to make threats."

"He was talking about Stephan. And that's the one thing, the one person, that could make her drop out of the election."

"Actually, I'm surprised he hasn't used the threat before."

She shrugged. "I don't think he took her serious-ly before. And he probably never imagined she'd fight fire with fire. Let's face it, boss, the verbiage on the wanted poster cut to the bone."

Especially the tattoo. "What does Tina say?"

"Stephan's staying with Paul. Paul said he didn't like effing Californians threatening his family and he'd keep an eye on Stephan. Tina says the posters stay."

"Tough lady. What's the next step for the Com-mittee to Elect Tina Breckenridge?"

"We're doing a snail mail-out. Abby got an ad-dress list of all the property owners on the island from a friend who works in the assessor's office. By the way, what were you and Angela doing walking in the dark on Roche Harbor Road last night about ten o'clock?"

"Who wants to know?"

"Lily MacGregor saw you. You didn't look like you were in trouble, and she saw Angela's SUV, so she didn't stop."

"Discretion is ever the better part of valor," I muttered, and headed upstairs.

"Incidentally, boss," she called after me. "I'm available if you need any more research on the Gundersen case. Meanwhile, I'm going to do some data mining and see if I can dig up anything *really* nasty on the Nazi."

I unlocked my office, turned up the heat, placed Bernie Morgan's message slip on my desk. The Seattle address for the Ronstad's, mother and son, was on 35th Avenue West. I sat and stared out the window at the yellow school bus disembarking a wave of students across the street. I spent several minutes trying to decide whether to call and ask for permission to visit Erika or just show up. The second option would avoid a 'no,' but could also result in a wasted trip and a door slammed in my face. The phone was answered on the third ring.

"Ronstad residence. Gretchen speaking. "

"I'd like to speak to Erika Ronstad. This is Scotia MacKinnon calling from Friday Harbor."

There was a slight hesitation, then, "Does Mrs. Ronstad know you, Ms. MacKinnon?"

"I'm investigating a matter regarding an old friend of hers. Captain Peder Gundersen. I'd like to make an appointment to talk to her."

"Mrs. Ronstad isn't–doesn't–doesn't usually have visitors. Her health is, umm, somewhat challenged.

"Would you please tell her I called and ask if she would be willing to talk to me?"

There was a lengthy silence. "She's sleeping just now. How can I reach you?"

I gave the office phone and my cell phone. "I could come over this afternoon or tomorrow," I offered. Since the rain was still sheeting on the windows, I hoped for the next day.

"I'll give her the message," Gretchen said softly, and rang off.

I unlocked my files and turned on the computer thinking about McCready's progression from smear tactics to intimidation. What would his next step be? Friday Harbor wasn't Caracas. Did he think he could get away with a kidnapping? The Wanted posters didn't appear to have slowed him down. The only new evidence we could hope for would depend on the memory and cooperation of a ninety-year-old.

There was also the other lead from Duane Ormdahl that I hadn't followed up on, so I spent the next hour searching for Dragomir Zorco. The internet had 175 items with his name in conjunction with the grounding of the *Polar Sea* over twenty years ago. Then nothing. No death notices, no criminal records. I submitted a formal request to DataTech, although without a known address or social security number I wasn't hopeful.

Among my e-messages I found one from Angela Petersen with the name of a private lab in Seattle that did DNA analysis. According to their website, Investigation Forensics Lab (IFL) was a full service facility in Seattle that tested Biological DNA, Latent prints, Firearms, Controlled substance identification, Infidelity testing – whatever that was --, Toxicology, and the one I was looking for: Trace Evidence, i.e., hair and fiber analysis. Perfect. All I had to do was pack up the evidence from the Storage Locker and ship it down to IFL.

Nothing from Carolyn Smith vis-a-vis the request to distribute the Petrovsky estate assets. I hadn't received any more calls from Hassan threatening imminent death or disposal of the hostages and in this case, no news could be bad news.

The last cryptic text from Melissa was the one advising that Shaun was en route to the Bay Area "to talk." I pulled up her Facebook page, found four new photos she'd posted of herself and friends, learned that her Contract Law course was a waste of time. No posts on pregnancy or sonogram photos of a developing fetus. There were three posts from Jewel Moon relating activities during Mendocino Quilting Week, her volunteer work with Deprived Children, and Giovanni's thoughts on a Greek Islands cruise vs. a visit to Corsica. Jumping right into the current, I posted two comments on Melissa's photos, praised Jewel Moon for her community spirit, stared at my phone for several minutes, hoping for a call back from Gretchen Storvik, then I went downstairs.

Zelda had left off meditating on her monitor screen and was smiling an evil smile as her fingers raced over the keyboard. "You are so not going to believe this," she chortled. "It might be made-up, so I'm going to have Cee Gee check it out."

Before I could ask what she'd found that would strain my credulity, the office phone rang. Zelda answered it, said, "She's right here, please hold," and passed the phone to me. "Gretchen Storvik," she said.

"Mrs. Ronstad would like to talk to you about the captain," Gretchen said. "She wants to show you pictures. She's feeling good now. Can you come this afternoon?"

It was nearly noon. I glanced out the window; the rain had diminished to a few random drops and the fog had thinned. I made an appointment for 2:30, which was cutting it close. I raced back upstairs, called Kenmore Air. They had a float plane leaving from the marina in 20 minutes. There were two vacant seats. I locked up the file cabinets, found the small overnight bag I keep for emergencies with toothbrush and clean underwear, and stuffed both in my carryall along with the Gundersen file to review on the plane. I accepted Zelda's offer of a ride to the marina.

Chapter 35

PORT OF FRIDAY HARBOR

to Lake Union Seattle

Kenmore Air is the largest seaplane company in the Pacific Northwest. They have both scheduled and charter flights, from Seattle to Victoria and the San Juans, and all the way up the Straight of Georgia. Their main workhorse is the deHaviland Beaver. I heard recently that Harrison Ford bought one of their refurbished birds.

Zelda dropped me at the top of the main dock. I asked her to please arrange a rental car for pick up at the Kenmore terminal. She promised to call me if she found any information on Dragomir Zorco or Lochlan McCready a.k.a. the Condor, and shared that she thought her relationship with Shel had come to an end. When I got out to the seaplane dock, the seven-passenger Beaver was bouncing in the waves while five arriving passengers gingerly made their way down the skinny ladder steps. The best way to disembark is backwards, like coming down a companionway or a hayloft, but most folks don't do that.

The pilot was Roseanne Gallagher, a former client. Last winter I'd helped her locate her son who'd gone incommunicado from Princeton. She gave me a wink as she encouraged the last disembarking passenger, a rotund gentleman, to lift his feet off the lower step and onto the swaying dock. The Seattle-bound passengers were a family of four: two harassed looking parents and two teenagers making eye contact only with their iPhones.

I followed the second teenager on board and took a seat in the back of the plane. Roseanne stowed the luggage, closed the door and climbed into the cockpit, from where she gave us a speedy passenger briefing. To my relief, she announced we would not be making the usual stop in Roche Harbor and were headed directly for Lake Union.

We taxied across the harbor and were airborne, out over San Juan Channel past Lopez Island, then southeast past Whidbey, the longest island in the U. S. Stretching away to our right were the rain forests and snowy glaciers of the Olympic Peninsula where white plumes of CO_2 swirled in the air currents above the Port Townsend paper mill. We taxied up to the dock at the Lake Union terminal at 12:57. When I turned on my phone, there was a text from Zelda: The Enterprise rental people should be waiting for me at the terminal. She'd reserved the car for 24 hours.

I was the last passenger off the plane. I thanked Roseanne for a good flight and asked about her son. "Jacob's back in school," she said. " Studying forestry this time."

I hurried up the ramp to the reception area and waiting room. The rental car associate was outside, standing beside a white Ford Fusion. We checked the vehicle for dents and gouges, I signed the requisite papers, and ten minutes later I was en route to 35th Avenue in Magnolia under the guidance of the vehicle's GPS nav system. My mind wandered to the upcoming interview with Erika Ronstadt and I was chastised by the GPS lady when I missed a turn at an intersection. I found a place to turn around, apologized, and continued on over the Dravus Street Bridge.

Magnolia is the second largest neighborhood in Seattle, a hilly peninsula northwest of downtown, connected to the rest of the city by three bridges over the tracks of the BNSF railway. The neighborhood is bookended by Magnolia Park to the South and Discovery Park on the northwest.

I found the Ronstad house in the middle of the block on 35th Avenue, a modest two-story, gray shingle dwelling probably built in the 1950's, surrounded by a crimson cloud of big leaf maple trees. Smoke curled out of the brick chimney. I parked the Fusion on the street, locked it, and went up the broad walkway bordered by two thick, neatly trimmed hedges. It was colder than Friday Harbor, the wind sharper.

The faded blue wooden door had a stained glass window in the top. I pressed the bronze doorbell and heard a chime inside the house. A minute or so later the door was opened by a blonde woman of some indeterminate age.

"I'm Gretchen," she said with a frown. "Please come in."

I stepped into the hallway. The fragrance of a wood fire filled the house. At the far end of the hallway there was a padded window seat below a leaded glass window. I handed Gretchen my business card. "How is Mrs. Ronstad doing?"

"She's in her room. She wants to talk to you. But . . ."

I waited, hoping I hadn't made the trip for nothing. "I'll try not to upset her, if that's what you're thinking."

She peered at my card. "You're a private investigator. I checked you out. What do you want to talk to Erika about?"

I provided a brief version of Tina Breckenridge's desire to clear her family name. About the conviction of a woman for murder without a body ever having been discovered. "A family friend of Peder Gundersen suggested Erika might have some information about what really happened before the captain disappeared."

"That was a long time ago, wasn't it? It's that she gets confused. About time. After you called, she told me she talked to Peder last week. Peder Gundersen. I've worked here for a year and I've never seen anyone with that name."

"Perhaps it will become clear when I talk to her," I said. "Time isn't always linear."

Her eyes widened. "It isn't, is it? Let me take your coat. Would you like some tea?"

I declined the tea. She hung my coat in the entryway closet and I followed her down the hall past a small living room whose bay window looked out on a back garden where more maple trees were shedding leaves. The hallway did a dogleg to the left and presently we arrived at a wood-paneled room with another bay window that looked out onto the same garden. A recliner chair and a love seat sat in front of the fireplace where a wood fire burned. There was a bed in an alcove.

"Erika sweetheart, Ms. MacKinnon is here to talk to you."

Seated in the recliner that faced a TV was one of the most beautiful women I've ever seen. Her skin was translucent and unlined. A nimbus of curly grey-white hair surrounded the face. She wore a lavender pant suit of French terry and she looked at me out of clear, ageless blue eyes. She extended a small veined hand. I clasped it carefully, feeling the bones beneath the parchment skin. Gretchen motioned me to the love seat.

"You have news of my Peder?" she asked. "Did he call you? Is he coming?"

"When did you last hear from Peder, Erika?"

"A long time." She frowned. "Six months? He wrote to me." She glanced at Gretchen who was standing in the doorway, arms folded over her chest.

"Tell me about the last time you saw Peder." I said.

"It was snowing. He came here." She looked around the room, frowned again and shook her head. "No, no, not here. The other house." She frowned and looked at Gretchen again.

"Erika lived in Ballard before she moved here," Gretchen said.

"Was your son with you when you saw Peder, Erika?" I asked, trying to establish a time frame.

"Oh, yes. Wolf was there. It was winter. It was too cold to fish."

"Was your husband there, too? Was Gus there when Peder came?"

She gave a mirthless chortle. "Gus was gone. Long gone. He went to live with that hussy in Pelican."

247

"How old was Wolf when you saw Peder?"

"He was . . . he was young." She furrowed her brow and twisted her hands in her lap. My question had fractured something in her memory. I tried to think of a way to withdraw the question, then she said, "He was twenty-four, maybe twenty-five. Why do you want to know? Why does it matter?"

"It doesn't matter, Erika," I said gently. "Tell me, how was Peder when you saw him? Was he well?"

"Well? How can you be well when you've almost been killed?"

Gretchen moved away from the door toward Erika.

"I'm sorry, Erika. Do you know who tried to kill Peder?"

She put her hands over her face and rocked softly in her chair. "My beautiful Peder," she whimpered. "His poor shoulder and all that blood."

Gretchen sat down on the arm of the recliner, put an arm around Erika, crooned to her. I moved over to the window seat and stared out at the garden where a soft mist shrouded the property.

Erika began speaking. "Wolf was very handsome. Like his father. I have pictures of them." Her face was calm now, the distress was gone.

"Peder was Wolf's father?" I asked, struggling with the captain's tangled relationships.

"Of course."

"May I see the pictures?"

She looked at Gretchen. "Where are my Peder's letters and pictures?"

"I'll get them." Gretchen went to a wooden cabinet in the alcove, returned with a large scrapbook. She handed it to Erika who put it on her lap and riffled through a dozen or so pages, then stopped. "Peder and Wolf," she said with pride. "Wolf's birthday." She held up a photo that showed a young version of the captain with a thin, blond teen-age boy dressed in a sailor top and dark pants. "He was sixteen." She turned more pages, read a newspaper clipping then another, closed the album. "No more pictures."

I was probably going to lose her again, but I had to ask the question. "What happened to Peder the last time you saw him? Why did he have blood on him?"

"There was a big fight."

"Who did he fight with?"

She shook her head. "He was afraid."

"Why was he afraid?"

"Because he killed him."

"Who did Peder kill?"

She looked directly at me, then looked away and pressed her lips together. "I can't tell you that."

I waited a few moments, then repeated the question. She turned to face me. The blue eyes were now empty. As clearly as if a curtain had dropped, I'd lost her.

"Where did Peder go after he was with you and Wolf?"

The curtain lifted for a brief second, then was replaced by something else entirely. "He wanted me to go with him. My darling Peder. He said he couldn't go without me. But I couldn't go."

"Where did Peder want you to go?"

She replied as to a very small child. "To Iceland, of course."

"Why did Peder want to go to Iceland?"

Another look of disbelief. "Because that's where the boys were."

"You mean his sons, the ones with his girl friend, Brette."

"No, no, no. His wife. She was his wife."

"Before he married Hazel?"

The named awakened something dark. "He never divorced Brette," she said. "He just married Hazel. She lied to him."

"Hazel lied to him."

She sneered. "She was a drunk and a slut and a thief. Peder was afraid for a long time."

"Afraid of Hazel."

"*No*. Peder was afraid of *Zorco*."

"Dragomir Zorco? The captain of the *Polar Sea*?"

"He was a drunk, too."

"Why was Peder afraid of Zorco?"

" He's dangerous."

"After Peder came to see you when it was snowing, where did he go?"

"Yes."

"Yes, what?"

"He killed Zorco."

"How do you know?"

"He had to run away before they found out, he had to go to Iceland. He wanted me to go with him, but Wolf didn't want to go and I couldn't leave Wolf."

"How do you know he went to Iceland?"

She stared out at the garden and her eyes went far away. "He didn't like Iceland, but he couldn't come back home."

"Tell me why he couldn't come back home?"

She shook her head and spelled it out for me. "He. Was. Afraid. Zorco. Would. Come. Back. And. Kill. Him."

I tried one more time. "Why was Zorco going to kill him?"

"Hazel was a bitch."

"Did Peder stay in Iceland?"

A long silence. Her chin dropped onto her chest, her eyes closed. The scrapbook slipped from her lap onto the floor. Several photos and a small white envelope slid out of the scrapbook. Erika's eyes remained closed. In the silence I heard the ticking of the tall clock by the fireplace. I asked again, softly, "Erika, may I see Peder's letters from Iceland?"

She raised her head and said, "Peder wants me to go to the islands."

"Could I see the letters, Erika?"

She turned to Gretchen. "I'm thirsty," she said in a petulant voice. "Bring my tea now. Then I have to pack."

Gretchen retrieved the scrapbook along with the white envelope and loose photos from the floor, gave me an unreadable look, and hurried out of the room.

"Peder is in Ecaria," Erika informed me. "Please go away now. I have to pack."

Chapter 36
FISHERMAN'S TERMINAL

Seattle

I knew there were no letters from Iceland. I didn't know where or what Ecaria was – perhaps a Norwegian word for the afterlife. Erika didn't enlighten me. Gretchen brought the tea, Erika retreated into a far away silence, and I made my departure. Back in the Fusion, I checked my phone, found a text from Zelda: *Dragomir Zorco deceased. Son Igor will talk to you. Lives aboard the Lisa Marie @ fishermen's terminal dock 8.*

It was ten minutes before four o'clock. The Fishermen's Terminal was founded in part by Norwegian fishermen and is home port for six or seven hundred commercial vessels that make up the North Pacific Fishing Fleet. It's located off Salmon Bay, at the base of the Magnolia neighborhood next to the Ballard bridge, not more than a five-minute drive from the Ronstad house.

The afternoon traffic was heavy and it took closer to fifteen minutes. I parked in front of the Chinook restaurant and walked out to the docks. I found the *Lisa Marie* half way down on the right-hand side of dock eight, a well-maintained fiberglass blue-hulled seiner or gillnetter– I wasn't sure which – at least 50 feet in length. I had no idea what Zelda had told Igor

Zorco. I stood for a minute beside the vessel, taking in the downriggers and the big drums used for reeling in the nets. When I see these boats, all I can ever think of is hard, dangerous work in icy seas. I was about to announce my presence by knocking on the hull when the side door opened. A large man in his late 40's leaned out the door. He wore a white T-shirt and ragged blue jeans tucked into black fisherman's boots. His brown hair going gray was collar length, his beard was bushy. "Hey, you must be Scotia. I'm Igor. Come aboard." He had a warm smile that showed one missing front tooth. A long white scar outlined the left side of his face.

I clambered on board. He gave my hand a hearty shake and I followed him forward to the wheelhouse. It was warm inside. The polished wood console below the windows above the bow had all the requisite tools for locating fish in Alaska waters: Horizon GPS, sounder and chart navigation. A ComNav autopilot. Radar and a laptop computer and a Satphone.

"Nice boat," I said. "A seiner?"

"Yes, ma'am. Been fishing out of Bristol Bay for twenty years."

"It's in really good shape."

"We rebuilt it two years ago."

"You have a partner?"

"The wife's brother. Couldn't do it alone. My son works with us in the summer."

"What's the engine?"

"3406 Cat main. Four hundred hours on it." He motioned to the small settee behind the helmsman's seat. "Have a seat. I was about to get myself a beer. Will you join me?"

I accepted the offer and Igor disappeared below. From the windows I could see hundreds of boats in the marina and the Ballard hills beyond. Igor reappeared, handed me a sweating bottle of Heineken, then sat in the helmsman's seat. "So. Your assistant said you're writing about that scumbag of a sea captain that got himself murdered." He took a long swig of the beer.

"He was a colorful character, wasn't he."

"They never found the body, I guess. I heard she ground him up into sausage. Served him right."

"Your father knew him."

He nodded. "Unfortunately, yes. It was a dark day he let that idiot on board the *Polar Sea*. And the man called himself a pilot. What a joke."

"I've read a lot of versions about the grounding. Can you tell me what happened?"

He looked away through the window for a long minute, took another swig of the beer, wiped his mouth with his hand. "The *Polar Sea* was bound for Vancouver. Gundersen came on board in Port Angeles. Everything was fine till the engineer said there was a problem with the engine. Dad went below for about twenty minutes. All Gundersen had to do was steer the boat around Stuart Island into Boundary Pass." He shook his head. "Next thing Dad knew, they'd rammed the island. Guess who got blamed for it and lost his job?"

"It must have been devastating for him."

"Hell, yes. Dad was an immigrant and he had all of us to support and nobody would give him a job. Nearly killed him."

More beer, then the cornflower eyes went dark. "We moved couple of times. Dad took to drinking, staying out late, started knocking my mother around." He rolled the empty bottle between his hands and stared at the floor. "I took him on one night when he came home drunk and started screaming that he was going to kill Gundersen. When my mother tried to hush him up, he started in on her and I couldn't take any more." He traced the scar on the side of his face. "When I was fifteen, my mom took me and my brother to live in Anacortes."

"A terrible time for all of you."

I remembered what Erika Ronstad said about Peder showing up at her house covered in blood . . . with a bad shoulder. That Peder was afraid of Zorco. "Do you think your father ever tried to make good on his threat?"

"You mean to kill him?" He gave me a long look. "*My father did not kill Peder Gundersen*. Don't go there."

We sat in silence. I finished my beer and Igor stared through the window. The boat in the next slip backed out into the channel. The *Lisa Marie* rocked gently in the wake. A few drops of rain spattered on the windows. "I wasn't suggesting your father killed him, Igor," I said softly. "I was wondering if the two of them ever had any actual physical . . . fights?"

The silence this time was longer. Igor stood up and moved toward the companionway. "Another beer?"

I nodded. I would drink beer all night if that's what it would take to find out what happened between Dragomir Zorco and Peder Gundersen all those years ago. Five minutes passed, then ten. It appeared the interview was over and I was opening the door to leave when Igor reappeared. "Sit down. Please. I'll tell you what happened."

He handed me another Heineken and I sat.

"It was after we moved to Anacortes, my mom and me and Leon. My mom worked nights as a waitress. It was in the winter. Me and Leon were leaving for school when Dad drove into the driveway in the old red pickup. He must've hit something because one of the front fenders was dented in and the windshield was broken. He sorta fell out of the truck, couldn't hardly walk, and we helped him inside. My mom was asleep. She almost fainted when she saw all the blood." He stopped, covered his eyes with one hand. "He was a godawful mess. Big ugly gash in his head and blood all over his face. My mom started to call 911, but he got into a rage and yelled at her. No doctor, he said. No doctor. He yelled at Leon and me to get out, to go to school." He stopped again, bit his bottom lip. "We left, and Leon wanted to go to the neighbors and get a doctor, but I was afraid of what Dad would do, so we just went on to school and didn't tell nobody."

"Did you find out what happened?"

"He was still there when we got home from school. My mom didn't go to work that night. I heard them talking, after Leon and I were supposed to be asleep. It sounded like Dad had gone to find Gunderson, out in the islands somewhere. They got into a fight, he said, and then the old bugger grabbed a gun and shot Dad. In the head and in the leg."

"Your dad never reported this?"

He shook his head, then shrugged. "My mom wouldn't talk about it. Dad stayed for a month, then started drinking again. My mom told him to leave or she would go to the police."

"He left?"

He stared blankly out the window. "We never saw him again."

"Do you remember what year that was?"

He did some silent calculating, then said, "Well, I was in the tenth grade and I was sixteen years old, so it must have been in 1982. Sometime after Christmas."

Although his disappearance hadn't been reported until six months later, Peder Gundersen apparently disappeared in January of that year. "Nobody ever talked to your mother during the murder trial? The sheriff or either of the attorneys?"

He shrugged again. "I was into football and chasing girls. I don't think I paid much attention. I do remember one night we were watching the news with my mom and something came on about a murder trial in Friday Harbor and she turned it off right away."

Igor's mood seemed to darken suddenly. He slammed the empty Heineken bottle down on the console. "Why the hell did you have to bring all this stuff up? It happened thirty years ago. Shit, I was having a good day 'till you got here."

I knew I should make a quick exit, but sometimes I get stupid when I'm getting close to what feels like a breakthrough in a case. "Igor, one of the main pieces of evidence in the trial was the blood spatters on the ceiling at the Gundersen home."

"So?"

"They couldn't do DNA analysis back then, but it sure would help my research if I knew whether the blood on the ceiling was the captain's or your father's."

He let the question hang for a minute, then his fist clenched, his face flushed, and I wondered if he was going to strike me. Instead, he started pulling hairs out of his beard and stuffing them into a plastic bag that was lying on the console.

"You want DNA? Here's your fucking DNA. Take these. And these. My father was not a murderer. Don't you dare write that he was. Now get your ass off my boat and don't ever come back."

Chapter 37
M/V ROGUE WAVE

Lake Union, Seattle

Without much effort, I'd managed to become *non grata* twice in one afternoon. Breathing hard, I hurried along the dock and up to the parking lot. In one hand I clutched the plastic bag of beard hairs Igor Zorco had thrust on me and unlocked the Fusion's door with the other. I slid into the car, closed the door, and sat quietly, taking long deep breaths, trying to calm my heartbeat. In the past two hours two people had told me stories, either of which, if true, could have turned the case of the *State of Washington v Hazel Gundersen* upside down.

First Erika with her tale of letters from Iceland and some place called Ecaria. Now Igor's narrative of his father's bloody fight with the missing captain. After which both men disappeared. Could both stories be true? Or had time and memory created illusions?

I stared at the bag of beard hairs and winced. But they were my only chance of identifying the blood spatters on the Gundersen ceiling. The rain had stopped and patches of blue sky were appearing to the west. If I could find it, I could drop the beard hairs at the forensics lab Angela had recommended, even though the rest of the evidence Angela and

I had purloined from the Sheriff's Evidence Storage was still in Friday Harbor, locked in the trunk of the Alfa Berlina. If I'd had my wits about me, I could have brought it all with me, but I seemed to be somewhat short on wits recently.

Investigation Forensics was simply listed as IFL with an address in downtown Seattle. I found a phone number for IFL, got a recording informing me that their business hours were 8:30 to 4:30 and if I knew the extension of the person I wanted to call, I could dial it at any time. It was 5:48, a fact which saved me a trip south into what would be horrendous late afternoon traffic. I would take the beard hairs back to Friday Harbor, collect the rest of the evidence, and overnight it all to IFL.

I called Kenmore Air, booked a seat on the 8:00 a.m. flight the next morning, then considered where I was going to lay my head for the night.

In earlier, happier times, I would have spent the night at Nick's condo. I hadn't heard from him since the evening last week when I'd turned down his offer of a sleep over at the Mt. Dallas house. I told myself I didn't have to spend the night. We could go out to dinner and I could get a room near the Kenmore terminal. He was probably still at the office. I dialed his cell phone. He answered on the second ring. There was music in the background, and the murmur of voices. Women's voices.

"Scottie?"

"Nick." I struggled for something intelligent to say, regretting the call.

"Nice to hear from you. How are you?"

"I'm fine. It's just that I was in Seattle on a case and I've got an early morning flight, so I thought . . . maybe . . . we could . . . have dinner. Or something."

There was a short silence. "Wish I'd known you were coming. Nicole is here. And her mother. We were just going out. I. . . uh, don't suppose you want to join us . . . "

"No problem, Nick, I'll just grab something to eat and get a good night's sleep. Sorry to have bothered you. Have a great evening. Catch you later." I hit the disconnect button before he could reply.

I mentally reviewed lodgings near the Kenmore terminal, remembered a B & B Nick and I had spent the night at several years back. In this case the B & B stands for "bunk and breakfast' and the hostel is the *M/V Rogue Wave*, a 54-foot tugboat moored on the south end of Lake Union. The innkeeper is a former Coast Guard captain. I pulled up the website on my phone, found the number. They had one cabin available. The rate was not cheap, but it included a full breakfast and private bath, and was a five minute drive to the floatplane terminal. I booked it.

Nagged by Erika's last words about a place called Ecaria, I did a quick on-line search. Ikaria, also spelled Icaria, had nothing to do with the Norwegian afterlife. It was an island lying just off the Turkish coast, about 20 km southwest of the island of Samos. Famous for its dark red wine, its thermal springs, and for the legend of Icarus who flew too close to the sun, Icaria was touted as a Blue Zone, one of the healthiest places on the planet, where most of the inhabitants live well into their 90's. The longevity was attributed to living in a place where nothing ever happens: no thumping nightclubs, no major airport, no high-rise condos. A perfect refuge for a sea captain fleeing from monsters, real or imagined. Now all I needed was evidence that Peder had actually gone there. Or gone anywhere.

I needed to get some fresh air and clear my head. Darkness would be falling in an hour. I turned the key in the ignition and headed out of the parking lot toward my favorite Seattle hiking spot.

Discovery Park is Seattle's largest public park, 500-plus acres on Magnolia Bluff. I parked in the lower lot, grabbed my backpack, locked the car, and headed for the Loop Trail that winds through forest groves and meadow lands and connects to the road to the beach. Thirty minutes later, I stood beside the West Point Light. The wind was brisk and a small sailboat tacked across the water toward West Seattle. To the south lay Vashon and Blake Islands, directly ahead to the West was the bedroom community of Bainbridge Island.

I found a bench overlooking the water, sat, and scolded myself for having called Nick. Having dinner with him last week was a silly regression into a relationship that for all intents and purposes had ended months ago. Then I berated myself for having been so easily talked into flying off to the Med with Michael Farraday like a dewy-eyed teenager. Except just now, the house in Scotland didn't sound bad. All it would take was one text. While I contemplated the consequences of such an action. I thought about my inquiry to DataTech and suddenly realized with a jolt that there had been two reports from DataTech but all I'd read was the one on Shaun Timmerman and gotten so worked up over my daughter's choice of a partner that I'd forgotten to download the second. At that point my phone rang. It was Jared Saperstein.

"I called your office. Zelda says you're in Seattle. What's up?"

"Chasing down some leads for Tina Breckenridge. I met with an old girl friend of Peder Gundersen and talked to the son of the Russian captain that lost his job after the grounding of the *Polar Sea*."

"Anything of substance?"

"Probably more dead ends. I'll be back tomorrow."

"I saw McCready today. He was at the Rotary luncheon."

"And?"

"He didn't like the editorial I wrote."

The editorial on negative campaigning. I'd forgotten to look for it.

"You probably haven't had time to read it. Anyway, McCready's exact words were, 'So you've joined the hatchet women.'"

"Hatchet women. Cute."

"He went on to say he didn't appreciate my editorial and that the posters were libelous and as far as Ms. Breckenridge was concerned, with her family history, wasn't it a case of the pot calling the kettle black?"

"I don't think the Coronas expected him to be overjoyed with the posters. They just want people to think about what he's up to before they vote. He came to the office this morning before I got there. Made some veiled threats about Stephan, Tina's son."

Jared was silent for a minute, then said, "Did you tell her?"

"I haven't, but I will. She's having trouble keeping him in line as it is."

"The election's next week. Could she send him off somewhere?"

"I'll suggest it. Hard to lock up a teenager."

"My nephew is in town. He's been lecturing at the University. Want to join us for dinner tomorrow? I'm doing clams and mussels."

I half-promised to show up around six o'clock. I called Tina Breckenridge, got her voice recording. Without mentioning McCready's threat, I left a call-back message. While I'd been talking to Jared the sun had disappeared and the wind off the Sound was cold. Cursing myself for having overlooked the second DataTech report, I shivered all the way back to the parking lot where the Fusion was the only car left.

The *Rogue Wave* was moored in a marina filled with yachts, both sail and power variety. A fireplace-warmed salon welcomed me on board. Captain Joanne signed me in and processed my debit card. After advising that the First Mate's Cab-in had a shower but no bathtub, she gave me walking directions to a pub called the Seventh Wave. The First Mate's Cab-in, a small but comfortably appointed space with a queen-sized bed flanked by red and green running lights, including a flat screen TV. Three large windows framed a view of the Space Needle, Queen Anne, and downtown Seattle. The head – no bathrooms on a tugboat – contained a tiled shower and a toilet. The sink with its brass fau-cets was placed below a bronze porthole. I opened the porthole, inhaled the breezy scent of iodine and diesel fuel, closed it again. It wasn't *DragonSpray* and there was no furry feline, but it would do for the night.

Calico. Oh, my God. I'd forgotten about her.

What would she do when I didn't come back? Supposing Redhead showed up and kidnapped her again? I grabbed the phone and found a text from Zelda that was slightly eerie. *Sheldon is being nasty and I don't want to go home. Cn I bunk on Dragon-Spray 4 the nite?* She knew where I kept the extra key at the office. I texted back with a happy face smiley: *Sure. Pls feed Calico & don't let her out.*

The feline crisis handled, I unpacked my tablet, logged onto the DataTech website, clicked on the Report Waiting button. And stared at the three lines of text on the Report page:

No records, public or otherwise, were found on Michael G. Farraday of Port Isaacs, Cornwall, U.K.

No records are available for related names of Donald Farraday or Talia Farraday.

All U.K. sources were searched.

Trying to wrap my brain around the possibility that everything I thought I knew about Michael Farraday, a.k.a. Falcon, was a hoax, I closed down my computer, bundled up, and headed out into early darkness. A short walk through heavy mist brought me to the Seventh Wave. Not in the mood for a 30-minute wait for a table, I found a seat at the bar between a large ginger-bearded man in a navy pea coat and a woman in a red satin shirt. After five minutes I was able to make eye contact with the bartender, an unsmiling Brad Pitt lookalike who silently took my order for vermouth and soda with lime. The bearded man wanted to discuss the provenance of my adult beverage. I told him it was called a MacKinnon, that I had invented it, then busied myself with the apps on my cell phone, only three of which I ever used, and he turned his attention to a friendlier fifty-something blonde with green eyeshadow on his other side.

I ordered the Parmesan encrusted rockfish which arrived with amazing swiftness. H alfway through the rockfish, my phone chirped with an incoming text. It was from Melissa and predictably cryptic: *We need to talk. Call u later.* I finished the rockfish and the broccoli, declined the chocolate volcano cake, and paid my bill.

The DataTech report on Falcon still running through my brain like an insistent movie trailer, I got back to the *Rogue Wave* at and joined Captain Joanne for a cappuccino in the main salon. She delivered the foaming cup, sat with me for five minutes, then was called away to sort out an anguished call from a man who had reserved the entire B & B for the following weekend, but had just realized he was marrying the Wrong Woman. Which, of course, brought me back to Melissa and the fervent hope that she had figured out that Shaun was a Wrong Man.

Just like Simon, Melissa's father.

And Nick Anastazi, still tethered to Madame-X.

The nonexistent Michael Farraday with his probably nonexistent dying wife and nonexistent highland Scottish castle.

On that high note I took my cappuccino back to the First Mate's cabin. I got the door open just as a call came in from Tina Breckenridge. Stephan was missing again. "I should be used to it by now, but I still worry."

"Could he be with his father?"

"Paul hasn't seen him for two days. He thought Stephan was with me."

"Did you install the tracker on his backpack?"

"I did, but he found it and we had an awful fight. He said I was a horrible parent and he was going to live with Paul and he never wanted to see me again."

We were both silent for a few moments then I asked, "If he's not with Paul, where do you think he would be?"

A long sigh. "Probably out geocaching."

"How does that work? Geocaching. An electronic treasure hunt?"

"More or less. They get GPS coordinates from sites on the internet, then they go looking for them. Or sometimes they hide a cache and post the coordinates."

"What's the treasure consist of?"

"It could be anything. Videos, CD's, books. The challenge is to find it and log in at the cache."

"Does Stephan have his own computer?"

"Yes."

"Did he take it to his dad's house?"

"Yes."

"Could you ask Paul to see if Stephan's computer is there and if it is, check for any browsing history on a geocaching site."

"I'll do it."

She called back twenty minutes later, her voice breathless. "His computer was there and most of his other stuff. Paul thinks he knows where he might be. Stephan posted for a new cache out near English camp. I'll go meet Paul out there soon as it's daylight."

I thought about McCready's not-so-veiled threats when he was at the office earlier and Jared's encounter with him earlier in the day. "How does Stephan get around the island? He's too young to drive, isn't he?"

"He just turned sixteen. He's harassing me about a license. Mostly he hitches, like all the kids do."

"Tina, there's something you need to know. It's about McCready. He was in the office this morning and told Zelda that if the posters weren't removed, you were going to 'lose something precious.'"

"Zelda told me. But I don't think Stephan's running off has anything to do with McCready. It's the stuff in school and the bullying on Facebook. Some idiot kid named Gorv has been harassing Stephan about Sage. And Stephan is still furious with me about the tracker. Then Ian came up for the weekend." She was silent for a minute, then asked, "You don't really think McCready would harm Stephan? Would he?"

"I think McCready will use whatever intimidation he thinks will win him this election."

She was silent for a minute, then said, "Ian wants me to withdraw from the election."

"Are you going to?"

"God, Scotia, I can't. Not now. I'm not a quitter. I know it's going to be close, but I *have* to win."

"No matter what the price?"

Chapter 38

LAKE UNION, SEATTLE

to Port of Friday Harbor

I slept dreamlessly and sometime during the early morning hours of Wednesday the rain moved on, leaving behind a large, almost perfect rectangular window of blue sky and gusty winds. I was up at 6:00 a.m., showered, dressed, and ready for breakfast at 6:45. There were no other guests about and Captain Joanne prepared a buckwheat crepe with spinach and feta cheese and promised to e-mail me the recipe. There were no early morning texts or phone calls. I'd tried to call Melissa after I talked with Tina and got her VM which advised me to "*Please hang up and text me I don't do phone calls.*"

I returned the Ford Fusion to the lot outside the Kenmore Air terminal on Lake Union and went inside to check in, then joined the three other passengers awaiting flight 110: a saturnine, olive-skinned, white-haired man in blue jeans, black leather jacket and black leather briefcase and a 20-something couple who told me they were headed to Deer Harbor on Orcas Island for whale watching. Black Leather Jacket had his phone glued to his ear and didn't look happy. Ten minutes later the pilot motioned for us to follow him down the boarding ramp.

"You should have waited for me," Leather Jacket said tersely, frowned, and pocketed the phone with a final "Sod all." I followed him onto the plane and took the back seat. The Beaver taxied away from the Kenmore dock precisely at 8:00 a.m. As we lifted off over the lake I peered out the small window and waggled a farewell to the *Rogue Wave*.

For the next fifty-five minutes I tried to intuit whether or not McCready would make good on his veiled threat to harm Stephan. I wanted to believe it was way too far fetched for anyone to commit a kidnapping over an island election, but knowing McCready's background -- and remembering his wife's comment about her husband's dark Third Element – it was possible he would use Stephan as leverage to get Tina to drop out of the race. If he thought he could get away with it.

After a quick stop at Deer Harbor, we took off again and hopped over the island, taxiing up to the outer float dock at the Friday Harbor marina at ten past nine. The harbor was white with wind-churned waves. The pilot retrieved our bags and I hurried up the main dock. I desperately wanted a change of clothes and to check on Calico, and if I was going to get the fiber and hair samples down to the Seattle lab, I had to move. Given the unique location of the islands, the UPS plane leaves at 11:30 a.m. Afternoon drop-offs don't go out until the next day.

I hurried over to "G" Dock. *Pumpkinseed* was buttoned up with the blinds closed. I found a note from Zelda on the galley counter top: *Calico had her breakfast. Almost out of kibble. I cleaned the litter box.*

From her preferred spot between the pillows on my bed Calico watched me change into a clean pair of jeans, then covered her eyes with one paw and snuggled deeper. I left the small porthole open for her, locked *DragonSpray*, and made my way up to the parking lot.

Chapter 39
OLDE GAZETTE BUILDING

Friday Harbor

The box with pieces of blood-spattered ceiling tiles and pieces of carpet we'd purloined from the Sheriff's evidence locker were sitting in a box in the trunk of the Alfa Berlina. I drove it up to the OGB, removed the box, added the plastic baggie with Igor Zorco's beard hairs, and went inside. A wood fire was crackling and piano music filled the downstairs. David Lanz or some facsimile thereof. I checked my cubby for mail, found a pink message slip from Car-olyn Smith that said, *Call me*. The coffee was brewed and Zelda sat at her workstation. "What's in the box?" she said. She clicked her mouse and the printer ut-tered a few discreet sounds.

"DNA samples."

"The Condor and his minions took down most of our posters. I e-mailed you some very interesting stuff."

"I'll look at it in a bit. Have to get this stuff over to UPS like now."

I grabbed a cup of coffee and raced upstairs, pulled up the website for Investigation Forensics Lab. IFL had special memberships for law enforcement agencies. Their services were available to the general public with the stipulation that samples for testing had to be submitted by an attorney.

I dialed Carolyn Smith's office. Her P. A. put me on hold for several long minutes, then Carolyn came on the line. "I have bad news on the Petrovsky matter, Scotia."

I took a deep breath. "They've killed Harrison."

"Nobody's heard from Harrison. It's about the judge. He refused to approve the special distribution."

I exhaled. "Any particular reason?"

"When he asked if any of the beneficiaries objected, Petra gave a big spiel about Harrison's disappearance and lack of communication and irresponsibility, so he rejected the petition." She sighed. "I tried, I really did. Have you heard anything from Harrison or the pirate negotiator?"

"Not a word from either."

"Luisa's tried to call Harrison every day. The call goes directly to voice mail. Any word from Michelle's father?"

"Mr. Bau was quite explicit about not wanting to hear from me."

"What about DuPont?"

"What's the point of bringing H & W back into it, if there's no money to negotiate with?"

"How long will they keep them alive if there's no ransom?"

"Some of the hostages have been held for over a year."

We were both silent for a couple of minutes, then I said, "Carolyn, there's another matter you could help me with." I explained what I was trying to accomplish for Tina Breckenridge with the DNA analyses and asked if she would submit the samples to IFL for me. And that we needed to ask that the analysis be expedited.

"IFL is super expensive. Can your client afford them?"

"Her aunt can."

"I'll call the lab and make arrangements for billing. What exactly are we sending?"

"Blood spatters on ceiling tiles and a bloody carpet and towels that we're trying to match to hair samples. Actually beard hairs."

"*Beard hairs?*"

"Yes."

"I see. You want this analysis when?"

"Before the Commissioner's election next Tuesday."

"In your dreams. Give me the lab's phone number."

Ten minutes later she called back. "Their usual turnaround time for the services you want is two weeks. If we overnight the samples today, and are willing to pay an extra $2500 expediting fee, they'll try to have the results to you by next Monday. But no guarantees."

"We'll pay the extra fee. I'm on my way to UPS right now."

"Bring it to me. We'll handle it."

Carolyn's office was only five minutes away and I was back at the OGB at ten o'clock. Zelda was fastening three large hand-lettered posters to the white board with big colored magnets. The professor peered over her shoulder reading the headlines aloud.

"Friday Harbor 1984".

"Don't Kill the 4th Amendment."

"Butterflies are not for killing."

"Very creative," I said, "But I don't imagine the minions will leave them up for long."

"We're not posting these. We're distributing them at the rally we're organizing on Friday. Lily just called. Nobody knows where Sage is." She returned to her workstation, clicked up a new file.

"Lily McGregor's niece?"

"Lily and Sage had an altercation on Monday afternoon, then Lily went over to Lopez for a gathering of goddesses. When she got home this morning there was no sign of Sage."

"Today is Wednesday."

"I know. Her calls to Sage go straight to Voicemail." She made a screen edit and clicked on the print button.

"Is Stephan still missing?"

"Yes."

"Has anybody notified the sheriff?"

"Lily and Tina went to his office this morning."

"What's Sheriff Bishop doing to find two missing teenagers?"

The professor's cell phone rang, he checked the LCD screen, then retreated to his office and closed the door.

"That was probably Abby," Zelda said, looking over her shoulder at the closed door. "The professor invited her to dinner."

I repeated my question.

"The sheriff said, and I quote, 'Probably just a couple of sex-raddled kids off on a lark.' If they haven't turned up by tonight, he'll order a search."

"By tonight." I compared my own Overly Protective I Want to Know Where You Are 24 Hours a Day style of parenting to the laissez-faire island style. "Why did Lily wait so long to report her missing? Wasn't she worried when Sage didn't come home Monday night? Or last night?"

"Sage was supposed to stay with Leslie.

"And Leslie's mother? What did she think when Sage didn't show up on Monday? Doesn't anybody care where their kids are?" I sounded shrewish, but I didn't care.

"Um, well, that gets complicated. Either Leslie forgot to tell her mother about the arrangement and/or the two girls got into a fight and Sage refused to go there. Lily tried to call on Monday, but she couldn't get a cell connection from Lopez. So nobody figured out Sage was missing until this morning when Lily picked up messages from the school."

I tried a new approach. "Has Sage ever gone missing before?"

"No, but she's been having nightmares since she and Leslie got lost up in the DNR. She insists the two men they saw are vampires, even though Lily told her the vampires are all on Lopez."

"Vampires on Lopez."

"Yes. They keep a low profile. Do all their hunting at night.

Is there a connection between vampires on Lopez and Sage getting into a fight with Lily?"

"Sage refuses to use her powers."

"Her powers. You mean she's precognitive, like her aunt." I'm not a big supporter of paranormal forensics, but Lily's "powers" had once been helpful in a previous case.

Zelda twirled around to face me. Her sweatshirt proclaimed, *Come to the Dark Side, we have Cookies.* "No, boss. Sage refuses to use her *witchcraft*. They got into a fight because Lily told her it's dangerous to ignore it."

"You're saying that Sage is a witch."

"Lily says she has the power."

"Is Lily a witch?"

"The gathering she went to on Lopez was with the coven, but she prefers the term goddess. She thinks McCready destroyed the cairns and that he kidnapped the kids to make Tina drop out of the election and she's going to cast a hex on him."

I felt my grasp of reality growing tenuous. "I hate to burst Lily's bubble, but I don't think a hex is going to stop McCready."

She rolled her eyes. "You don't know Lilly's hexes."

"And I seriously doubt that Lochlan McCready is running around knocking down piles of stones."

"Yeah, well, there's one more thing. Last year Sheriff Bishop received a fee of two hundred thousand dollars for his work on the BSI board. Don't ask me how I know."

"Wouldn't think of going there."

Chapter 40

OLDE GAZETTE BUILDING

Friday Harbor

Zelda left at noon to walk Dakota and stop at the print shop to print the posters for the Friday rally. She promised to call with news of Sage or Stephan and bring back a non-Paleo ham and cheese panini, whatever that might be.

I'd hit a wall on Tina's case until I had the results of the DNA analysis. I couldn't help thinking that if I'd spent more time focusing on finding something to stop McCready instead of delving into the 30-year-old Gundersen murder file, Stephan might be safe at home right now. Assuming, of course, that McCready had anything to do with his disappearance. I couldn't see any connection between McCready and Sage Mc-Gregor. Maybe Nigel was right: just a couple of over-sexed kids on a lark. Or hunting for an elusive geocache.

So I sat at my desk and stared out the window at the dark green sedan parked across the street from the OGB. The early morning blue sky I'd awakened to in Seattle had given way to overcast gray over San Juan Island, which exactly matched my mood. I speculated about Harrison Petrovsky and Michelle Yee and the Somali thugs and considered calling and asking Hassan for proof of life. Or calling Yee Bau for an update. I decided that both calls would be futile for different reasons. That some situations are money-dependent. I was brooding over Melissa's dysfunctional relationship with Shaun and the phantom Michael Farraday when I heard the door downstairs open, and then a minute later I heard it close and then heard quick, light footsteps on the stairs. I turned around. Elyse Montenegro stood in my doorway. She looked nearly as distraught today as when she first appeared in my office several years ago to enlist my help in finding her husband's murderer.

"I was afraid you wouldn't see me if I called," she said from the doorway. She was hugging a manila envelope against her chest with one hand.

"What can I do for you?" I removed my rucksack from the chair beside my desk. "Sit."

She sank into the chair, took a deep breath and started talking. " I want to apologize for what I said to you last week. It was rude and I'm sorry."

"About Lochlan McCready."

"Yes. It wasn't . . . I didn't know . . . I heard something last night that I wasn't supposed to and I started putting two and two together. This morning Leslie told me Stephan is lost and nobody knows where Sage is and I think they might be in danger."

"Why do you think they're in danger?"

"I overheard Loch talking on his cell phone. He saw me listening and got really, really angry."

"You were at his house?"

"Yes."

"Do you know who he was talking to?"

"His name is Griffin. He's one of the BSI directors. He was supposed to come up last week but he got delayed and Loch was really upset. He flew up this morning."

"Does he wear a black leather jacket?"

"I've no idea."

"What was the gist of the conversation you overheard?"

"Something like, 'I don't care how you wanted it. You weren't here.' And then he said, 'Nigel's not going to do shit. She'll be out in twenty-four hours.'" Then he saw me listening and he went into the bedroom. I think they were talking about some project he's got on his computer. It's about a factory he's building. Or some kind of lab. I think it's here."

"On San Juan Island?"

She nodded. "When he saw me looking he closed up the laptop." She opened the envelope she'd been hugging and pulled out two sheets of paper. "I went through his briefcase when he was in the shower. I found the minutes of a board meeting last fall. Read it, please."

The minutes were succinct and questions that had been plaguing me the past week got answered. And a few I hadn't thought of emerged.

At the November 15 meeting of BioIntel Systems Inc. held in Bellevue, Washington, CFO Merritt Griffin reported that both the City of Bellevue and the City of Redmond have turned down BSI's business license applications. Whereupon the following Resolution was unanimously approved.

RESOLVED that director Lochlan McCready is hereby ordered to enter into a contract with the Washington Department of Natural Resources for the purchase of fifty acres of land in San Juan County as shown on Exhibit A. . . .

I stopped reading and riffled through the papers. "There's no Exhibit A."

"I know. I must have missed it. Keep reading."

"... for an amount not to exceed ten million dollars, said land and any attached structures to be used for the purpose of pilot testing miocroaerial vehicles and other related projects."

I stopped reading. "MAV's."

"Yes. Baby drones."

"You know about them?"

"Baby dragonflies and moths and God knows what else."

"Ten million dollars."

"Yeah."

"Can you get Exhibit A?"

"He's coming over tonight. I might be able to get it."

"How do you think this is connected to Stephan? Or Sage?"

"It took me a while to figure out how much Loch hates Tina Breckenridge. The night you saw us at the Bistro? He said he didn't care how many scumbag investigators Tina hired, he was going to win the election. That elections aren't won at the ballot box. And now the kids have disappeared."

"What do you know about McCready's military background?"

She sighed. "He told me about his assignments

in Africa." Tree branches brushed against my window and a shower of leaves blew into the street. She stood up. "I have to go. There's a storm coming in and we have a load of hay being delivered today. I don't want Loch to know I was here. I'll e-mail you if I find out anything else." She glanced out my window. A man in a black leather jacket and blue jeans was approaching the dark green sedan parked on the street below. Just before getting into the car, he glanced up toward my office. "That's him," she said. "That's Merritt Griffin."

The downstairs door closed behind Elyse and I watched her get in the brown SUV with the Ravenwood Stables decal on the door. She backed out onto the street and headed west on Guard Street. Exactly one minute later the green sedan made a U-turn and followed Elyse's vehicle. I tried to recall the brief one-sided conversation I'd overheard as we were boarding the float plane this morning. Was Merritt Griffin watching my office? Tailing Elyse? If not, why was he parked there?

Two children missing for two days should have triggered an Amber Alert and a notification to the NCIC and nobody was taking the disappearance seriously. To calm my increasing jitters over the two missing teenagers, I logged onto my bank website, verified my checking account balance and scheduled bill payments for my moorage and electricity. I logged off the bank website and checked my e-mail. Among 28 spam messages I found one from Captain Joanne of the *Rogue Wave* with the promised buckwheat crepes recipe, and a message from Zelda. The subject line said, *Read the forwarded message from Cee Gee.*

So I did. The message from *cryptowhite@aol.com* consisted of an attachment which was a document from the State Department of Natural Resources. The document was an agreement from the DNR to accept an offer tendered by *BioIntel Systems Inc.* to purchase a parcel of land in the County of San Juan for the amount of three point nine million dollars. It was dated the previous November. The legal description for the parcel was, of course, based on the grid system created in the 19th century: township, range and section numbers. I had no idea what part of the island it referred to, or even if it was San Juan Island. It could be anywhere in the 400 islands that make up the San Juan Archipelago.

I printed out the attachment and then read the rest of Zelda's message. *Pretty interesting, eh, boss. I didn't know it was legal for the DNR to sell public land to private enterprise, but apparently they can sell and resell to whoever they want. With one caveat: The County Council has to unanimously approve any sale of DNR land in the county that's not intended for public use. The current Council refused to approve the sale to BSI by one vote. That one vote was the District 2 commissioner who is now deceased. Since the Council has been shuffled and reshuffled three times in as many years, McCready has to get on the Council or risk losing the land. Oh, BTW, check the signature on the Acceptance.*

I pulled the document from the printer. It was signed by L. Lionel Bishop. The Sheriff's brother.

I spent way too much time trying to suss out the implications of the BSI acquisition of DNR land in

San Juan County and at three o'clock my phone rang. It was Jared Saperstein. "Seth missed the morning ferry and he won't be in till 6:30, so don't rush over. "

I didn't immediately know what he was talking about, but I recovered quickly. "Your nephew. Tonight. Okay. What shall I bring?"

"Pick up a couple bottles of Evolution White."

"Will do. Is Seth staying long?"

"We'll find out." He chuckled and cut the connection.

The downstairs door opened to the accompaniment of women's voices – Zelda's and Abby's – and canine toenails. I heard a knock on the professor's door and a few seconds later Zelda pounded up the stairs.

"Tina and Paul went out to English camp. They found the geocache. Stephan and Sage had logged in."

"What does that mean?"

"The caches have a kind of record book. When you find a cache, you put in your name and date."

"But no kids?"

"No kids. Then Tina got a text about eleven o'clock."

"From Stephan?"

"From an untraceable cell phone. Something like, *Get out of the election by tomorrow night, put an ad in the Sounder and the Gazette, don't contact the police.*"

"No mention of Stephan or Sage?"

"No."

"What's she going to do?"

"She said the text could have come from anyone

who didn't like her and there was nothing to link it to the kids or to McCready. Paul says the whole thing is Tina's fault and if she doesn't withdraw, he's going to get a court order to force her."

"Men like to threaten court orders."

"Yeah, makes them feel powerful. Anyhow, Paul called Nigel Bishop and demanded that he send out the deputies to look for the kids. Nigel was about to leave for some freaking meeting down in Oak Harbor, so he turned the whole thing over to the under-sheriff. The deputies are out searching now."

"Does Lily MacGregor know about the text?"

"She's cool. She says that Sage is okay. She can see her. She'll call when she figures out where Sage is and she's going to focus on putting a hex on the Nazi. Um, boss?"

"What?"

"You think Condor would, you know, actually harm them?"

I didn't answer for almost a minute. "Desperate men commit desperate acts. Something is making McCready desperate. I saw the message from Cee-Gee. And I just had an interesting visit from Elyse Montenegro."

"What did the Ice Queen want?"

"She found this in his briefcase." I handed her the copy of the BSI Board meeting minutes.

She read the minutes and smiled. "Buying DNR land. Another nail in his coffin. Wait 'till I tell Abby. You think he kidnapped the kids?"

"It's possible and if he did he might be playing a game of chicken. Or not."

"He's counting on Tina to cave and drop out of the election," Zelda said.

"Possibly."

"When she does, the kids reappear and McCready becomes Councilman for San Juan Island."

"BioIntel gets their fifty million dollar contract."

"And life goes on."

"That's about it." I shrugged. "As long as the kids can't identify their kidnapper."

"Given McCready's history, Tina doesn't have much choice does she?"

"The intimidation factor is a bit high."

"I told her about the wet operations. Wish I hadn't."

"Few parents would gamble with a child's life. I doubt she's tough enough to call his bluff for very long."

Just now the deputies would be searching every cove and trail and thicket of the island. I reached for my phone, scrolled through People, found Angela Petersen's work number. She answered on the third ring. I told her I was with Zelda and switched to speaker phone.

"We've searched every inch of Lime Kiln park," she reported in a tired voice. "Including all the secret little canyons most people don't know about. Ditto Deadman's Bay, English Camp, the Roche Harbor watershed and Mt. Young."

"You heard about the threat?" I asked.

"What threat?"

I told her about the anonymous text message.

"Why the hell didn't Nigel tell us? That's a whole

different scenario. You think McCready's behind this?"

"I would say the probability is about 90%."

"Where does he live?"

"Mineral Heights."

"Tina is fucked," she said quietly. "She will have to withdraw." I heard the radio dispatcher in the background. "Something coming in," she said. "Gotta go."

"Unless . . . " is from Zelda, who'd heard the whole conversation.

"Unless what?" I said, pressing the End Call button.

"Unless we find the kids before tomorrow night."

"We?"

"Me and T.J."

"Cee Gee's gorgeous older brother."

"Yeah."

"You think he can find Stephan and Sage? When the deputies haven't been able to?"

"He worked in Death Valley. Got some kind of Park Service award for finding the most lost people."

"Lost, as in couldn't find their way back to camp?"

"Kids who wander away from their parents. Grannies who get tired and decide to take a short cut. Out-on-the-edge wilderness types who want to blaze their own trail."

"Sage and Stephen, even if they're together, could be anyplace. It's not like they went for a walk at English camp and got lost. These kids grew up here. Where's T.J. going to start?"

"You ever hear the expression, 'Cutting for sign'?"

I shook my head. "Anything like cutting for stone?"

"Sign is all the stuff the trackers find: footprints, tire marks, thread, bits of clothing. If he can't find them, at least he can tell where they went."

"Can you get ahold of T.J?"

"With pleasure."

She clattered down the stairs. My phone rang. It was Melissa.

I took a deep breath. "Hi, sweetie."

"Hi, mom." Her voice was slow and tired.

"How's Shaun's visit going? You two talking?"

"Yeah." Silence. "He told me about the thing with the woman in Evanston. He said it was all a mistake and the D.V. thing --it happened because he was– um- high and she overreacted."

"He was high."

"Yeah."

"As in high on drugs."

"Yeah."

"What kind of drugs? Weed? Cocaine?"

More silence, then, "Meth."

I felt a jolt in the pit of my stomach. Crystal meth, whether snorted, smoked or injected, is the world's most addictive drug. I remembered how Ben Garcia, my husband, had tracked the biggest meth dealer in San Diego for months, built an airtight case, then was felled by a burst of automatic weapons fire when he went in with the DEA. Involuntarily I directed my attention to the shadowy Spanish sidewalk café in the old print on the wall Jared had given me for my birthday. I focused on the shadows cast by the wooden chairs. On the cracks in the pale cobble-stones. And mostly on the warmth of the interaction between the blue-shirted waiter and the woman in the apricot sweater that Jared said looked like me and I heard Melissa's voice coming from very far away.

"Mother? Are you there?"

"Was it just a one-time occurrence or is he addicted?"

"He's addicted. He can finally admit it. I'm proud of him for that."

"How long has he been using?"

"Um, about fifteen years."

"So he started in what, high school?"

"He was on a class trip in Sweden and their advisor let them run around on their own and somebody gave them some stuff. He said it was totally amazing. But he didn't use it much until he got into med school and then he just used it like when he had to prep for an exam and needed to study all night."

"Melissa. Do you know what crystal meth does to the body?"

"I know, mother, it's really bad. He's going to rehab. I was hoping you would be more supportive."

"It's beyond bad and only seven percent of meth users ever recover. You need to get this man out of your life. Now. While you can."

"I can't *believe* you are so negative. I am *not* going to abandon him. He's going to rehab and then we're going to live together while he finishes med school. I'm applying to Northwestern. Stop trying to control my life. Why do you always have to overreact?" The phone went dead.

In the past decade the percentage of drug treatment admissions due to meth addiction have tripled along with a growing rate of Domestic Violence cases. During my last year in San Diego the city was called the Meth Capital of the U.S. and I recalled the growing rate of meth-associated calls from users coming down from a binge. And now my daughter was bonded with one of these guys?

I glanced again at the Spanish print and longed to race down the narrow cobblestone passage and hide in the shadowy old café. Or steal away into an old Scottish castle.

Chapter 41

OLDE GAZETTE BUILDING

Friday Harbor

Classical guitar music drifted up from New Millennium. A phone rang and I heard Zelda answer. A few minutes later the door opened and closed with a slam. Across the street the green sedan was back, Black Leather Jacket in the driver's seat, cell phone to his ear. The day had turned darker and grayer. A burst of rain spattered against my window.

For the moment, there was nothing more I could do.

Not for Harrison Petrovsky.

Not for Tina Breckenridge.

Not even for my own daughter.

I locked my file cabinet, put on my parka, locked the door and went downstairs. The note on the whiteboard advised that *Life is an impenetrable fog of mystification.* There was a note from Zelda in my mail cubby: *I'm meeting T.J. at 6:00. He wants to start tracking tomorrow early.* I wondered if the rain would help or hinder Cutting for Sign. I dropped the note in the wastebasket and headed for the door as the professor came out of his office.

"Scotia. Just the person I wanted to see. Abigail is joining me for dinner tonight. Would you know what her favorite restaurant is?"

"You can't go wrong with the Bistro."

"That was my choice too."

"How are the Africa plans going?"

"Abigail is interested. Have my fingers crossed. We might be in Tanzania a month from now."

He opened the door for me and peered out. Rain was falling steadily. "That green sedan's been there most of the afternoon. Know who it is?"

"I'm told he's connected to Lochlan McCready. He seems to be keeping an eye on the Old Gazette Building."

"I'll keep an eye on him."

I drove down the hill and parked behind the market. I was walking inside when a call came from Jared.

"Scotia, it's been a bad day. My nephew got delayed. He's not coming up until late tonight. I just spent two hours with one of my stringers who's in the midst of a child custody fight. I'm beat and not in the mood to cook tonight."

If Jared expected me to offer to cook, I wasn't rising to it. "Not a problem. A raincheck is fine." "May I take you to the Bistro instead?"

We agreed to meet at 6:00. When I got back to *DragonSpray*, it was already Calico was not around. I turned up the heat and closed up everything except the one small porthole. There were lights behind the curtains on *Pumpkinseed*. I went over and knocked on the stern transom. Sounds of TV leaked from inside and presently Henry opened the door. He was unshaven, wearing a faded blue hoodie with black lettering that said *I'm Single and Disease Free*.

He was carrying a bottle of Heineken and his neighborliness had improved.

"Hey, Scotia. Time for a beer?"

"Love to, Henry, but I'm meeting Jared. Just wondering if you'd seen Calico today."

He smirked. "And you want to know if Lindsey's been around." " That too."

"Yes to the first. No to the second. Lindsey and I are mutually *non grata*."

"When did you see Calico?"

"About three o'clock, she was sitting up on your bow watching fish in the water. Then that scruffy black cat from C dock came by and they had an un-friendly conversation." He took a long swallow of beer. "I'll keep an eye out for her."

I thanked Henry and climbed back on board *DragonSpray*, poured a dry vermouth and soda, powered on the TV. I sat for a few minutes on the settee, listening to the King 5 news update: Mt. Sakurajima volcano was erupting. A white rhino had been shot dead by poachers in one of Kenya's most heavily guarded wildlife parks. And in London, a futuristic looking skyscraper was inexplicably causing temperatures at street level to soar to over 150 degrees Fahrenheit. On the local Pacific Northwest scene, a 6.4 earthquake had occurred south of the Queen Islands. I changed into a clean pair of blue jeans, the one pair that fit my new Paleo body, and my favorite black zip-up polar fleece sweater. I brushed out my hair, applied moisturizer and taupe eye shadow, a spritz of Jo Malone. Victoria weather radio was predicting heavy rain overnight, and for Thursday, a high of 55, with mostly overcast skies.

I heard a so 'meow' as Calico landed in the middle of my bed. Her fur was dripping wet and I was toweling her o when my phone rang. It was Angela Petersen. "Nigel refused to even discuss a warrant to search McCready's house. Jeff and I are doing an end run."

Jeffrey Fountain was the Undersheriff. " Find anything?"

"The only people coming and going were Elyse Montenegro and some dude in a black leather jacket."

"Was the dude driving a green sedan?" "How did you know?"

"Name's Griffn. CFO for BSI."

"What's BSI?"

"BioIntel Systems Inc., McCready's company. Griffin was sitting outside the high school most of the afternoon."

"Right across from your office."

"Yes. Elyse came by and when she left so did she. Then he came back. What's your plan?"

"I'll let you know if we turn up anything."

I pressed the End Call button as the incoming text icon flashed. It was from Falcon. *Heading 4 Invergary House next wk. Will u join me? M.*

I went back to toweling Calico, then found my foul weather jacket, locked up, and headed up the dock. e rain was a steady drizzle and all I could think about was summer on the loch and warm scones with strawberry jam for tea. Except it wasn't summer there now and the same cold rain was most likely falling on the loch. Or a colder rain. If I went there, what would

I do after? How many years would I have to spend as the Other Woman? When would I find out who Michael Farraday really was?

Chapter 42

THE WATERSIDE BISTRO

Friday Harbor

Candles flickered above red checked tablecloths. Only three tables were occupied. Jared was sitting at the usual corner table, idly twirling a glass of red wine. Beyond the rain-spattered window the *Chelan* was loading for the 6:25 sailing.

I stood for a minute at the entrance alcove, watching Jared, absorbing what his friendship meant. Comfort. Dependability. No drama.

The restaurant owner came out of the kitchen, took my dripping jacket and nodded toward Jared's table. "He's waiting for you."

Jared stood up and pulled out my chair, gave me a kiss on the check. "You smell good. Sorry about all the aborted plans. Weird day."

"Indeed."

"You too? Any word on the Breckenridge boy?"

"None." The waitress brought our menus and explained the evening specials. Ginger soy salmon. New Zealand lamb chops in a ginger soy marinade. And my favorite, a dish called Evil Jungle Prince. Jared ordered the Mushroom Sampler appetizer for two, filled my glass and topped his from the bottle of Three Angels zin.

"No Evolution Red?"

"They're out. I like this better. How are you?"

"I'm really depressed." I hadn't meant to say it and I was slightly stunned by my words.

Jared reached across the table and laid a hand over mine. "Tell me."

"Everything I've touched since I got back has turned into a fiasco. Harrison Petrovsky is still a hostage in Godforsaken Somalia. I wanted to help Tina clear her family name so she could win the election and I haven't accomplished a bloody thing. I'm no closer now than I was a week ago to finding anything that will stop McCready's mudslinging. And now two kids are missing for three days."

"*Two* kids?"

"Sage MacGregor, Lily's niece."

"Are they together?"

"Elyse Montenegro thinks so."

"She and McCready an item?"

"Apparently. Not for much longer, I think."

"Time to bring in the F.B.I."

I nodded. "Thing is, Tina got an anonymous text explicitly warning against the F.B.I. and giving her until tomorrow night to announce she's withdrawing from the election."

"Is she going to do it?"

"Apparently not. The deputies searched all the obvious places. Lime Kiln, English Camp, American Camp, Mt. Young."

"If the kids' disappearance is linked to McCready, none of these places make sense."

"Because?"

"Assuming McCready hired somebody to kidnap them," he said thoughtfully, "then they're stashed away on private property."

"Even someplace off island."

"For sure they're not sitting out at Jackson Beach smoking a joint."

"The deputies are spinning their wheels," I said.

"That may be Nigel's intent."

"Now you know why I'm depressed."

"I know you, Scotia MacKinnon," he said in a low voice. "You'll find a way to rescue the two missing kids. And the sailor." With his eyes still on mine, he took a sip of the wine. The mushroom sampler arrived and we ordered: Evil Jungle Prince for me, lamb chops for Jared.

"You said you met with Gundersen's old girlfriend yesterday," he said. "You learn anything that might clear the family name?"

"If I can believe Erika, the captain showed up at her house in Ballard one snowy winter night covered in blood and wanted her to flee to Iceland with him."

"*Iceland*?"

"So she claims."

"Was he fleeing from Hazel?"

"She says he was fleeing from somebody he killed. Or from someone who was going to kill him."

Before I could recap my meeting with Igor Zorco, Tony Bolton and Abigail Leedle were standing beside our table. I introduced Tony to Jared, who invited them to join us.

"I just wanted a quick word," Tony said. "Scotia, after you left, I was on the phone and I heard someone going up the stairs."

"The stairs to my office?"

"Yes. I called out to him. It was that chap in the green sedan."

"Griffin? McCready's CFO?"

"Said he had an appointment with you. I told him he should call back and sent him packing. Made sure everything was locked up when I left."

Jared and I looked at each other. "You don't exactly have a state of the art security system," Jared said. "Let's check it out after dinner."

The professor said he and Abby would be at the C & S in case we wanted to join them. The waitress delivered our orders. Jared watched me pick at the Jungle Prince for several minutes, then said, "Anything else depressing you besides Breckenridge and Petrovsky?"

"Melissa's boyfriend is a drug addict."

"That's very depressing. Cocaine?"

"Crystal meth. She thinks he can spend a few months in rehab and it will be happy ever after. They're going to live together after she graduates next spring." I speared a piece of chicken.

"Meth is nasty. You'll have to walk away."

"It gets worse."

"Worse how?"

"She's pregnant."

"So you can't walk away."

Chapter 43

S/V DragonSpray

Port of Friday Harbor

So you can't walk away. Jared's words bounced around in my brain for the rest of the evening while we finished our dinner. Outside, the rain was diminishing and we hurried to Jared's car parked half a block away uphill on Spring Street. Three minutes later we were parked in the driveway at the OGB. All was dark and quiet.

"There's no outside light here, MacKinnon. If you continue taking on interesting cases, might be wise to get one. With a motion detector."

The entry door was locked. There was a FEDEX flat envelope on Zelda's desk, but nothing appeared disturbed. Upstairs my door was still locked. Inside all was as I had left it. Whatever Griffin had been after, it didn't appear he'd returned. Not yet.

Ten minutes later we were back at the C & S to join Tony and Abby for Irish coffees. Abby reported that the unofficial island pollsters were predicting Tina to win the election by one point. On an island with less than 7,000 inhabitants, a one-point difference might be a game changer. I kept thinking about Melissa and had a hard time focusing on the chitchat. A little after nine Jared said he was heading down to the ferry dock to meet his nephew. I declined his invitation for yet another after dinner drink with the nephew from Edinburgh and took myself back to 'Spray.

A heavy mist lay like a cloak over the waterfront and the night seemed exceptionally dark. The main dock was deserted and the liveaboards were tucked away. I collected my bathing paraphernalia and headed up to the shower. Half an hour later I was back on the boat I brewed a cup of chamomile tea, took it into my cabin, spent a long time telling myself that I couldn't control my daughter's life. Then I re-read Falcon's last message, fantasized about spending long nights tucked into one of the big beds in a castle bedroom in the glow of a wood fire. Did it really matter that Farraday was just another alias? It only made sense that an MI6 agent would protect his identity, and the identity of his family. But when two people become lovers, when do the walls come down? At 11:30 I texted back. *Invergary House is tempting. Hav to clear 2 cases. Will keep u posted.*

I was awakened at 12:09 by a heeling of the boat to port. There wasn't enough wind to cause the heeling, and it was very late for a boat to be leaving the harbor. After a few seconds the boat flattened out. I almost convinced myself I'd dreamed the incident when Calico leaped off the bed. She stared upward, toward the bow, her tail twiching madly.

In the silence the rigging creaked. *DragonSpray* heeled slightly again, this time to starboard, then leveled.

There was an intruder on the boat.

It is an ancient law of the sea that you do not board a vessel without permission and unlawful boarding constitutes an act of war or piracy. Theft of dinghies or unsecured engines is not uncommon in the marina, but only an idiot or someone intending malice boards an occupied vessel in the middle of the night. Should I wait to see if the intruder would leave or would attempt to force my flimsy lock on the hatch covers? Or go topside and confront?

I slid out of bed, quietly pulled out a drawer, pulled on a pair of sweats and a hooded shirt. I searched in the darkness for my boat shoes, couldn't find them. There was no further motion topside. I moved into the salon and stood silently for several minutes, my heart thudding against my breastbone. Whoever had boarded the boat was motionless, but could be anywhere from the bow to the stern. Waiting for me to emerge from the cabin.

I took several deep breaths, removed the cushions from the port-side settee. I lifted the cover to the storage locker underneath, let my fingers find my surveillance rucksack and the little Beretta in the very bottom. The side curtains in the salon were open. In the faint light I checked the chamber, removed the safety, and moved over to stand for a few moments beside the companionway. All was silent above. Very slowly, I unlocked and opened the hatch covers, knowing I would be a target the minute my head emerged from the companionway. I stared upward, searching the darkness. I took a steadying breath, went up quickly on bare feet and leaped into the cockpit, scanning forward with the Beretta. The bow section of the boat was in deep shadow. For several seconds I could make out nothing, then one of the shadows moved.

"Put the gun down, MacKinnon." It was a man's voice, with a faint British accent. "If I'd wanted to wipe you I had lots of earlier chances."

"Get off my boat, whoever you are."

"Or you'll what? Shoot me? And then explain to the sheriff why you shot an unarmed man?"

"Get the hell off my boat. Now." I began to move forward along the starboard side, praying my bare feet wouldn't slip on the cold wet deck. As I got closer to the bow, the figure moved out of the shadows. In the light from the dock lights I could see the outlines of his face. It was Black Leather Jacket, he of the green sedan.

"We need to talk, MacKinnon. That is, if you care a whiff about your client."

I paused amidships at the stays, holding the Beretta with both hands. "Talk, Griffin. Make it fast. No one is going to convict a captain of defending herself against a midnight marauder." *And you wouldn't be the first to go to a watery grave in this harbor.*

"The thing is, my associate is getting a little bit annoyed with Mrs. Breckenridge. Given her family history, she doesn't have a snowball's chance in hell of winning the election. And those posters your associates put up around town are libelous."

"I believe they were all fact-checked."

"He's given her several chances. Now she's got less than twenty-four hours."

"Or what?"

"Do Mrs. Breckenridge a big favor. Convince her to withdraw from the race tomorrow."

"Tina Breckenridge is not going to withdraw."

"Too bad. If she listens to reason she's still got a nice life ahead of her."

"I don't make Tina Breckenridge's decisions for her."

"Perhaps you should."

"If you're holding either Tina's son or the Mac-Gregor girl, I will personally guarantee the F.B.I. is going to be all over you. Get off my boat and tell your associate this is San Juan Island, not Venezuela."

I cocked the Beretta's hammer, leveled it at his chest. Griffin moved along the deck until his face was only inches from mine, the barrel of the Beretta against his chest. My finger poised in front of the trigger, itching to pull it.

"Have you heard from Melissa this evening?" he asked softly.

I stared at him, feeling my blood turn to ice. "If anything happens to my daughter, I will kill you."

Chapter 44
ABOARD S/V DRAGONSPRAY

Port of Friday Harbor

After Black Leather Jacket climbed off the boat with a triumphant smirk, I sat in *Spray's* cockpit, trembling in the black fog, Beretta at hand, scanning the shadows, listening or any returning footsteps along the dock. By two o'clock I was drenched to the skin. I went below, locked up, peeled off the wet clothes and put on flannel P.J.'s and thick socks. I placed the Beretta within easy reach on the bedside table and fell into bed.

For a long time I stared wide-eyed into the darkness, assessing the seriousness of McCready's threats, the possibility of two children being used as undeclared hostages. Of the possibility that they could get to my daughter. Finally, at 3:30, I called Melissa. She answered with a yawn. I told her I'd had a bad dream and wanted to make sure she was okay. She was fine, she assured me sleepily. Did I know what time it was? Yes, Shaun was with her. She was sorry she'd hung up on me. Could we talk in the morning?

For the first time ever I was grateful for Shaun Timmerman.

I was still awake at 4:30 when Tina Breckenridge called. Lily's dog was barking nonstop. She thought someone was prowling in the woods behind her cottage.

"Where's Lily?"

"She's not answering her phone. I think the coven is putting a hex on McCready. Do you think he's sent someone to harass me?"

"Time's running out. He's desperate. Threats and intimidation haven't gotten him anywhere. It also might just be a raccoon in the woods."

"I don't think I can take much more."

I told her about Griffin's visit to the boat. She muttered something unintelligible. "You think I should withdraw from the election."

I was silent for a minute, then told her, "I can't predict what McCready will do. Or has done. He's a wildcard. It's possible he has the kids. And if you think there's a prowler, you call 911."

"I already called. All the deputies are out on the West Side. A car with some teenagers went over the cliff. I can't stop thinking Stephan might have been with them."

"Where's Ian?"

"In Seattle. He'll be back on the ten o'clock ferry."

"It's been 72 hours since you or Paul last saw Stephan. You have to call in the F.B.I. And keep your lights turned off."

"I'll talk to Ian when he gets back this morning."

There must have been a cloud of insomnia hovering over Friday Harbor. The phone rang again a few minutes after six. My eyes felt like I'd been sleeping in sand. This time it was Jared.

"Sorry if I woke you. Couldn't sleep and I kept

thinking about Griffin trying to get into your office, so I got up and took a stroll."

"To make sure the OGB was still standing?"

"Something like that."

"And?"

"Just as it was when we were there. All locked up."

"Griffin visited me last night."

"Visited '*Spray*?"

"Yep. A little after midnight."

"You okay?"

"I'm okay. He made some threats, then he departed. I didn't sleep much after that. Feel like I've been run over by a truck."

"Threats against you?"

"Against me, against Tina, against my daughter."

"I'll pick up some fresh pastry and coffee. See you in twenty minutes."

"Excellent." To hell with the Paleo diet. "Give me half an hour."

Sitting in the cockpit in the cold black dampness had done nothing good for my joints. My face in the mirror did nothing to uplift my spirits. I found clean underwear and my cleanest pair of blue jeans and a warm sweater. I put on KING 5 news and threw cold water on my face until I was gasping, toweled off, applied BB cream which was supposed to cause my skin to metamorphose into luminous porcelain. It didn't. I brushed my hair and realized I hadn't seen Calico since last night's incident with Griffin. I opened the aft porthole for her, put on the weather channel and caught the end of the local forecast: Fog changing back to rain by noon, rain tapering off by evening. Winds of 20 knots with gusts to 25 and 30. Becoming windy overnight.

I turned off the TV and rummaged in the cooler for some fruit to accompany the pastry. I found a bunch of red grapes and was clearing the table in the salon when Jared knocked on the hull. He came below with two tall containers of coffee and white bakery sack. "Tell me more about your intruder."

I uncovered the coffee container, peered in the sack, pulled out a warm almond croissant, and summarized the visit from Griffin. "Mentioning Melissa was meant to jolt me and it did."

"They're upping the intimidation. Is Melissa okay?"

"Okay as of 3:30 a.m."

"Anything new on the Gundersen matter?"

"When I was in Seattle I had a conversation with the son of the ship captain who lost his job after the *Polar Sea* went aground."

"That would be Zorco,"

"Igor Zorco. He claims his father was involved in some kind of shooting fracas in January of '82. Corroborates what Erika Fredericksen said about Peder turning up with a bloody shoulder, although she was vague about when that was."

"But the captain wasn't reported missing for several months."

"Arne Ormdahl made the first report in May of '82."

"Maybe Captain Zorco came back for a second try and succeeded."

"In which case, there would have been a body."

"Not hard to deep-six a body in twelve hundred feet of water."

"Point taken. Igor says his dad refused to talk about it, then he disappeared. Never was seen again."

We sipped our coffees and munched on the pastry in silence for a while.

"So the dog and the cat," Jared finally offered, "Maybe they ate each other up."

"So it would seem."

"Did any of the attorneys talk to Zorco *pere*?"

"No record of it. He certainly didn't testify."

"What's your next step? Or do you have one?"

I told him about the beard hairs. "I sent the hair samples, along with the carpet pieces and towels and blood-spattered ceiling pieces to a private lab for DNA analysis."

"And you hope for either a match or a mismatch with the blood on the pieces of evidence."

I shrugged. "Best I can do."

"When do you expect the results?"

"Hopefully by Tuesday."

"Kind of late to influence an election on Wednesday." His phone rang and I reached into the sack for another croissant. I felt nervous and helpless. Two kids had been missing for 72 hours. If McCready didn't have them, the scenario was even worse, and my mind flew to the hundreds of teenage runaways that wandered the streets of Seattle. Fugitives from their parents, their homes, their lives. Victims of pimps and drug dealers. Stolen youth. Please, God, don't let Sage and Stephan have left the island.

Jared put down the phone and reached for his jacket. "That was my new editor. Car crash out on the west side early this morning. Three teenagers. I'll call you later." Neither of us voiced the obvious.

After Jared left I made a fresh pot of coffee and called Tina Breckenridge. The call went directly to VM. I left a message to call me soonest. It was nearly eight o'clock. Zelda and her Navajo tracker would be out at English Camp, picking their way through the wet grass. Cutting for sign. I rummaged in the fridge, found a carton of blackberry Greek yogurt. As I ate it, I tried to piece together the fragments of the 30-year-old tragedy that was about to bring my client to her knees.

For reasons we might never know, Peder Gundersen had fled the old homestead on Orcas one snowy winter day. Fled the threat of a crazed wife, or fled from a man who was intent on killing him, or with the belief that he had killed a man whose life he had ruined. He arrived in Seattle in a bloodied state and tried to persuade Erika to run away with him to Iceland. As far as I knew, she declined and Peder had departed for Iceland. Or not. Maybe Peder Gundersen and Dragomir Zorco did have a subsequent encounter and one of them killed the other, neither to ever be seen again.

A little before nine, Calico appeared, ravenous and loquacious. She devoured half a can of white meat chicken primavera with garden greens, washed her whiskers, then disappeared into the aft cabin. I tidied the galley, made up my bed, considered doing a batch of laundry and immediately discarded the idea.

The fog had disappeared. Spring Street bustled with activity. Outside the bakery, Abby and Tony Bolton had their heads together and I caught a glimpse of Lily MacGregor bolting out of the garden shop. She climbed into the small gray Subaru parked at the curb and sped away. I wondered how the hexing had gone. I turned the corner on 2nd street and saw Elyse Montenegro, phone to her ear, standing in the doorway of George's Tavern. She held up one hand, spoke a few more words, then pocketed the phone and glanced across Spring Street. A gray Range Rover with tinted windows was parked in front of Coldwell Banker.

"Here, take this," Elyse said quickly, pulling a small plastic card from the pocket of her jeans. "I don't know what it's for, but Loch went ballistic when he couldn't find it. And I saw a text from Griffin, something about a dome. I sent you an e-mail."

She sprinted across the street and climbed into the Range Rover. I pocketed the card and moved into the doorway of the tavern, watched the vehicle reverse out of the parking space and motor downhill to the roundabout at the foot of Spring Street.

The OGB was dark and cold. I turned up the heat and brewed a pot of coffee. Upstairs my door was still locked. If Griffin had returned and managed a B & E before invading *DragonSpray* at midnight, there was no sign of it. I downloaded my email, and found the message from Elyse Montenagro:

A forwarded message from Lochlan McReady to Nigel Bishop. The message was sent the night before. There was no text, only an attachment. I downloaded it and read the confirmation of a fifty thousand-dollar deposit made by BSI to a bank account in the Cayman islands FBO Nigel Bishop.

The deposit confirmed what Zelda had discovered earlier: that our Sheriff was on the payroll of McCready's company. I thought about what Elyse had said: Something about a dome. There are a number of geodesic domes on the islands. Was the dome connected to Tina Breckenridge? To Nigel Bishop? Or just BSI business?

I called Zelda's phone. No answer. I left a VM. I tried Tina's number and got her VM again. I was about to call Jared when Zelda called back. She was with T.J., calling from the Horse Trail parking lot. "We didn't find Stephan and Sage. We tracked them to Mitchell Hill, then we lost them. I have to pick up my car and go to the clinic."

"Why are you going to the clinic?"

"I slipped in the mud and got twisted up with some rocks and kind of tore up my arm. T.J. is taking me to Lily's where I left my car, then he wants to keep tracking. But it's government land and posted. I thought you two might meet up."

"Slow down. How do you know it was Stephan and Sage?"

"We found some stuff." "What kind of stuff?"

"I'll let you talk to T.J."

A few seconds of silence, then a masculine voice "Ok. So we started at sunrise this morning, at the geocache location at English Camp, and we followed two sets of tracks out to Bell Point on Westcott Bay, then back past the campground and up to the road."

"West Valley Road?" I asked.

"Yep. They crossed the road at the intersection of Yacht Haven and West Valley. I think they walked along West Valley Road up to Horse Trail Road, and up to the parking area. We tracked them on the service road and then followed the trail up towards Mitchell Hill. "

"It's posted as government land."

"DNR is government land."

"Zelda says it was always posted, but it was open to hikers. Now it's fenced off and posted. No Trespassing."

I considered what the implications of that might be, then asked, "How do you know the tracks were Sage and Stephan?"

"What we know is there are two pairs of athletic shoe tracks, probably one male, one female. Because of all the recent rain, tracking in the mud wasn't difficult. We found some small signs along the trail, we're taking them over to Lily's to see if she can identify anything."

"What kind of signs?"

"A candy wrapper. A button. Couple pieces of green plastic. Piece of red wool, like from a blanket.

Credit card receipt from the Little Store. A key on a black spiral band with a tag that says Ravenswood."

"Either of you see anything that looks like a dome? A geodesic dome?"

"The only structures we saw were at English Camp. No domes anywhere."

"I'll meet you in an hour at the parking lot at the top of Horse Trail Road."

I checked the rucksack I keep in the bottom drawer of my desk: binoculars, handheld GPS, first aid kit, bottle of water, camera. I thought about the posted sign on the gate at Mitchell Hill that Zelda and T.J. had found. Once T.J. and I breached it, regardless of whether we found the missing children, we'd be totally on our own. I dialed Angela's phone. No answer. I turned off the computer, locked up, went downstairs, locked the front door, and headed down to the Port to get the Alfa Berlina. Either we found the two kids before night or I, personally, would call in the FBI.

Chapter 45

HORSE TRAIL HILL

San Juan Island

Eleven o'clock came and went. 11:15 and 11:25. I paced around the parking lot, checking the time on my phone every few minutes. The earlier blue sky had disappeared; a heavy mist filled the air. The kind of dampness real estate agents hate but that keeps our islands so green.

I pulled a map from the box near the gate and studied it. The area was crisscrossed by service roads and trails. I knew from past experience almost all the trails were loops, and at certain times of the year the service roads were so overgrown it was impossible to distinguish them from the trails.

11:35. Down the hill and across the road, the lake below Blazing Tree lay flat and metallic, a ragged piece of wet slate. From overhead came the drone of a small plane preparing for a landing at the Roche Harbor airport.

11:45. I was about to call Zelda when my phone chirped for an incoming text. It was from Carolyn Smith: *Follow this link for latest on Petrovsky matter. Hope you're sitting down.* I stared at her words for a long minute. Whatever she'd sent me probably meant more hassles with the pirates which I wasn't in the mood for.

I tapped the link and watched the screen fill with an article from *The Guardian*.

She Shan Flying Tigers Free Hostages from Pirates in Somali Raid.

NAIROBI, Kenya - Around 1:00 a.m. Tuesday, elders in the Somali village of Addado reported hearing the sound of helicopters. Ten minutes later a daring raid by around 30 members of Shanghai's prestigious SWAT team, locally known as the She Shan Flying Tigers, was under way. The focus of the raid was to rescue two hostages – an American sailor and his Shanghainese first mate - held by Somali pirates for over three weeks. The commandos parachuted into a camp on the outskirts of the village, where they had intelligence that the hostages were being held. Then, reported one of the surviving pirates, the visitors began launching missiles.

Although he has refused to discuss the raid with the press, it is believed the mission came about at the behest of Shanghai banker Yee Bao, whose daughter, Michelle Yee, was being held along with Captain Harrison Petrovsky of the S/V Ocean Dancer, a yacht that was highjacked a month ago off the Seychelles. According to Captain Petrovsky's online postings, the couple were headed for a diving resort on Mafia Island owned by relatives of Ms. Yee.

Apparently a San Francisco (Ca.) hostage negotiator began ransom negotiations with the pirates, then the matter was taken over by Yee Bao and his brother-in-law Reginald Archer, an instructor with the Flying Tigers. The pirates had recently refused an offer of $3 million, and were threatening to kill the hostages. Ms. Yee, who is a trader with a Shanghai investment firm, reported she had been repeatedly beaten, had fractured ribs, and for several days was separated from Captain Petrovsky. Apparently negotiations were also under way to sell the hostages to al-Shabaab, the terrorist offshoot of Al Queda that claimed responsibility for the 2013 siege and massacre at the Nairobi Westgate mall and a number of other recent bombings. The negotiation, according to Ms. Yee, fell apart and deteriorated into warfare between the two terrorist groups.

There are differing reports as to whether the Flying Tigers captured any of the Somali gunmen, with local Addado officials saying three had been captured, and our source reporting that "nine were killed and four were taken alive." A spokesman for the Tigers was adamant that no prisoners were taken.

Captain Petrovsky declined to accompany Ms. Yee to Shanghai and is currently in Mogadishu where he hopes to arrange repairs to Ocean Dancer and then continue his voyage through the Mediterranean and back to the States. Upon arriving in Shanghai, Ms. Yee was met by her parents and transferred to a private hospital.

I didn't know whether to laugh or cry. Captain Petrovsky was on the move again.

The time was now 12:10. I scanned the road below and started to dial Zelda's number. Midway through, an incoming call interrupted. It was Angela Petersen.

"I don't have any good news. We haven't found the kids and we didn't learn anything last night. Nigel's put me on security detail for the Senator. And he's using the 'copter so the Senator can go sightseeing."

"What Senator?"

"Some friend of McCready's. He's got another rally planned tonight."

"He's bringing in the big guns."

"In more ways than one."

"Meaning?"

"The Senator's nephew and two friends got here last weekend. They've been closing up the bars the last few nights. One of them is a minor with phony ID. Last night they were in the car that went over the cliff out on the West Side."

I breathed a sigh of relief. Stephan Breckenridge wasn't in that car.

"Any fatalities?"

"None. But the boys are a bit roughed up. Scuttlebutt is somebody sold liquor to the minor."

"So the caca's going to be flying."

"Yeah. The senator is flying in with the whole family at noon."

"When did the Sheriff get a helicopter?"

"He bought one from Islands Airlift."

I thought about the 50K deposit in the Cayman Islands account. "How many geodesic domes do you know about in the islands?"

"Quite a lot, actually. There's one at Three Meadows, one out at the Wold Road Retreat Center. One over on Stuart. Two or three on Lopez. Quite a few yurts. Why d'ya want to know?"

"Any new ones constructed in the last year?"

"Can't think of any."

"I'm heading out to do some trespassing."

"You want to tell me where?"

"Zelda and T.J. Tahoma, the new Park Ranger, think they tracked Stephan and Sage to a security gate at the bottom of Mitchell Hill. I plan to find out what's on the other side of the gate."

"Why are you– oh, shit. Here comes Nigel looking like a thundercloud. Gotta go."

I pressed End Call. It was 12:23. Still no so sign of T.J. The Alfa Berlina was still the only vehicle in the parking area. A light rain began to fall. I wiped the raindrops from the face of my cell, which now had zero service bars. I paced for another ten minutes, then zipped the phone into the rucksack and proceeded up what I thought was the service road, on my own.

The road was bordered with Red Leaf maples, the ubiquitous Oregon grape, holly, salmonberry, and all around, big patches of nettles. I didn't see any critters, human or otherwise. I'd worn my foul weather jacket when I left the boat, so I was mostly dry on top, but the rain was soaking through my jeans. The trail became increasingly muddy and slick. In several places puddles covered it completely. Despite my thick-soled boots, I slipped a couple of times and bruised my right elbow on a boulder. I passed several forks in the trail and hoped I was choosing the one that would lead to where Zelda and T.J. had tracked the two kids and that I was not walking in circles. After an hour I was still climbing uphill. The woods were heavy with the scent of dampness. Molds and lichens covered stones and boulders. Half an hour later, I came to a stop in front of the fence at the bottom of Mitchell Hill. Two signs were very visible.

Government Facility, No Trespassing.
This property is under Video Surveillance.

The fence was a serious obstacle. Galvanized mesh, commonly referred to as hurricane fence or cyclone fence. Which has always mystified me since it wouldn't stop either one. The fence was installed on posts of steel tubing set in concrete. The mesh was tied to the posts with aluminum wire. What this fence was designed to do was detract or discourage or intimidate legitimate hikers from any thought of gaining access to the gravel road on the other side of the locked and posted gate. I couldn't see a video camera, but that didn't mean it wasn't there. It could be wireless or solar-powered.

Wireless cameras have changed the face of security, and what concerned me was the possibility of a video of S. J. MacKinnon Private Investigator breaching a posted government fence that could be delivered instantaneously to a phone, e-mail, or web portal. In which case there would be a welcoming committee waiting on the other side of the hill. And S.J. MacKinnon with no back-up.

One way or another, I had to get over the fence and onto the gravel road that lay beyond it. I considered a run-and-climb approach and immediately abandoned it. The fence was not topped with razor wire, but it was at least six-foot high and I wasn't current with my run-and-climb practice.

I peered along the length of the fence in both directions. To my right the fence ran downhill and the area was clear on either side as far as I could see. To the left the fence followed the steep uphill slope into a densely wooded area. I chose the up-slope, trying to remember the last time I'd tried to climb a Douglas fir. Or a Western red cedar. The hillside was steep and rocky, the rocks covered with thick green moss that slithered underfoot. I scrambled through the thick undergrowth of salal and Oregon grape for what seemed like forever until I reached a large Gary oak tree that overgrew the fence. On my side of the fence, the branches of the old tree grew close to the ground. The bark was rough and uneven. On the other side of the fence, high up in an old snag, a large raven commented on my presence and was answered by a second in a neighboring snag. I wondered if they were Edgar and Lenore. Supposedly crows and ravens are smarter than horses and I thought about what Abby had said about their facial-recognition ability. The bigger bird produced a deep "quark" and I wondered if I could learn to speak Raven. I suspected Abigail Leedle already did.

I burrowed around in my rucksack, for a pair of leather gloves. I pulled them on and hoisted myself onto a low branch. When I got to the trunk I began climbing from branch to branch. I climbed what I calculated to be about seven feet up, then began wriggling my way out on a branch above the fence. The ground sloped steeply downhill away from the fence, and I was beginning to have doubts about my plan. Or my lack of a plan. In the Police Academy I'd been trained to leap out of buildings far higher than this tree branch. That was then and this was now.

I took a deep breath, put both hands around the branch and dropped. What-ever procedure I'd been taught failed. Instead of a nice springy landing and roll, my right ankle took all of my weight and I ended up with my right leg twist-ed backwards under my hip. The pain that shot up my leg and into my back brought tears to my eyes. I lay on the wet ground, on top of my rucksack, trying to assess the damage.

Broken bones?

A sprain?

A pulled ligament?

In slow motion I unfolded my leg and stretched it out. The pain seemed confined to the inside of my right knee. I rotated my ankle. Nothing seemed bro-ken.

I unzipped my rucksack and checked my phone. The protective case had a long crack on its face. The service bars were alternating between one and two. There was a text from Zelda, which did nothing to improve my mood. Or my situation.

TJ got drafted into doing security @ Lime Kiln 4 visiting senatr. Nobodys hrd frm Tina. Elyse is in trble. I texted back a request for more information, but the signal had disappeared. I tucked the phone back in the zippered pocket.

Grabbing onto the fence for support with my right hand, I pulled myself to my feet, took one cau-tious step. Then another and another. My locomotion was more a hobble than a walk and it took an eternity to make my way back downhill to the gate. Both ra-vens found my struggles hilarious, gave a final cackle, and flew away, up over the hill. In the same direction I was headed. And where hopefully I would find a dome.

An hour later I made it to the top of Mitchell Hill. The pain in my knee was worse. I stopped at the edge of the woods, found a huge boulder to rest against. The gravel road I'd been following continued down into a flat valley. Two long open sheds with metal roofs, the kind contractors use to store equipment, stood to one side of a large, flat, paved clearing. A late model black pick-up truck sat in front of the farthest shed. On the opposite side of the clearing was a large cage-like affair that seemed to enclose three trees, maples or oak trees, I couldn't tell which.

The gravel road continued beyond the sheds and disappeared behind what appeared to be a large mound of earth surrounded by a grove of Gary oaks. From where I stood, the mound looked like a large anthill. There were no dogs. No alarms. No indication that a camera back at the gate had recorded my illegal en-try. The woods ended at the bottom of the hill where I would be in full sight of anyone approaching from below. I stood for several minutes at the top of the hill, aware of a distant buzzing sound. Like the sound of a chain saw. Then it stopped and quiet returned. A few minutes later the buzzing resumed, but seemed to be moving away.

I waited five minutes, then began edging my way downhill, keeping to the thinning cover of Douglas firs, following a path behind the sheds. Away from the protective canopy of the trees, the rain was a downpour. The two ravens flew over my head and took up a perch in two young fir trees at the edge of the compound. Once again, I was their person of in-terest. I thought about Edgar and Lenore again. The birds watched me, but made no comment. I stopped behind the last shed and peered around the corner and stared at the mound of earth that was actually a brown-shingled geodesic structure of seven or eight sides.

I'd found McCready's dome.

Chapter 46
BioIntell Facility

San Juan Island

For several minutes I scanned the brown geometric structure and the big caged enclosure across the clearing. The roof of the dome, a grayish brown color, was clearly visible. Creeping closer, I realized there were actually two domes: The larger dome rested on a flat concrete foundation and was connected to the smaller one by a wooden bridge. A wooden door with clear glass side panels was set in the front of the larger dome, facing onto the clearing. Above the entry door were five triangular skylights, but no other windows. To the right of the entrance a bronze plaque proclaimed *BioIntel Systems Inc. Research Laboratory.* A smaller sign advised, *Authorized Personnel Only.* Nothing about a government facility. A narrow wooden deck encircled the large dome.

Nothing moved in the clearing. I pulled my phone from the rucksack, snapped a photo of the dome, and focused the camera on the caged enclosure. As I stared at it through the camera lens, took in the wire mesh sides and top, the black birds perched on the branches of the enclosed trees, I realized what I was looking at. I snapped another photo and sent both photos to Zelda and Angela with a text: *McCready's compound at the foot of Mitchell Hill. Could use some backup when available.*

The buzzing noise was audible again, like a giant buzzing insect. The sky grew darker. A gust of wind hit me in the face. I stared at the big aviary that backed up to a third structure, another windowless, brown-shingled geodesic dome. I checked my watch: 2:40. Pondering my next move, I heard my phone announce an incoming VM. It was from Angela, but there was only one service bar and the message on the screen directed me to call a 425 number to retrieve it. Which, with one service bar, wasn't going to happen.

The buzzing noise disappeared. The only sound was the wind soughing through the fir trees. Pain shot through my knee. I reached down to massage it and winced. My hand came away covered in blood that was seeping through my jeans.

I wiped my hand on my jacket and stepped under the overhang of one of the open sheds. As I stood there, contemplating my next move, two large ravens swept past me and came to a landing on top of the cage structure. Then three things occurred: From the dome behind the aviary, a wooden door opened and several objects were flung into the cage beneath where the birds had landed. Simultaneously, the top of the cage structure where the birds were perched opened and the two birds quickly lowered themselves to the floor picking at whatever had been deposited. And finally, the two ravens who'd been surveilling me all afternoon began a noisy harangue from the fir trees at the edge of the clearing. Did they belong in the aviary? Was there a reward waiting for them as well? Or were they upset at the captivity of their feathered cousins?

The depositing of food in the cage was the only movement that might be attributed to humans. There was a security keypad beside the main door, the kind that required a security card to be swiped, and then I remembered with glee the card Elyse had foisted on me earlier in the day. But even assuming it would open the door, it was unlikely I'd find the dome unoccupied. Someone was feeding the birds.

I crouched at the side of the dome and heard a telephone ring inside. It rang three times and then stopped. I glanced back at the black pick-up parked in front of the shed, noticed the green Honda ATV sitting beside it.

I pulled the security key card from my pocket and began edging my way around to the back of the dome, staying below the circular walkway. In the very back, a set of wooden stairs ascended to a metal door where an identical security box guarded the back entry.

Two minutes later I was inside a large open space surrounded by a circular corridor that ran completely around the interior with glass-enclosed rooms opening off from it. Shades or blinds hid what was behind the glass of each room. Each of the doors had a decal that said High Security Laboratory. Authorized personnel only. Each had a locking device that required a key card. I moved along the corridor, reading the sign on each door: Moths. Beetles. Mosquitos. Dragonflies. Butterflies. Under each printed sign was a colored illustration of that insect. I moved closer to read the fine print on the Beetle graphic: *cochlear implant batteries . . .microcontroller - 62mg . . . implanted counter electrode . . .2 x implanted wing neural simulators.* Alongside the photo of a Velvet Pink Moth was the following note: *neural probe tied to wireless simulator onto ventral nerve cord.*

I stared around the circular corridor, saw one open door at the far end. And then a woman's voice: "Yeah, everything's on schedule . . . eleven and twelve just came in . . . no problem. . . . The packages are totally concealed . . .Yeah, I'm fixing it now. What time's show and tell?"

The voice was getting clearer. And closer. I scanned the corridor for a place to hide, thinking about the Beretta I'd left on the stand beside my bed at 2:00 a.m. The door immediately to my left looked like a closet. It wasn't locked and it wasn't a closet, but a small windowless office with a desk, the only light coming from a small skylight in the ceiling. I darted inside, closed the door only seconds before I heard the woman's voice again just outside the door. "Max's checkin' the road. We'll be ready, boss." I opened the door a crack and glimpsed the hefty back of a very tall, sturdy woman wearing black trousers and a black long-sleeved shirt. Her hair was inky black, secured in a severe ponytail. She had a phone to one ear. With a final comment that I couldn't make out, she shook her head, pocketed the phone, and disappeared through the back door I'd just come through.

I listened to the heavy door close with a click, then I listened to the silence for a couple more minutes. The back door didn't reopen. I carefully closed the office door and began quietly opening the drawers in the desk, searching for anything more useful than my flashlight that I could use for defense or that might tell me anything about two missing kids. I found several 3-ring binders, a carton of Marlboro cigarettes, and a cell phone in a purple case. It appeared to be charged, but had no signal. I tucked it into my rucksack and continued rummaging in the bottom drawer where I hit pay dirt: An H &K semi-automatic P2000 SK. Two boxes of Cor-Bon ammunition lay alongside. I checked the magazine, found it loaded, checked the safety, slipped the pistol in the waistband at my back. I leaned against the door, heard nothing but silence, and slipped back outside to the corridor.

I desperately wanted to see what was in the room at the end of the corridor where the woman's voice had been coming from, but I had no idea if there were more personnel and I'd already pushed my luck way too far in the last twenty-four hours. I tried the purloined key card on one of the lab doors, then was asked for a security code. Ditto the room next to it and the one next to that.

Merde.

From outside came the roar of an engine, the vroom-vroom of what I'd bet was the dark green ATV. Black Shirt must be going for a ride. After a few more revs of the engine, the sound passed the dome and receded down the hill.

It was now or never. Either the kids were here somewhere in the compound or theyweren't. With a final glance at the back door, I headed around the corridor to where I hoped to find the bridge to the smaller dome and hopefully a door that wasn't locked. Luck was still with me and I hurried across the short wooden bridge between the two structures and found another unlocked door. The inside of the small dome was pitch black. I switched on the flashlight. The structure was a garage or storage area with a concrete floor and six sides. The only item being garaged was a flatbed trailer with a Washington state license plate that was stacked with six empty cages.

I didn't know how soundproof the structure was, but I had to risk it. "Stephan? Sage? Are you here? Stephan?" I listened to the silence, then called again. And again, all I heard was silence and a far away buzzing noise.

I'd been wrong: the kids weren't here. The hike up the mountain and injuring my knee was all a wild goose chase. I wasn't helping my client, and if I got caught trespassing, things were going to get worse very fast.

About to retrace my steps to the main dome, I heard a faint scuffling sound. Then another. The sounds seemed to be coming from below the floor. Tracking the sounds, I shuffled along the perimeter of the dome and nearly fell when my toe caught in something on the floor. The something was a heavy iron ring attached to a trapdoor. It took all my strength to lift the door. All was black below. I moved quickly to one side, aimed the H & K and my flashlight downward, and stared down at the gaunt, bearded face of Stephan Breckenridge and the terrified eyes of a pale young woman who had to be Sage McGregor.

Chapter 47

BⁱᵒIⁿᵗᵉˡˡ Fᵃᶜⁱˡⁱᵗʸ

Mitchell Hill, San Juan Island

The trapdoor was attached to a folding stairway that led down to a cellar. The kind of cellar where in generations past people kept root vegetables and canned foods through the winter. It was dark and cold and damp. There was no railing on the stairs and descending the steps was a lot worse on my knee than climbing hills. Both Sage and Stephan were bound to a long wooden bench, with duct tape on their mouth, hands tied with plastic restraints. Sage had a jagged bloody gash on her forehead that was leaking over her right eye.

There's no painless method of removing duct tape from human skin and Sage whimpered as I threw it on the floor. I did the same with Stephan, then found my knife in my jacket pocket and liberated the two teenagers from the bench. By the time I was done the blood on Sage's face was mixing with the tears streaming down her face. I was glad neither Tina nor Lily was present at that moment.

"Who are you?" Sage's voice was a hoarse whisper. "Are you going to kill us?"

"Ms. McKinnon! Oh, my God," Stephan whispered. He turned to Sage. "She's cool. She's not going to kill us."

I slid the H & K into my waistband. "I'm Scotia MacKinnon. I'm working for Stephan's mom and I'm here to get you back to your families." I cut the plastic ties on her hands and legs. For a minute she seemed unable to move her arms. I massaged her shoulders and cut Stephan's ties. He slowly brought his arms to the front of his body and rotated his shoulders. "I didn't think anybody would ever hear us," he said in a hoarse voice. "Or would care."

"We have to get out of here," Sage said rubbing her wrists against each other. "Before they come back to kill me."

"Who is they?" I asked.

"The vampires. I know they're going to kill me."

"They're not vampires, Sage," Stephan said in a hoarse voice, "They're just a couple of thugs pretending to be lab techs."

"They're going to kill me. I could tell the way Stella looked at me this morning."

"I won't let them kill you, Sage. Let's go." I put an arm around her waist and propelled her toward the stairs. "Stephan, give us a hand."

He stood up slowly, grimaced, and together we half-carried her to the top of the stairs. She cringed as we climbed into the darkness above. I shined the flashlight around the floor of the dome. "Is there a light in here anywhere?" As I posed the question I heard the buzzing noise again, closer now.

"That's Max," Sage said and began to cry. "He's back. He'll kill all of us. It's all my fault."

The incessant buzzing noise was growing closer, like a roar now, and Stephan closed his eyes and shook his head. "Oh, fuck. It's the ATV's. Both of them. Max went out couple of hours ago."

"Do you know where he was going?"

He shrugged. "Before they moved us to the cellar I heard Max say a delivery truck went off the road trying to get up here. I think something big's supposed to happen here this afternoon. Like some VIP's are visiting or something."

"Are they armed? Stella and Max?"

"Stella is. She likes to flash the gun around. How weird is that: lab techs carrying guns."

"The only thing Stella cares about is the birds." This from Sage. "And drinking beer."

"You mean the ravens in the aviary?"

She nodded. "She had a total hissy fit when she found out how McCready got them. She said she'd never have signed on if she'd known the baby birds were stolen. They're all wired, you know."

"Wired how?"

"They're programed. They have cameras. Tell her, Stephan."

"I don't know if they did something to their brains like I heard they did to the dragonflies and the moths, but the birds fly out and do surveillance and the cameras send pictures back to Stella's computer. Pictures from all over the island. Then the birds fly back at a specific time. Each cage of birds is programmed differently. Stella controls everything from her keyboard. Like when the meat gets dumped and when the cages open. "

"Did either of you ever actually see McCready?"

They both shook their heads. "They put us in

the dungeon both times when he was here," Stephan said. "But we heard S and M talking. About how Mc-Cready had the idea of wiring the birds, like some pigeon project in New York. About how crows and ravens are smarter than pigeons. Stella refused to wire them, so McCready did it himself. We could hear the birds screaming even inside."

I took a deep breath. The ATV's were a constant roar that was setting my teeth on edge, but with the Stella and Max headed back and McCready scheduling a show and tell, I had to make a decision.

There are different levels of bad choices. They range from stupid to moronic to insane. The level beyond insane is fatal. Choosing to stay and confront two armed thugs, male or female, fell somewhere between insane and fatal. I already knew Stella was bigger than I, Max mostly likely the same. And I was injured. If they were working for McCready, they were used to tying up loose ends. And they would be in a blood rage when they discovered the empty dungeon. I wasn't prepared to slay dragons. Or vampires.

"Is there any way out of here except going back through the main dome?" I asked.

"There was some kind of weird double door in here that was open when they brought us in," Stephan said.

"It's like the door at the stables," Sage put in. "It slides."

"Don't move. I'll find it." I crept to the nearest wall and began moving around the circular space, exploring with my hands. Half way round the room my fingers found metal. Corrugated metal, the kind that's used for roll-up doors in storage units. The lever or rope or whatever was used to raise it would be on the bottom. I knelt down, found the protruding metal flap, and heaved it upward. It wasn't quiet. I prayed the ATV engines would cover the noise. When the door was all the way up, there was a wall behind it. A wall that let in a crack of light and moved when I pushed against it. There was a track at the top, and one or two long minutes later I found the metal handle. I turned the handle, pushed against the sliding door, slid it a few inches to the left. It opened silently and I peered out. I couldn't see the ATV's but the sound was just below the hill. A steady rain was falling. Both kids were wearing sweat shirts and blue jeans with no jackets.

The door opened onto a concrete pad at the back of the two domes, with access to the road that went downhill and probably ended at the Roche Harbor wetlands. I was 90% sure the ATVs would come past the dome and the bikes would get parked back in the shed. After that Stella and Max would probably head directly for the main entry door at the front of the larger dome. In which case we might have a minuscule window to slip out and head downhill. What I couldn't guess was how Stella and Max would react once they discovered the empty dungeon. Would they call McCready? Call Griffin? Start searching for us?

The roar of the ATV's was virtually on top of us. "Get ready," I said.

Stephan stood up, took Sage's hand and moved toward the door.

"Wait 'till they get around by the shed, then we'll make a run for it. We need to get off the road fast, into the woods. It's raining. It'll be rough going." I opened the outer door wide enough to slide through.

"There's an old trail that parallels the road," Stephan said. "I'll show you."

I pulled the H & K from my waistband. We huddled at the door, sound-tracking the machines as they passed by the dome. There were several final vroom-vrooms, then silence. "Go, go, go."

We slid through the opening, and I raced after Sage and Stephan into the dense thicket of bushes and trees. She who runs away, lives to fight.

Chapter 48

MITCHELL HILL

San Juan Island

"What did you mean, this was all your fault?" I asked Sage in a low voice. We were ten minutes into the deep woods, following a narrow dirt trail through the omnipresent salal and Oregon grape. There was a pungent scent of wet earth, although the thick canopy of Doug firs and Red cedars protected us from most of the falling rain. Hopefully we were far enough off the service road to elude S and M and their spiffy toys if they decided to give chase. At least if they followed us on their spiffy toys, the noise would give us warning. I carried the H & K down at my side.

"It's because I lost my new phone," Sage said.

"How did that happen?"

"It was a week ago. When Leslie and I got lost with the horses. Stephan said he would help me find it."

I pulled the purple phone out of my pocket. "Is this yours?"

She grabbed it with a little cry, pressed a button on the top, swiped her thumb across the screen. "Oh, my God. It still works."

"Did your aunt know you lost your phone?"

She shook her head. "I didn't dare tell her. It was a gift for my birthday."

"You told her you and Leslie got lost on Cady Mountain."

"Yeah. We didn't exactly get lost, but we spent a lot of time looking for the phone. I thought I probably dropped it when the horses got spooked by the ATV. Les and I were on our way back then the big jerk grabbed us. Like five minutes later."

"You did see the sign at the gate about video surveillance?"

"When we came in with the horses, the gate was open."

Up ahead Stephan halted, turned around. "We came up here Monday," he told me. "Sage and me. The trouble started when we ran into the two thugs and Sage started whistling."

I looked at Sage. "Whistling?"

She looked down at the ground. "I was practicing."

"Practicing what?"

"She was trying to whistle up a wind," Stephan said.

"Excuse me?"

"A witch wind. She almost did it. Like both the ATV's turned over, but the wind wasn't big enough and that cow Stella went ballistic and hit her. She's a scarey piece of work."

"A little knowledge can be dangerous," I muttered. "Let's go on."

"We can't," Stephan said. "The trail's run out and somebody's been cutting trees." He pointed ahead where two humongous freshly cut Red cedars blocked our path. On both sides I saw only a dense thicket of underbrush. He glanced at my bloodstained pant leg. "We'll have to follow the service road down." He nodded to the right. "It's over there."

"Are we still on BSI land?"

He shrugged. "Who knows? This all used to be DNR." He stared at my pant leg again. "Your leg's bleeding really bad. Maybe we should go back."

"I'll be fine." I looked around. There was no sound from uphill, no outbursts of rage or roar of ATV's, which could only mean that Sage and Stephan's escape hadn't been discovered yet. "We can't go back. Going down is the only option. Lead on."

For the next ten minutes we fought our way through the dense underbrush and finally emerged onto a graveled road. The rain had diminished, but a wind had come up, icy and biting. "How far down to Roche Harbor Road?"

"Probably two miles," Stephan said. "Can you make it? If you can't, you and Sage could stay here and I could go get help."

I stared down the road, trying to make up a lie, when I saw the front end of a gray SUV silently emerge from around a curve just a few feet away to my left. It was McCready's Range Rover.

Stephan grabbed Sage and virtually leaped back into the brush. I couldn't react that fast and instead raised the H & K, steadying it with both hands. The SUV came to a jarring halt beside me. The front seat passenger was Elyse Montenegro. She was staring straight ahead. Lochlan McCready was holding a gun to her head, a twin to the one I had in my hands. The passenger side window rolled down.

"Put the gun down, MacKinnon. Toss it into the woods. Don't turn around. Do it now."

Slowly I lowered the H & K and let it drop a few feet behind me.

"Now get into the back seat."

I opened the rear door and climbed onto the smooth leather seat. I had to lift my right leg with one hand to get it onto the seat. The wound on my knee was still weeping. I glanced at the spot where Stephan and Sage had disappeared. Nothing. Would they have the sense to stay out of sight? Would they continue down to the main road?

"I'm very good at driving with one hand," Mc-Cready said. "Don't even think about doing something cute."

I watched my bloody pant leg make a big smear on the leather seat, fastened my seat belt, and leaned back against the headrest. Now McCready had two new captives. Life was sure to get interesting when he discovered the previous two had disappeared. Probably going to get interesting as well for the two thugs. He shifted into gear with his right hand and we began climbing the steep road. Two switchbacks and ten minutes later the SUV glided to a stop next to the black pickup. Two dark green Honda FourTrax were parked in the shed closest to the dome. The rain had diminished and a light wind ruffled the tree branches. There was no sign of Stella or Max.

McCready shifted into Park, transferred the gun to his right hand, retrieved a communication device from the side pocket of the door. He thumbed a button and spoke into the mic, eyes on me. "Need you two outside. Now."

I wanted to think that McCready's weapon was a bluff, that he wouldn't actually shoot Elyse. Or me. But everything I'd learned about the man pointed toward a sociopathic personality disorder. Or possibility psychopathic. Kidnapping is a federal offense and a long, long time could pass before anyone would discover two or three or four properly covered graves in the dense foliage of the deep woods on Mitchell Hill. Or four skeletons in the dank cellar under the floor. And if the cellar were sealed off, San Juan Island would have a new murder case: four missing people and no bodies.

A muffled voice came through the speaker of McCready's walkie-talkie. "Yeah, boss. Whadya need?"

"Bring a pair of restraints. Do it now."

Elyse made a motion as if to turn around. McCready slammed the barrel of the H & K into the side of her head. "You move when I tell you, bitch."

She shivered and stared straight ahead through the windshield. The main door to the larger of the two domes opened. A very tall, extremely thin man with a long, jet black ponytail came out. Max, Thug Number Two. His skin was very white and I wondered if he'd been living underground. I wondered if he and Stella were siblings. A pair of plastic restraints dangled from one hand and in the other he held a half empty beer bottle. Without Elyse in the picture, I could have created some mayhem, but we were out-manned and out-maneuvered.

I thought about my daughter and wondered if I'd ever see her again. About my mother down in Mendocino, expecting me to help with the Thanksgiving pies. I thought about Falcon and Invergary House, about strawberry jam with hot scones I wondered what would happen to Calico and couldn't bear the thought that she'd end up with the Redhead.

McCready hit the remote window control and yelled through the open window. "Max, lose the fucking beer and get your ass over here and watch the one in the back seat." Max put the bottle down on the deck, wiped his mouth, and came to stare at me with small black eyes while McCready got out and walked around the car. "Where the hell is your idiot sister?" he yelled, as he reached for the door handle.

Max shrugged. "Said she was going to fix the security system. Camera's not working. And she's got to feed the fucking birds."

Behind me I heard a plopping noise, then a grating sound, and simultaneously two large black birds were winging down the hill toward the aviary, barely missing our heads. I risked a glance behind and saw the two ravens swoop into the open top of one of the aviary sections and flutter to the floor of their cage. The top of the cage grated closed.

Programmed indeed.

I turned to watch McCready. Something overhead was attracting his attention. He scanned the darkening sky for a few more seconds, then jerked open my door, grabbed my right arm, and dragged me out of the vehicle. I screamed as pain streaked through my knee and would have fallen if he hadn't been holding me so tightly. He looked down at my blood-soaked pant leg and smiled. "Can't read,

MacKinnon? I would have thought you were smarter than to breach a surveilled perimeter. What were you thinking?"

I tried to take a deep breath over the pain. "The deputies are on their way up here, McCready." I tried to keep my voice calm.

"You're a lousy liar. Hands behind your back." He tucked the gun into his waistband. "You and Ms. Troublemaker here can go have a little tete-a-tete with the delinquents in the cellar. Not the way you planned to spend the evening, is it?" He shoved me toward Max and opened the front passenger door. "Cuff her and take both of them down to the cellar. Tell Stella to get her ass out here."

"Sure thing, boss."

Max didn't know. Maybe S and M had been so thirsty they hadn't bothered to check on the prisoners. Max twisted my arms viciously behind me and snapped on the plastic restraints. The wind was rising again. I shivered, wondering if Sage and Stephan had made it down to the main road. In the Range Rover Elyse was staring straight ahead, her back unnaturally stiff from her bound hands. McCready hauled her out of the car and pushed her ahead of him toward the dome. I wondered how long she'd been captive and if McCready had discovered the message she'd forwarded to me. The one showing the deposit to the Sheriff's Cayman Islands account.

As Max began dragging me around the SUV I tried to anticipate what was going to happen when McCready discovered the empty cellar, and then the main door of the big dome burst open and Stella came flying out. "Number eight and nine aren't eating," she shouted at McCready. "They're trying to get out of the camera harnesses and they're going to peck themselves to death. The camera on number four has a cracked lens."

"I don't give a flying fuck what Numbers eight and nine are doing. Help us get these two skags inside and."

McCready was interrupted by the sound of grating, but it was the grating of all the sections of the big aviary, all opening at once, and suddenly there was what seemed like a humongous black wave fluttering and flapping around us. I knew there weren't more than a dozen of the big ravens, but the raucous screams of the shiny black birds multiplied their number and I drew in my breath, preparing for the scraping of claws on the back of my neck, the pecking on my skin. I twisted away from Max who was trying to fight off the birds with both hands, and stumbled my way back toward the SUV. Stella gasped and covered her head with her hands, but the birds weren't attacking her. Like a cloud of demonic black minions from Lucifer, their target was McCready and his pony-tailed sidekick. I stared in horror as the little beaks stabbed and pecked at the two men's faces, watched McCready hurl Elyse away from him and try to pull the gun from his waistband. He got the H & K out, got one shot off, only to have three of the ravens descend directly onto his face, talons flexing. Cursing, blood running down his face, he pulled off his jacket and hurled it at the birds who simply circled and returned to attack. Elyse had made it back to the SUV, but like me, was unable to get inside because of the restraints on her hands. As she cowered there, tears poured down her face.

Stella suddenly broke away from the melee and bolted for the shed where the ATV's were parked. Max was crouched on the ground now, arms over his head, his and McCready's shouts mingling with the furious screams of the birds, and I realized this was not some end of the world attack on the human race, nor the harbinger of a dark Arctic winter. Millions of years of memory were stored in these proud feathered brains, along with the memory of being plucked from the nests of their parents and turned into robotic Smartbirds. This was avian revenge, pure and simple.

Another shot rang out, one of the ravens plummeted to the ground. The ATV roared to life and Stella was tearing out of the clearing. "Don't forget to feed them," she screamed over the noise. Gravel spinning, she roared away down the road. There was hoarse cawing from the birds as they circled the downed raven and lifted as one and soared overhead in a cloud. Long black hair flapping around his face, Max raced for the remaining ATV and seconds later roared out of the clearing after Stella. McCready shouted an unintelligible curse after the Fourtrax, then made a run toward the dome, scanning the sky overhead. He backed up against the door, frowning, blood tearing down his face. He scanned the sky, weapon pointed toward me and Elyse. And then I heard it: The sound of an aerial vehicle. The birds headed as one toward the tall Douglas firs at the edge of the clearing, lining up on the branches.

As we all stared up at the rain-drenched sky, a green and white helicopter circled over the clearing once, then twice, then, buffeted by the wind gusts, began to descend toward the center of the clearing. The rotors scattered the gravel around us and the AS3502 settled onto the ground. With a sinking heart I stared at the big gold star and the bold black letters that said **San Juan County Sheriff**.

Chapter 49

BioIntel Facility

Mitchell Hill, San Juan Island

The rotors were still whirling when one of the copter doors opened and the first black jacketed figure, a medium height brown-skinned female, leaped to the ground, gun aimed on McCready. The black jacket said F.B.I. in big white letters. The first figure was followed by a second, male, also armed, wearing a similar black jacket. Both agents had hard faces, the kind you'd prefer not to run into in the small hours of the morning unless they were on your side. McCready stood on the stairs of the dome, one hand still holding the H & K, the other swiping at the blood on his face.

"Lochlan McCready," the female agent said loudly, "You're under arrest. Drop the gun and put your hands above your head. Do it now."

"You've got the wrong person, ma'am," McCready said. He nodded toward me and Elyse. "These are the two you want. They were trespassing and destroying government property. I was just about to take them into town and turn 'em over to the Sheriff."

Both agents edged closer to McCready, both weapons aimed at his chest. "We have the right person, McCready," the female agent yelled, cocking the hammer on her weapon. "Drop the gun. Do it now."

McCready glanced toward the SUV where Elyse was still crouching against the passenger side door. She had a large red welt on the side of her face and her skin was the color of parchment.

"On what charges are you arresting me?"

"We are arresting you under Title 18, U. S. Code, Section 351, Kidnapping and Assault. Drop the gun and get down on the ground."

"You have no idea of who I am. Unless you are off this property in three minutes, both of you are going to be looking for new jobs by tomorrow morning."

Both agents moved closer. Faster than my eye could follow, McCready lifted his gun. The two agents leaped apart at the same moment, three shots rang out and McCready was twisting on the ground holding his right thigh. In an instant both agents were on him, he was face down in the gravel, and the restraint was in place. "Lochlan McCready, anything you say . . ."

When the female agent finished the Miranda, both agents hauled him to his feet and I heard the sound of a motor coming fast up the hill behind the domes. McCready looked hopefully toward the noise and then the Sheriff's white SUV was in the clearing and Undersheriff Fountain and Deputy Petersen were out of the vehicle with weapons drawn and headed toward the dome where the door seemed to open on its own.

The female F.B.I. agent hustled McCready toward the waiting helicopter while the male agent approached McCready's SUV. He removed our restraints, looked ruefully at my leg. "We'd like to lift you out of here right now, Ms. MacKinnon, but we want to get McCready behind bars ASAP. One of our colleagues is standing by at Roche Harbor Airport. If you can wait ten minutes, we'll send the pilot back for you. And then we'd like your statement."

"We'll wait," I said. "By the way, McCready is very devious." I nodded toward the plane.

"We've read the dossier," he said. "And we're all grateful to those two kids." Before I could ask, he sprinted across the clearing and Elyse and I watched as the rotors on the helicopter revved up and the green and white bird lifted up and over the trees. As the sound faded, Angela Petersen and her partner came out of the dome. They weren't alone and I stared in relief at the disheveled countenances of Stephen Breckenridge and Sage McGregor. "Not a trace of anyone else," Angela said. "What do you know about the two who disappeared on the ATV's?"

"Tall female, thirtyish, large, long black hair. Male, fortyish, six foot two, long black pony tail. Both driving green Honda FourTrax ATV's."

"They're vampires." This from Sage.

Angela and Deputy Fountain turned to stare at her. Sage shrugged. "Just saying."

Angela hid a smile. "Let's get you all back to town."

"Take the kids," I said. "Sage should go to the clinic, get checked over. Elyse and I'll wait for the helicopter." I turned to Stephan. "It was you. You liberated the ravens."

He produced a sheepish smile and we exchanged

high fives. "Yeah. Cool, huh?"

"Better call Wolf Hollow soonest. Somebody's got to feed them. And relieve them of the cameras." I turned to Angela. "How did you find us?"

"We were trying to get coordinates from the geomarks on the photos you sent," Angela said, "Then Tina got a call from Stephan. He gave her excellent directions. Now we need to find the two missing , uh . . . vampires."

"Who called in the F.B.I.?" I asked.

"Tina Breckenridge. Early this morning. They were already looking for McCready. Something about a woman from Venezuela who disappeared a few weeks ago."

I thought about the little vignette McCready's wife had related, about the pregnant woman who showed up at the winery, the one whose father was a Minister of something.

"When the woman didn't answer her phone for three days," Angela continued, "Her papa flew to San Francisco, got the F.B. I. involved, got AT&T to provide info on phone calls. She had three phone calls from McCready and some texts setting up a meeting in San Francisco. Then she disappeared. Ergo, when Tina's call came in, they got right on it."

I glanced at Elyse. She was slowly shaking her head from side to side, both eyes closed. I knew what she was thinking.

"Tina's okay?"

"Now she is. Ian got to the house just as Griffin was forcing his way in. There was a bit of a scuffle and Griffin ended up with a nasty GSW."

I smiled. "Good for Ian. How did the F.B.I. wrest the helicopter away from the Senator and his entourage?"

Angela and Jeffrey exchanged a long expressionless look. "The Senator's visit did not go well," Angela said. "We won't bore you with the details."

Jeffrey added, "When the two Feebs arrived, Nigel was more than happy to turn over the keys to the 'copter. Rumor has it he may be resigning."

A sudden gust of damp wind swirled the gravel around our feet. From beyond the tree tops I heard the welcome drone of the returning helicopter.

Chapter 50

MITCHELL HILL

to Friday Harbor

We took off to the northwest, banked in a wide circle over Briggs Lake, followed Roche Harbor Road back into Friday Harbor. As we swept over the Sheriff's Office storage shed where Angela and I had purloined the Gunderson evidence, Elyse explained how she had raided McCready's briefcase yet again, found BioIntel documents and drawings of the mountain research facility we'd just left. She'd put them in her bag, pleaded a veterinary appointment, and headed back to the stables. An hour later McCready had shown up. She took a deep breath and touched the welt on the side of her face. "I guess people show their true colors when they get mad. He was vicious, Scotia. I may have some bruises, but I might have made a worse mistake."

"Yeah, you might have gone to join the Venezuelan girl friend." I explained about the pregnant girl friend and the unannounced visit to the winery. Elyse shook her head. "There but for you . . ." she murmured, rolling her eyes. "What's going to happen to McCready?"

"It's my understanding when the FBI take someone into custody, they get photographed and fingerprinted. They'll attempt to get a voluntary statement and he'll remain in FBI custody at least until the ini-tial court appearance."

Below us lay the solid waste center, then we were over the school grounds and the post office and the OGB. I scanned the harbor, found *'Spray* bobbing on her lines. As we came back into cell tower range, my phone chirped. There were two new texts. The first was Melissa. *Shaun refuses to go to rehab. We hd a big fight. He's gone 2 work in S.D. GR2BR. Im going 2 Mendocino tmorow. Gram wants 2 do erly Thnksgvg. Will u cm? H&K*

My mother's text was in the same vein. "*Cn we do Thnksgvng this Sunday? Giovanni booked us on a cruise in the Med nxt wk. Bring your Brit friend.*

Five minutes later we descended to the runway at Friday Harbor municipal airport and taxied up to the EMT ambulance. The rotors slowed and came to a stop. The pilot climbed down, walked around to the other side of the copter, opened the door. Elyse crouched her way to the passenger door, slid down to the pontoon step, and onto the ground. Peg O'Reilly was waiting for her behind the security gate. I took a deep breath. I crawled to the door, took another deep breath, put my good leg out the door, and knew I didn't dare try to move the bad leg. How the hell was I ever going to get back aboard *DragonSpray*?

"Welcome back, MacKinnon." It was Jared Saperstein. He pulled me into his arms and lifted me out to the ground, onto the waiting EMT gurney. "First stop the E.R. Then to Franck Street for ver-mouth and soda. Dinner and a bed await."

"Have to feed Calico," I mumbled. "Have to give a statement. Have to go to Mendocino and make pumpkin pies."

"Calico is waiting for you at the house. Zelda brought over a new Sherpa bag for her to sleep in. And she grabbed your toothbrush and other necessities."

It was after seven when we got to Jared's house. I'd been x-rayed, all parts of my leg were unbroken, but badly bruised and lacerated. My knee and elbow were encased in bandages and I was supplied with a set of crutches and a vial of hydrocodone. The female FBI agent was waiting for us when I emerged from the ER and I described where I'd found Sage and Stephan and what had transpired thereafter. The rain had stopped, the temperature had dropped about ten degrees, and a brisk wind was blowing out of the southeast. While we drove up the hill I filled Jared in on the texts from Melissa and Jewel Moon.

"So Melissa's boyfriend is on the lam and you get family Thanksgiving in California." He pulled into the driveway and killed the ignition. "All's well that ends well."

I turned in my seat and studied the face of my best friend. The strong jaw, the fringe of graying hair that circled his well shaped head. The strong hands on the steering wheel with a ruff of dark hair over the knuckles. Brown eyes that were really more black than brown. "Jared, how would you like to spend Thanksgiving in Mendocino? We have to be there by Saturday night."

"Perfect. Your mother is a delight. My new editor will love having me out of the way. We'll take Calico with us."

"I need a shower."

"That can be arranged."

"I'll need stuff from the boat."

"I'll get whatever you need."

Inside, he installed me on the sofa, put on Channel 2 Northwest news. Calico strolled into the living room, adjusting to the change of residence in admirable Zen fashion. For a few seconds or maybe as long as a minute, I thought about Michael Farraday and Porto Sollér and the invitation to the Scottish Highlands, but it was hard to focus and it all seemed part of something long ago and far away.

Our small island does not usually make the evening news, but the whole day had been one long exception. Or more accurately, the whole week. Jared went to the kitchen to fix drinks and I listened to the anchor's version.

. . . the F.B.I. made an arrest this afternoon of a former CIA operative with an interesting dossier. Following up on a missing persons report of the daughter of a Venezuelan diplomat, the agency had been tracking LT. Colonel Lochlan McCready of Santa Barbara, California for several weeks. Today they received a tip that the subject of their search had allegedly kidnapped and was holding hostage two children from San Juan Island. One of the hostages is the son of a candidate for

San Juan County Council, against whom Mc-Cready was running in an upcoming election. Apparently the children were being held in a dungeon-like cell in a geodesic dome on a mountaintop on San Juan Island, where they were discovered by a local private investi-gator. Lt. Col. McCready was expelled from Venezuela in 2012 on allegations of espionage. After a shootout between two F.B.I officers and McCready on what was previously DNR land, McCready was taken into custody at 5:10 this afternoon. McCready refused to make a statement and is being held without bail in Seattle on pending charges from the U.S. Attorney General's office or Department of Justice. It was also rumored the geodesic dome is the site of a research facility called BioIntel Systems that is piloting a new generation of miniature cyborg drones. The anchor exchanged a long glance with her co-anchor who added his own comment: "I've also heard there will be an investigation into the sale of DNR land to a private corporation."

Jared came back into the room and handed me the vermouth and soda. "Appears that your client's little problem is solved. To bad they didn't give you more credit."

"Thank God for small favors."

I took a long sip of the drink and leaned back against the sofa. Calico was curled alongside my good leg, purring in her throat. Jared moved around behind the sofa and massaged my shoulders. As he leaned down, I inhaled a scent of musk from his skin. I wondered if it was a new aftershave or if I'd just never noticed. Or never gotten close enough to notice.

"By the way," he said. "Zelda called. Said you have a package at the office."

I rotated my shoulders under his hands. "She say who it's from?"

"Has a Seattle address. You want her to bring it by tonight?"

I sipped the vermouth and felt my shoulders softening under Jared's strong hands. "I don't think I can get my brain around anything else tonight. To-morrow will be fine."

"In that case, we'll have dinner in half an hour or thereabouts. Pan seared scallops and bok choi, Evo-lution White, vanilla bean gelato for dessert."

"I love you, Jared."

"I know you do, MacKinnon." He arranged a blanket over my legs, smoothed a lock of hair off my forehead, leaned over to kiss me. It was a slow kiss that started out softly and slowly evolved into an embrace that rocked my tiny insular world.

Chapter 51

THE HOUSE ON FRANCK STREET

Friday Harbor

We ate pan-seared scallops and baby bok choi and drank Evolution White from crystal glasses at 1:15 in the morning in Jared's dining room with big candles, and made plans to take '*Spray* up to Otter Bay for a weekend before winter set in, and didn't get to sleep until three a.m. In the morning I awoke to the scent of coffee. The deep dark aroma of coffee grown at a high altitude in a tropical climate along the Equator. Also to a dull pain in my right knee that called for another hydrocodone. I stared through the French doors at the wisteria vines moving lazily in the light morning breeze and considered the events of the previous twenty-four hours. Jared came into the room with a large wicker tray.

"I didn't want to wake you, but it's ten o'clock and you have three new calls on your phone, all from Carolyn Smith. Zelda just dropped off the FEDEX package. Maybe something you want to look at be-fore we head south. Or not.

Jared dropped the box on the bed and put the wicker tray with the two cups of coffee, orange juice, and the plate of almond croissants on the wooden ta-ble next to the bed. He arranged two pillows behind my shoulders and leaned down to plant a kiss on the back of my neck. I reached for the coffee and held it in both hands with my eyes closed, savoring the kiss.

Then I considered the box: maybe something nice I'd ordered and forgotten.

The return address was a UPS store in Seattle. I ripped open the box and emptied the contents onto the bed: two envelopes, two post cards, and a folded page of note paper. Jared reached for a croissant and watched me unfold the note paper. It was adorned with pale pink roses. The handwriting was neat and slightly backhand. *Dear Ms. MacKinnon, After you left yesterday, Erika talked about Iceland again. Her mental state seems to be deteriorating, almost as if she's slipping away. She said there was another box of letters. I found it and we read them together and she cried. This morning she asked me to burn the letters. Please don't tell her I sent them to you. Respectfully, Gretchen Storvik.*

"Gretchen Storvik is Erika Fredericksen's care-taker." I passed the note to Jared and examined the envelopes. Two were postmarked Reykjavik. The remaining envelopes and the postcards carried fad-ed postmarks that I thought were either Cyrillic or Greek. I extricated the letters from the envelopes and checked the handwritten dates. "These were written in July and November of 1982." I scanned the first let-ter. "There must have been earlier letters. This seems to be a continuation of something."

"Read it."

"My dearest, please do not say I made you sad. You know how much I wanted you to come with me.

You know it was to dangerous for me to stay ther and I try to explain last letter I come to Iceland to see the boys. There is no romance with Brette. She has fiance. I send her money all the years only for the boys. I will stay here some months until you come but you know I prefer a warm place like Greece, and I am almost out of money here. I am in contact with cousin John in Ikaria. Please come and bring Wolf. Imagine blue water and warm winds. All my love from your Peder.

"The island of Ikaria," Jared said softly. "Where supposedly everybody lives to be a centenarian. So he got away. What does the second one say?"

"Erika my darling I can no longer get work here because my arthritis very bad and winter has come down. Brette told bad things to the boys and they do not talk to me. I am out of money. I must leave soon. Always your Peder."

"Iceland in November. No wonder he wanted to go to Greece."

I studied the photos on the postcards. The first showed a white sailboat anchored off a small village of whitewashed houses with red roofs. The second was a shot of a secluded beach lapped by pristine blue water and surrounded by rocky hillsides. I turned the cards over. The ink on one postmark was too faded to decipher and I couldn't read the date on other one. Both were addressed to Erika Ronstadt at an address on 56th Street in Seattle.

"Erika, my love, I count days until you and Wolf arrive. Ilse painted the little bedroom and we arrange a small room over garage for Wolf. Flowers are bloom-ing. I working with John at the shipyard. Brette mar-

ried her boyfriend. His family has big fish oil business. They bottle and sell to U.S. He said I should not send more money so I can help with your tickets. I will call you tomorrow. Hard to believe I will hold you in my arms in a few weeks. Your Peder. P.S. I do not want to know about Hazel's problem."

"Hazel's problem." I shook my head. "Reading this gives me goose bumps."

"Like wandering into a parallel universe. Or a wrinkle in time."

The second postcard was the last correspondence: *"My darling, I think of you every day and pray your return. Summer is passing. Come soon. My heart aches for you. P."*

"Let me see that."

I handed Jared the second postcard. He studied the postmark. "This was mailed in July of 1983."

"I didn't know you knew Greek."

"Little Latin and less Greek. There's a lot you don't know about me."

"I look forward to knowing more." I nibbled a croissant and we stared at each other over the love letters. Erika had declined to accompany Peder to Norway and Iceland, but apparently she had joined him on Ikaria with Wolf. Who may have been Peder's son. Or not. For how long we did not know. A few weeks? A month? Were there other letters? Had she had ever returned to the island? Did Peder die there? He would now be well past one hundred.

"The DNA analysis of the blood spatters is sort of academic now, isn't it?"

I nodded. "After all those years of making his life

hell and threatening to kill him, Hazel was convicted of a murder that never happened."

"Poetic justice," Jared murmured, "With her lift-ed scale."

We finished off the coffee and croissants in si-lence. Jared brought me his laptop and my phone. "In case there are any loose ends you want to gather up before we head down to Mendocino. The password is 'infinity.' Rest as long as you want. Calico's been fed. I should be finished up at the office by noon. Then we'll get what you need from '*Spray* and head over to America."

I heard the front door close. Calico sauntered into the bedroom and leaped to the foot of the bed. Carolyn had called twice and left one text: *Send me your final bill. The judge has approved a distribution of the assets. Luisa will hold Harrison's portion pending his return. LOL. Case cleared.*

I doubted the last statement.

Calico stretched out alongside my good leg and I considered Jared's parting comment: any loose ends. There was only one important question that would always haunt me, and the answer might never be forthcoming. I entered "infinity" on Jared's laptop when prompted, clicked up his browser, Googled for the Chief of Police of the Island of Ikaria. Along with categories for petrol stations, internet cafes, current weather – clear, 13 degrees Centigrade, – a video cam of the Ikaria Ridge and the Castle at Kapsalino, I found a directory of municipal and emergency contacts. The contact for Municipal Police was Christos Kazantzakis. I composed a brief inquiry to Mr. Kazantzakis, requesting information on a resident or former resident of Ikaria, formerly of Iceland and the United States, approximate age if still living, 107 years.

As I pressed the Send button, my phone rang. It was Zelda. "You're okay? Can you walk?"

"With the help of Vicodin, I'll be okay. How's your arm?"

"A lot of blood, but nothing serious. Jared says you're going to Mendocino and meeting Melissa there."

"That's the current plan. Thanks for bringing the FEDEX packet by."

"Any good stuff in it? Sexy underwear? I hear you and Jared are now an item."

"You *heard*?"

"There is no mistaking the eyes of a man who's spent the night with the love of his life. So, anything in the FEDEX packet I need to know about?"

"Let's just say the contents provide most of the missing answers relative to *State of Washington vs. Hazel Gunderson.*"

"As in, the missing body?"

"Watch for a special edition of the *Gazette.* "

"That's cruel, but I'll wait. Guess what. Sheldon said he's given up on me and he's leaving, taking a job in Alaska with Exxon. His aunt's selling the house."

"That will leave you homeless."

"I'm moving in with Cee Gee and T.J."

"Sounds cozy."

"She's my best friend and I'm learning a lot from her that will be very helpful with my new career. And

T.J. is, um . . . "

"Gorgeous and smart and good in bed."

"Yeah. I just talked to Abby. She's decided to go to Tanzania with the professor as soon as she finishes the Raven Chronicles. She's talking with a couple of magazines about photo assignments for Africa. I'm meeting her for lunch. Shall I stop by the boat and get you some clothes? Stuff for the kitty cat?"

I gave her a list of necessities I'd need for the stay in Mendocino: blue jeans, warm shirts and sweaters for beach walks, boots, hiking shoes. "And the long garnet-colored velvet skirt."

"Got it. In case you're wondering, a crew of volunteers from Wolf Hollow rescued the ravens in the cages. They're going to try and save the one that M shot in the wing. Abby went with them and photographed the whole thing."

"What will happen to the birds?"

"I hear they're going to a sanctuary in Eastern Washington."

"Raven rehab. Sounds good. What about the flying insects? The cyborgs?"

"Um . . . there was an item on King 5 this morning . . . a DARPA spokesperson swears the cyborgs were never shipped to BioIntel. There's a lepidopterist from the University en route to the island to check out the situation."

"Anyone heard from Elyse Montenegro?"

"Saw her this morning at the market. Still in shock, I think, but mostly okay. Peg Reilly stayed out at the ranch with her last night. Her dad's on his way up. He's going to buy Ravenswood for her. Oh, I

heard this morning two people were arrested on Lopez. Names are Max and Stella. Ring any bells?"

Chapter 52

ABOARD THE S/V ELWA

Friday Harbor

On Saturday morning, after settling Calico in her Sherpa bag in the back seat of Jared's SUV on the car deck of the *Elwa*, we took the elevator to the upper level. Jared went to the galley in search of coffee and I wandered slowly to the back of the ferry and onto the outside deck. I'd replaced the Vicodin with valerian root. My hobble had diminished to a small limp and Zelda was returning the crutches to the hospital. I found a bench to sit on as the Elwa began a slow back to port.

As we moved away from the dock, Friday Harbor grew smaller and smaller until it was a postcard village hovering above the morning mist. A white power boat motored along the breakwater toward the fuel dock. To the north of the Port building, on the balcony of the yacht club, a tall man in a red shirt came out the door and leaned on the railing, checking out the widening patches of blue sky. From high above the trees at the University lab, two black feathered streaks swept across the sky and came to a landing atop the two pillars in Fairweather Park.

The ferry completed the turn, passed the Reid Rock buoy to port, and headed out into San Juan

Channel. My phone chimed. It was Carolyn Smith.

"I just got a call from IFL. They've got your results. Shall I e-mail them to you?"

"I'm on the ferry. Could you read them to me?"

"Using two techniques they call polymerase chain reaction and restriction fragment length polymorphism . . . sorry, that's a mouthful . . . the blood on the ceiling could not have belonged to the parent of the person who grew the beard hairs. As for the blood on the carpet, they found a 99% probability that it came from the parent of the person who grew the beard hairs. I'll e-mail this to you and you can peruse it at your leisure. So what did you think of the *Guardian* piece I sent you?"

"It always helps to have friends in high places. At least the She Shan Tigers didn't leave Harrison behind."

"Maybe someday he'll actually make it home. Talk later. Have to be in court in ten minutes."

Behind me the door opened and Jared came outside, handed me a container of coffee.

"You look pensive," he said.

I told him about the DNA results. "Are you planning to do an article for the *Gazette*?"

"Absolutely. I'll put it together while you and your mother make the pumpkin pies. My new editor will run it on Monday, although I doubt that a majority of the San Juan electorate will vote for a candidate who's in FBI custody."

My phone chirped a text from Melissa. *Cant wait to c u. Cn I come up and stay with u @ at Christmas vacation? Do u have room on DragonSpray?*

I showed the text to Jared. He read it, smiled, leaned over and kissed me.

"I just heard back from the realtor," he said. My offer on the North Bay house was accepted. Fortuitously, it has a separate mother-in-law unit."

EPILOGUE

The Friday Gazette
Special Online Edition
Editor's Letter

Orcas Island Horsewoman Exonerated

In 1987, following a notorious five-week trial in Friday Harbor, an Orcas Island woman was convicted of first degree murder. The alleged victim was Captain Peder Gundersen, a retired ship pilot who disappeared sometime in the early part of 1982. The woman was Orcas Island resident Hazel Kortig Gundersen, owner of Dolphin Bay Stables. The couple had a long history of domestic battles and Hazel Gundersen was convicted despite the absence of either a body or an eye witness to the alleged crime. She was sentenced to life in prison, where she died six years ago.

This week, thanks to the diligent investigation of Friday Harbor P. I. Scotia MacKinnon on behalf of her client, Tina Breckenridge, new evidence has surfaced which, had it been available at the time of the trial, would have produced a different outcome.

The evidence consists of a number of letters and

postcards sent by Captain Gundersen from Iceland and from the Greek Island of Ikaria months after the date alleged by the prosecution that Hazel Gundersen shot her husband and disposed of the remains. The letters were sent to a Seattle friend of the Captain who visited him in Ikaria and were kept secret by her until a few days ago.

Additionally, analysis of biological DNA and trace evidence (blood spattered fibers from carpet and ceiling) indicate that while the blood in the carpet could have come from the Captain, the blood in the ceiling -- deemed the result of a gunshot wound by the expert who testified at the trial – could not have. Who the blood spatters on the ceiling belonged to may forever remain a mystery.

Finally, this week P. I. MacKinnon received verification from the Ikaria Keeper of Public Records that Captain Peder Gundersen died on the Greek island of Ikaria last year, at the age of 110 years.

Hazel Gundersen was the great-aunt of Tina Breckenridge, who is a candidate in tomorrow's special election for San Juan Island County Council. This editor and this paper fully support Ms. Breckenridge's candidacy.

—Jared Saperstein
Mendocino, California

The End

Acknowledgments

My deepest thanks to the following people and organizations for providing me with the information and support I needed to write this novel: Donna Donahoo of San Juan island and Nairobi, Kenya; San Juan County Undersheriff Jonathan Zerby (Ret.); San Juan County Evidence Manager Chuck McCarty; Ruth Offen of the (Friday Harbor) Waterworks Gallery; the wonderful staff of the San Juan Island Library; and the following faculty and facilitators of the 2012 Naples (Florida) Citizens Police Academy: CSI Sarah Vasquez, Communications Officer Marie Reese; SWAT Team Officer Jeffrey Perry, Master Officer Buddy Bonollo, Community Policing Officer Linda Lines, and Chief of Police Thomas Weschler.

I am also indebted to Ann Rule for her book *No Regrets* and to Paul and Rachel Chandler's *Hostage: A year at Gunpoint with Somali Gangsters*. And for those readers, parents or otherwise, still puzzling out any of Melissa's cryptic texts, please refer to Randall C. Manning's Texting Dictionary of Acronyms.

The references to and portrait of the She Shan Flying Tigers are sheer fantasy.

As usual, I could not have completed this project without advice from my generous First Readers: Donna Donahoo, Sabrina Duncan, Marilyn Kussick, Rosalie McCreary, Sandy Pellegrino, Don Thompson, Kris Zerby, and Jonathan Zerby.